A CENTURY
OF STORIES
NEW HANOVER COUNTY PUBLIC LIBRARY
1906-2006

Sandwiched

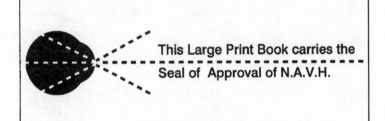

This Large Print Book carries the
Seal of Approval of N.A.V.H.

Sandwiched

Jennifer Archer

Thorndike Press • Waterville, Maine

Published in 2006 by arrangement with Harlequin Books S.A.

Thorndike Press® Large Print Americana.

The tree indicium is a trademark of Thorndike Press.

The text of this Large Print edition is unabridged.
Other aspects of the book may vary from the original edition.

Set in 16 pt. Plantin by Carleen Stearns.

Printed in the United States on permanent paper.

Library of Congress Cataloging-in-Publication Data

Archer, Jennifer, 1957–
    Sandwiched / by Jennifer Archer.
       p. cm. — (Thorndike Press large print Americana)
    ISBN 0-7862-8588-5 (lg. print : hc : alk. paper)
    1. Single women — Fiction. 2. Mothers and daughters — Fiction. 3. Large type books. 4. Domestic fiction.
    I. Title. II. Thorndike Press large print Americana series.
    PS3551.R337S26 2006
    813′.6—dc22   2006004731

Like the women in *Sandwiched*, I lived under one roof with some fabulous females for many years. This book is dedicated to them with love and gratitude:

My mom, Joan Browder, who is patient and supportive, loving and wise. You mean the world to me.

And

Linda Heasley, Charla Walton and Angie Prince — sisters by fate, friends by choice. My life would not be nearly so fun or interesting without you.

As the Founder/CEO of NAVH, the only national health agency solely devoted to those who, although not totally blind, have an eye disease which could lead to serious visual impairment, I am pleased to recognize Thorndike Press* as one of the leading publishers in the large print field.

Founded in 1954 in San Francisco to prepare large print textbooks for partially seeing children, NAVH became the pioneer and standard setting agency in the preparation of large type.

Today, those publishers who meet our standards carry the prestigious "Seal of Approval" indicating high quality large print. We are delighted that Thorndike Press is one of the publishers whose titles meet these standards. We are also pleased to recognize the significant contribution Thorndike Press is making in this important and growing field.

Lorraine H. Marchi, L.H.D.
Founder/CEO
NAVH

* Thorndike Press encompasses the following imprints: Thorndike, Wheeler, Walker and Large Print Press.

Thanks to my editor, Gail Chasan, who is a dream to work with; and to Tara Gavin and all the other wonderful people I've met at Harlequin.

Thanks to my agent, Jenny Bent, who challenged me to make the proposal stronger, and stuck out the tough times with me.

Thanks to the Thursday night Divas, who offered wine and whine sessions, encouragement and their invaluable expertise and suggestions: Dee Virden Burks, Jodi Koumalats, Marcy McKay, DeWanna Pace, April Redmond and honorary Diva (whether he likes it or not) Robert Brammer. And to the long-distance Divas, Britta Coleman and Candace Havens, who encouraged from afar.

Thanks to my friend, Ronda Thompson, who met me at Schlotsky's and saved my sanity by helping me figure out how to structure the dreaded synopsis.

And as always, thanks to my husband, Jeff, who didn't complain when the alarm went off every morning at 5:00 a.m.; and to my son Jason who sometimes remembered to call and let me know he was going to miss his curfew (again); and to my son Ryan, whose funny phone calls from college gave me nice breaks away from the writing.

Chapter 1

Cecilia Dupree
Day Planner
Saturday, 11/1

1. Unpack Mother.
2. Grocery store.
3. Shop for Erin's concert dress.

Instead of filing for divorce, I should've buried Bert in the backyard, in the spot beneath the willow where our bulldog likes to pee.

I realize my mistake on a Saturday morning while driving home from the Donut Hut. The sun shines bright in a lapis-blue sky; the autumn air is as sweet and crisp as my mother's famous gingersnap cookies. It seems a shame to go back to the house so soon on such a gorgeous day, back to Mother and a bedroom full of boxes containing her things. So I decide, instead, to take a little drive.

After rolling down the windows, I choose

a chocolate long john from the doughnut sack then proceed to lick off the icing. Which might give you a fairly clear idea of what's lurking at the back of my mind, though I have a difficult time admitting, even to myself, why nibbling the pastry gives me such an inordinate amount of pleasure. I pretend I'm only attempting to satisfy my sweet tooth but, after more than six months of sleeping alone, deep down I know better.

Since the separation, I've spent my days and nights trying to keep up with my teenaged daughter, checking on my widowed mother, putting in long hours at a demanding child-and-family counseling practice. No time exists for sex; at least that's what I tell myself. So I avoid anything and everything that might remind me of what I'm missing.

It isn't easy.

In case you haven't noticed, sex is everywhere these days. Television. Movies. Books. Doughnut sacks. Even my late Friday and Saturday nights of safe, celibate solitaire have turned traitor on me. After a couple of months alone with the card deck, the King of Hearts has started to look appealing; I'd swear he has a frisky gleam in his eye.

But back to Bert and why I should've buried him.

Somehow or another, I wind up on his street this Saturday morning. And just in time to see him step onto the front porch of his condo with a young, buxom redhead attached to his side. The girl doesn't look much older than our daughter Erin, the only worthwhile thing Bert ever gave me during our nineteen years of marriage.

It's the kiss that does me in. I can't tear my attention away from their passionate lip-lock, from Bert's hands kneading and caressing that tight, round, voluptuous butt. Because of that kiss, I don't see the curve in the road. I hit the curb, run up onto the sidewalk, jerk to a screeching halt only inches from a mailbox in front of the condo across the street from Bert's.

That forces my attention away from the kiss. Bert's too, apparently, because before I can catch my breath, he's beside my window, looking down at me with the smug, disdainful sneer I know so well.

Swallowing a creamy bite of pastry that, luckily, I didn't choke on, I meet his gaze and attempt to act as if nothing is at all unusual about my minivan, aka "the grocery getter," being parked on his neighbor's walk. "Hello, Bert."

"Cecilia." His eyes shift to my lap where the prior object of my desire now sits in a

11

smear of chocolate, soiling my gray, baggy sweats.

Bert, I notice, wears boxers. No shirt. His feet are bare. He's lost weight and bulked up since the last time I saw him barelegged and bare-chested. Muscles bulge I never knew existed. My once soft and pudgy soon-to-be ex looks buff and disgustingly great, which only makes me wish all the more that I'd chopped him up into little pieces and planted him beneath the willow tree. Maxwell, our bulldog, would've loved me for it. The dog never cared much for Bert. I imagine he'd take great pleasure in a daily tinkle over the remains of the guy who called him "girly-dog" and once kicked him for eating out of the trashcan.

When I realize Bert sees me sizing up his pecs, I shift my attention to beyond his shoulder where a little red convertible backs out of his drive. "How upstanding of you to volunteer to teach the Girl Scouts mouth-to-mouth resuscitation."

Bert doesn't even flinch. I guess nothing embarrasses him anymore after being caught by me in the arms of Tanya Butterfield, our neighbor's twenty-one-year-old daughter.

"You're looking good," he says, eyeing my sleep-mussed hair and the pimple on my chin, compliments of my frequent flirtation with chocolate. I always thought blemish-free skin would be one of the few perks of perimenopause. I thought wrong. This morning, I left for the Donut Hut straight out of bed and didn't bother to use a comb or wash my face, much less put on makeup to cover the zit.

Bert sweeps a finger across the side of my mouth and comes away with a glob of icing. "I see you gave up on your diet."

Before I can think of a barbed comeback, an old man steps out of the house in front of the mailbox I barely missed demolishing. He stands in the yard wearing his pajamas, arms crossed, glaring at me over the tops of his reading glasses.

"Hello, Mr. Perkins," Bert calls out. "Everything's okay. She missed your box. I'll have her off the sidewalk and on her way in no time."

Bert steps away from the van, and I put it in Reverse then back out into the street. I consider shifting into drive, slamming on the accelerator and leaving him choking on exhaust. But Bert's arrogant declaration to pucker-faced Mr. Perkins changes my mind. He'll have me on my way in no time? We'll see about that. No one controls Cecilia Dupree. Not anymore. I press on the brake and wait for him to walk back over.

"So . . ." Bert bends down to look into the window again, leveling one forearm on the edge and his gaze on mine. "What brings you to my neighborhood at 8:00 a.m. on a Saturday morning, CiCi?"

Birds twitter and cheep, serenading my humiliation. "Yesterday Erin and I moved Mother out of Parkview Manor Retirement Village and into the spare bedroom. Today we're unpacking. I went to get breakfast."

"I'm not exactly on your route home."

There is no way in Heaven or Hell I'll admit that I've ended up on his street because I've been thinking about him day and night for the past week. Our wedding anniversary passed uneventfully three days ago and, the truth is, I'm having a tough time learning to live single.

Seeing Bert doesn't help matters. While he has obviously been working out at a gym, dating, *having a life,* I've been paralyzed. Unable to move forward. Wallowing in the predivorce doldrums while feeding my face with whatever I can find in the fridge to fill the hollow spot inside of me, the gaping hole Bert left behind.

Don't get me wrong; I stay busy. During the day, my life is chaos. And most every evening, I'm at the kitchen table studying patient files. When I've had enough of that, the King of Hearts and I fool around a little until Erin comes home from wherever she spends her spare time these days. When it's time for bed, old movies on late-night TV keep me company until I drop off to sleep.

It's not so much that I miss Bert; I miss what felt familiar. Being one half of a couple. Having a warm body in the bed beside me at night. Lately, I've even been tempted to give in to Maxwell's sad eyes and let him sleep on the bed at my feet.

Determined to salvage my pride, I lift my pimpled chin and meet Bert's stare straight-on. "It's been so long since Erin's heard from you, I was afraid you might've skipped town. I thought I better swing by and make sure your car was still in the driveway." I hope it doesn't occur to him that I could've just picked up the phone.

"Erin's cell's always busy. I'll try her again today."

Shifting the van into drive, I motion toward the old man who still stands in the yard, arms crossed, watching us. "Tell your neighbor I apologize."

Bert smiles. "Say hello to Belle for me. I'll miss her cooking this Thanksgiving and Christmas. She's okay, isn't she?"

"Mom's fine. For the most part, anyway."

15

He frowns. "For the most part?"

"Her eyesight's getting worse. I think she's depressed about it. She doesn't socialize at all. She's stopped cooking for the other apartment residents, and you know how Mom loves to cook. Anyway, Erin and I talked it over and decided she'd probably be happier and more active living with us. We've hired a woman to come over and be with her during the day."

"That's a big step. I admire you for it."

"Yeah . . . well." I shrug. "I do my part for the elderly of the world, you do your part for the youth."

"Youth?"

I nod toward his condo. "The mouth-to-mouth?"

Bert surprises me with a blush, which gives me a small measure of satisfaction as I drive away, this time leaving *him* alone and embarrassed.

Sweet justice.

Around 11:00 a.m., Erin declares her work duties done, blows her Nana a kiss and takes off for her best friend Suzanna's house. They plan to eat lunch at the mall, then spend the afternoon shopping for a dress for Erin's yearly holiday orchestra concert. I'd planned to go along, but too much is left here to do, and Erin didn't seem to mind if I begged off.

Mother shakes her head as she watches Erin go. She mutters something about families eating together, about homemade meals and how life was better back in the old days when my brother, Jack, and I were kids.

The mention of Jack makes me want to crush the box at my feet. Nothing's changed. Even as a kid, my brother could always find clever ways to weasel out of his responsibilities. I have to give it to him this time; moving eight hundred miles away just before Dad's heart attack is his best scheme yet. I want to be here for Mother. Still, some backup would be nice. Even long distance, you'd think Jack could help with the decision-making, with trying to boost Mother's frame of mind. But, no. His idea of involvement is a fifteen-minute phone call once per week.

As I drag the box to Mother's bedroom and start unpacking clothing, knickknacks and books, my early morning drive-by comes to mind. So. Bert has a life. Not only a life, a *sex* life. Women actually find him appealing. Maybe he really wasn't just a mercy lay or a boredom diversion for our neighbor's not-so-innocent young daughter.

And that pisses me off.

All these months while I've been raising our child alone, coping with all the stress that goes with having a teenager, juggling family and career, struggling with ending our failed marriage and putting it behind me, Bert and his penis have been out on the town. Literally.

Mother's humming drifts to me from the kitchen where she's putting away her gourmet cooking utensils, pots, pans and bakeware. The sound makes me pause. I can't recall hearing her hum like that since Dad died almost a year ago. The anniversary of his passing is a week away. Next Saturday.

The humming pleases me . . . and makes me feel guilty. The truth is, I haven't come to terms with her moving into my house. I love her and want the best for her. But is her moving in best for Erin and me? I haven't lived full-time with a parent since I left home at the age of eighteen for college. I'm accustomed to doing things my own way, not Mother's. And Erin is finally starting to have friends come around. She likes her independence and privacy, and so do I. But did all that walk out the door when Mother walked in?

"You okay in there?" I yell.

"I'm making headway, Sugar, but it's

going to take a while," she calls back. "Your cabinets are a mess! You could die of starvation before you found a pot to boil water in or a pan to scramble an egg."

"Which is why I don't boil water or scramble eggs."

"For heaven's sake! What do y'all eat?"

"Takeout." I pry open a box filled with colognes and bubble bath and other bathroom stuff. "Frozen dinners."

"What about breakfast?"

"Breakfast? What's that?"

Even the two walls separating us can't block her sigh. "No wonder Erin's so skinny, poor thing. Now that I'm here, I'll take care of that."

I drag the box toward the adjoining bathroom, reminding myself that this is what matters. Family pulling together during tough times. My mother's happiness in the winter years of her life. Not my pride or privacy or independence. And most certainly not Bert's extracurricular activities.

I groan. *Bert.* I can get over the fact that he has a social life and a sex life and I don't; I *will* get over it. Nothing good ever came of sex anyway. Well, nothing but babies and orgasms, but I'm long past the baby stage of my life.

As for orgasms, let's just say Bert never

put much stock in the motto "it's better to give than to receive." So, while I could argue that some is better than nothing at all, I haven't really given much up in that department. Anyway, if not for raging hormones, Bert would've lost interest in me when the first date ended. It wasn't my brilliant mind he probed in his bachelor apartment when we were seniors at the University of Texas.

Hefting the box onto the bathroom vanity, I start pulling out floral-scented bottles and small brown medicine vials.

"CiCi?" Mom calls from inside the bedroom.

"In here."

My petite, plump, pink-cheeked mother appears in the bathroom doorway, a bright smile on her face, her eyes unnaturally huge behind the magnified lenses of her glasses. She holds my thick, white plastic cutting board, which she lifts up in front of her. "Not that it's any of my business, Sugar, but don't you think it's time you threw this ol' thing away?"

I blink. Rarely, if ever, do I use the board, but still it's mine, and after her previous criticism of my kitchen organizational skills, I'm starting to feel a bit defensive. "What's wrong with it?"

"I'm blind as a bat, but even I can see there's mold growing on it." Mother wrinkles her nose. "It isn't sanitary."

"It's sanitary. I bleach it after every use. The green just won't come off."

"Surely you can afford a new cutting board."

"Why should I spend the money when that one's still perfectly functional?"

Mother gives me The Look. You know, The Look? Head tilted to the side, one brow raised, lips pursed?

I realize how ridiculous I sound, a forty-one-year-old woman arguing with her mother over a moldy cutting board I haven't seen in months, maybe years. So what if her scrutiny of my life and home makes me feel fifteen again? I don't have to act fifteen. "Okay, okay. Get rid of it," I tell her.

Mother's sweet countenance returns. She steps toward the trashcan by the desk in the corner and drops the plastic board inside. "Thank you so much for making space for all my things. I can't wait to start cooking for you and Erin, and it isn't the same if I don't have my own pots and pans."

I reach into the box, run my hand across smooth, cool glass, over peeling labels and bumpy plastic. "It'll be great having your home-cooked meals again. Cooking's just another of your many domestic talents I didn't inherit."

With my gaze still on Mother, I pull out another item.

Mother's gasp is quick and sharp. The color drains from her face, then rises again, bright red now rather than pink. Her eyes blink. Rapidly.

I glance down at my hand and immediately drop the object I'm holding. I'm no expert on vibrators, but I'm pretty sure I know a neck massager from . . . well . . . the *other kind.* The one on the floor at my feet is not for sore muscles, I can promise you that. Flesh-colored, it has a switch on the side that must've engaged when it hit the bathroom tile because the dismembered member pulses and vibrates and buzzes.

"Um . . ." I can't tear my gaze from the quivering body part, which fake or not, is quite impressive in size and energy. "Uh —"

"Well, for heaven's sake!" Mother's voice is high and panicky. "How did my bread beater get packed with my bathroom things?"

"Your *bread beater?*"

The next thing I see is her hand wrapping around the *thing,* which is an action I would've been happy never to witness in this or any other lifetime. She lifts it from the floor and turns off the switch while I reluctantly peer up at her.

My mother no longer blushes or blinks. In the space of a few seconds she has pulled herself together. She couldn't look any more prim or proper if she stood in front of her church choir to lead a hymn. Squaring her shoulders, holding the "bread beater" in front of her chest like a baton, she meets my eyes.

"That's right. My bread beater. Haven't you seen them advertised? It's a clever new device that kneads dough, easy as you please."

"Well . . ." I clear my throat. "Isn't that . . . something."

Mom turns and starts off through the bedroom. "I'll just go find a place for it in the kitchen."

I watch her go, then shift my attention to the mirror and stare at the dumbfounded expression on my face. I picture Erin going after a fork and finding Mom's newest kitchen gadget in the silverware drawer.

First Bert, now Mother. Wouldn't you know it? At the age of seventy-five, even she has more of a sex life than I do.

Later in the evening, after a trip with Mother to the grocery store, she cooks a

23

dinner that brings back memories of all those childhood meals she mumbled about earlier. She, Erin and I actually sit at the kitchen table rather than at the coffee table in the den, my usual place to dine. We carry on a conversation instead of watching the news.

Afterward, stuffed with savory fried chicken, garlic mashed potatoes and fresh green beans, Erin and I clear the table while Mother takes off to watch *Wheel of Fortune.* An apple cobbler bubbles and browns in my oven; Mother left the oven light on, and I glance at her culinary masterpiece with longing each time I pass by. I'm not sure why, maybe it's the foreign aromas of cinnamon and spice drifting through my kitchen, but I'm unusually relaxed and content as my daughter and I load the dishwasher together.

"I'm going to rent a movie, then watch it at Suzanna's," Erin declares when we finish.

"Before you leave, I want to see your concert dress."

"I didn't find one. I'll try again tomorrow or next week."

"Make it some time I can go with you."

Erin crosses her arms; her eyes shift away from mine. "It's no big deal. Suzanna will help me."

Okay, I admit it; for the second time in one day I feel like an overemotional teenager. Only now, instead of butting heads with my mother, my best friend is replacing me with someone else. I can't help it; silly or not, I'm jealous.

"What about that book report you said was due on Monday?"

"I'm not doing homework on a Saturday night. I'll work on it tomorrow."

"Be home by eleven." I eye her tight hip-hugging jeans, the inch of bare flesh between them and her T-shirt. Revealing so much skin is a new look for Erin. A fashion side effect of her friendship with Suzanna, I imagine. Though I don't like the change, I've decided not to make a big deal of it. I counsel families with kids younger than Erin who are promiscuous, have alcohol problems and worse. If an exposed navel is the most I have to deal with, I count myself lucky. I'll just keep an eye on her and make sure that's as far as it goes. "Got your mace?" I ask.

She gives me the eye-roll she spent middle school perfecting. "You know it's on my key ring."

"Just make sure you keep it in your hand if you're returning the movie and walking through the store parking lot after dark."

"I know, Mom." She hugs me and laughs. "You've only told me a million and one times. Anyway, there's a movie drop. I won't even have to get out of the car."

"Let Maxwell in and feed him before you go."

After Erin leaves and *Wheel of Fortune* ends, Mother and I watch *CNN* together while eating ice-cream-smothered pie. Maxwell peers at us with pleading eyes. He sits in front of the sofa, whining quietly each time I lift my spoon. Mother gives me The Look again when I place my bowl on the floor to let him lick it. I laugh at her and proceed to fold a couple of loads of laundry.

I'm placing a stack of clean underwear on Erin's dresser when I see the novel on her bedside table. I figure it must be the assigned book for her report since I've never known my daughter to read a novel unless it's required. I hope she's not getting sidetracked by her newfound social life and putting off the report until the last minute. But I remind myself that, though she's spending more time with friends these days, it's still not in Erin's nature to procrastinate. She's a typical only child. Fairly responsible as teenagers go.

I walk over, pick up the paperback, read the title. *Penelope's Passion.* A hazy cover creates the effect of looking through steam at a woman's naked back. A man's hand lifts the damp, curling tendrils of hair at the nape of her neck. I have my doubts Erin's English teacher chose this particular read.

Settling at the edge of my daughter's bed, I open the book to a random page.

Penelope sensed rather than heard the captain's approach. Pulling the sheet to her breast, she watched the door . . . and waited. Her heart fluttered like hummingbird wings, her stomach felt as unsteady as the ship, tossed and swayed by the turbulent sea.

Flickering candlelight painted shadows on the walls. For only a moment, Penelope glanced away to watch them dance, and when she looked back, he stood there . . . filling the doorway . . . his dark eyes devouring her, looking more a pirate than captain of a ship. His unbuttoned shirt revealed a powerful expanse of muscled chest. The sight of it made Penelope aware of her own chest, bare beneath the bed sheet. Her only garment had mysteriously disappeared while she bathed, so she'd had no choice but to retire naked.

Penelope lifted her chin. "Do you intend to rape me, Sir?"

The captain pulled off his shirt as he stepped into the room and closed the door behind him. "Since you now share my name, I intend to consummate our marriage."

She kept her gaze on his face, too nervous to glance lower at his body, afraid if she did he might see the excitement in her eyes when she looked up again. "And if I refuse you, Captain?"

He chuckled, his smile quick and heart-stopping. Then he reached for the buckle on his belt and moved closer to the bed.

Penelope could no longer refrain. She glanced at his broad chest, then lower still, down his flat, muscle-corded belly to the thin line of dark hair that trailed to the top of his breeches. Her breath caught, her stomach tightened involuntarily and a warm, sweet ache spread like heated honey through her limbs. To her shame, she yearned to touch him, yearned for him to touch her in all the places no man ever had, or should.

"Dear Lady," he said, his voice a deep, arousing caress, "you won't refuse me."

"Well, hell," I mutter, closing the book.

Penelope isn't the only one with a warm, sweet ache.

First Bert, then Mother, now Erin.

Maybe the person who came up with the old saying, "if you can't beat 'em, join 'em," knew what he or she was talking about.

Tucking *Penelope's Passion* beneath my arm, I leave Erin's room. At the end of the hallway, I poke my head around the corner into the den where Mother sits knitting and watching TV, with Maxwell snoring on the rug at her feet. The knitting needles click out a rhythmic beat.

"I think I'll turn in early and catch up on some reading."

Mother's needles pause. The clicking stops. She looks up at me. "I hope for once you're reading for pleasure instead of for work."

The corner of my mouth spasms as I think of Penelope's captain. "Purely for pleasure tonight, Mother. You have my word."

Chapter 2

To: Erin@friendmail.com
From: Suz@friendmail.com
Date: 11/1 Saturday
Subject: Tonight

Hey. Meet me at the mall at 11:30. We'll eat, then shop for something to wear out tonight to The Beat. You're going. No excuses.

I look at the outfit spread across Suzanna's bed and wish I'd never checked my e-mail this morning. The skintight, one-sleeved red-and-black striped top will leave one shoulder completely bare, while the pleated black pinstriped miniskirt is barely long enough to cover my scrawny butt. But the worst of it all sits in an open box; a pair of ankle-high, pointy-toed red boots with buckles on the sides and short spiked heels.

This afternoon at the mall, I gave into Suzanna's arm-twisting and bought it all. It seemed like a good idea at the time. The outfit was great for laughs in the dressing room. But the thought of actually wearing it in public makes me want to puke up Nana's fried chicken.

My stuff has been in the trunk of my car since I left the mall. It's bad enough having Mom to deal with, but now I have Nana, too. It's not like I don't want her to live with us; I do. But I'm afraid if the two of them saw these clothes, Mom would go ballistic and Nana might have a heart attack. And two against one makes it that much harder to defend yourself. I'm sure Mom didn't have this sort of outfit in mind for my concert. Which, now that I think of it, I totally forgot to shop for. The concert, that is.

"This all goes back," I say, shaking my head and turning to face my friend. "It's not me at all. It's more like something you'd wear."

Suz grabs the top and holds it up in front of me. "Oh, get over it. You're just nervous. You're gonna look *amazing*."

"I'll feel like a skank."

"Are you saying I dress like a skank?"

"No. I'm saying that you can pull off wearing slutty things *without* looking skanky. I can't."

Suzanna tosses the satiny top in my face. "That's just stupid."

I catch the shirt and start to refold it. "It doesn't matter what I wear tonight. If I'm with you no guy's going to notice me anyway." Not that they pay me much attention when Suz *isn't* around. It's just worse when she is.

"That's only because you're so quiet. They probably think you don't *want* to hook up."

"Okay." I sit at the edge of her bed, wishing she'd turn off the rap music, which I hate. "Then explain why it is that guys who've never met me, guys who don't know I'm quiet or that you're outgoing, completely look past me whenever you and I are together? Even before we ever open our mouths?"

Suz rolls her eyes. "As if."

"It's true."

"If it is true, which it isn't, then maybe it's because . . ." She pauses to nibble her lower lip. "Well, I hate to say this, but maybe it's because you dress like an orchestra member."

"I *am* an orchestra member."

"Exactly." Suzanna flips back her long blond hair.

"Playing the cello doesn't have anything to do with the way I dress. Lots of girls who aren't in orchestra dress like me."

"They probably can't hook up, either."

"What's wrong with my clothes?" I glance down at my jeans and T-shirt, bought last week, though they aren't my style. "I'm showing skin." I point at my belly button. "See?"

Suz eyes my jeans. "At least they aren't your usual. Baggy, khaki or black."

"Samantha Carter dresses like a *nun* and she has boyfriends. My clothes aren't the problem."

"Then what?"

I lay the folded skank-top on the bed beside me, cross my arms and stare straight at her chest. "Remember yesterday after school when you ran up to me in the parking lot while I was talking to Todd Blackburn about our science project?"

She nods. "What about it?"

"When he saw you coming, he forgot I existed. At first I thought it was your bouncing ponytail that threw him into a trance. Then I realized your hair wasn't the only thing bouncing."

Her eyes widen. *"Shut up!* I wasn't bouncing!"

"Yes you were! And Todd wasn't the only guy in the parking lot who noticed. Instead of 'follow the bouncing ball,' it was 'follow the bouncing boobs.' "

"That's disgusting." Suzanna's face flushes, which is a total surprise since nothing much embarrasses her.

"Well, if that's the problem," she says, "I can solve it."

"If you tell me to stand up straight and stick out my personality, I'm out of here." Back before Nana quit sewing, she'd say that to me. She'd be fitting a dress or whatever, pinning it at my shoulders or under my pits and getting all bent out of shape because I was slumping.

Suz makes a face and starts for the door. "Wait here."

While she's gone I turn off the music and swipe a piece of mint gum from her dresser. I think how weird it is that two people so different wound up friends. I moved to Dallas as a sophomore two years ago when Dad expanded his business. Since then, I've been pretty much alone when it comes to a social life. I hate my school with all its little groupies. Until Suz transferred in at the beginning of the year, I didn't have a best friend. The truth is, I didn't have any close friends at all. Just kids I hung out with sometimes. Other girls from my orchestra class, usually. Most of them quiet, goody-two-shoes nobodies. Which is probably how people think of me, too. I didn't share secrets with anyone or talk on the phone 'til late at night. I never laughed so hard I peed my pants. Mainly, I studied a lot, practiced my cello, made the honor roll and spent time with Mom.

Then Suzanna showed up and everything changed. She lives nearby in a Dallas suburb. Suz isn't exactly honor roll material, but she knows how to have fun. She should've graduated last year, but she didn't pass a couple of classes. Instead of retaking the first semester of her senior year at her old school and being totally humiliated, her parents let her transfer. I still can't figure out why she chose to hang out with me. At her old school, she was a cheerleader with more friends than she could keep track of. She says they've all taken off to different colleges. I'm pretty sure some of them made her feel stupid for not graduating, though she's never come out and said it.

Some friends.

I think she realized that. Or maybe she's just had enough of the whole "high school popularity" thing. Whatever the reason, she latched on to me the second she heard me playing cello in an empty classroom one day after school, and she's never let go. Okay, so sometimes I feel like her ugly stepsister. But at least I have fun now that I'm not hanging with Mom 24/7.

I'm dabbing some of Suz's spicy perfume on my neck when she walks back into the room and hands me two pale pink oval blobs. "What are these? Dead jellyfish?"

"Silicone inserts," she says. "They're Katie's. She takes after Dad. I take after Mom."

Katie, Suzanna's fifteen-year-old sister, is so flat she's almost concave. "She actually wears these?" I press the blobs against my 32-A's. The inserts even have nipples. Hard ones.

"Sometimes she does."

"Well, I can't," I say. "I won't."

"Why not?"

"It's false advertising for one thing. For another," I pinch the nipples, "I'd look like I'm chronically cold."

Suz snickers.

"Besides, if a guy's only interested in me because he thinks I have big boobs then maybe he's not worth knowing."

She sits beside me. "Let me explain guys to you. They can't help it. They're drawn to ta-tas like flies are drawn to picnic tables. It's the way they're wired."

I lay the blobs on the bed beside the red boots. "In that case, I have no hope."

"Not true. You just have to trick them into noticing you so that they'll stick around long enough to get to know you better. Once they do, and they realize how funny and smart you are, your booblessness won't matter so much."

I stare at her. "Yeah, right."

Suz sighs. "Okay, maybe not. I've never met a guy our age that mature."

I think of Dad. Mom doesn't know I figured out about him and the sleazoid who lives next door. But I'm not stupid. I saw how his eyelids got all heavy-looking whenever he saw her out in the driveway wearing only a little bikini top with her short shorts. I heard how his voice changed whenever they spoke, how his deep drawl got deeper and more drawn out, like the words were coated with molasses. "I'm not sure they're ever that mature," I say to Suzanna. "Even the old ones."

Suz sighs. "We'll have to concentrate on something besides funny and smart then." She studies me. "You have great eyes. I wish mine were big and brown. And your hair . . ." She twists it up on top of my head then lets it fall. "I like the color."

"You have a thing for muddy brown?"

She makes a face. "It's chestnut."

"Whatever you say."

Suz picks up an insert. "Quit being so negative and just have some fun with these, why don't you?" She tosses it at me. "At least try them on with the clothes."

Five minutes later, I strut back and forth in front of Suzanna's full-length mirror laughing like a crazy person. "Hey, dressing like a slut is sort of fun."

"Ohmigod! You're *so* not slutty-looking. I swear! You look like a model. You *have* to buy some of those thingies to wear all the time. They look *real!*"

Jumping up and down, I watch them jiggle. I laugh so hard tears run down my cheeks. I admit to Suzanna that I think I might like pretending to be the girl in the mirror for just one night.

"Then let me change clothes and we'll get out of here," she says, clapping her hands together.

My stomach twists. I wipe my eyes. "I want to, but I can't."

"What now?"

"My mom. She'll freak if she finds out I went to The Beat."

"We won't be drinking. If you're under twenty-one, they put a band on your wrist so the waiters won't serve you."

"I'm not eighteen yet. I can't get in."

"My cousin Trevor works there. He'll be taking cover at the door tonight. He'll let you through."

"I don't know. I could be eighteen and swear not to drink, and Mom still wouldn't let me go."

"Come on, Erin. Please? All the college guys go there. When I went with Trevor last weekend on his night off we had a blast."

"I want to. . . ."

"Then do it! I like your mother, but she's so strict. You're not a little girl anymore, and if you don't stand up to her and make her see that, you'll never get to have any fun. What does she expect you to do? Sit around with her and your grandmother on weekends? You might as well just skip the next twenty years of your life and go straight to the old folks' home."

"I can't stand up to her. I know my mother. I'll lose."

"I think you should try. It's either that or go behind her back."

I imagine telling Mom I'm going to The Beat. After she gets over the shock of it she'll forbid me to leave the house. I imagine saying that she can't stop me. Then I think of my car, which she bought, the gasoline, which she pays for, the allowance she puts in my pocket. She has plenty of ways to make my life miserable.

"I choose going behind her back."

Suz raises her brows. "Ooh-kay."

"It's my only chance of going." I glance at my watch. "We're not going to have much time. I have to be home by eleven on weekends, and it's nine now. By the time you get ready and we drive out there, we'll have to leave again."

"Eleven? Your Mom *is* strict." Suzanna frowns. "Things don't really even get going until after eleven. But don't worry." She thinks for a few seconds then smiles. "I have a plan."

It's easier than I thought to sneak the sack of new clothes into my bedroom.

"Erin? Is that you, Sugar?" my grandmother calls from the den when the front door slams.

"Hi, Nana. Be right there." I stuff the sack under my bed.

Even before I get to the den, I hear music playing. The kind with a lot of brass and piano, with some guy's silky voice weaving through it. I'm sort of weirded out when I find Nana on the floor with Maxwell tucked up beside her. Leaning against the sofa, she scratches his belly, her eyes closed, her glasses on the coffee table beside her. Socks cover her feet, and her toes tap the air to the beat of the song. I don't know why seeing someone her age sprawled out on the floor with her shoes off seems strange, but it does.

For a minute, I just stand and stare at her, afraid to break the mood. It's like her mind is someplace besides this room, in a different time, a happy one if the smile on her face is any clue. It may sound stupid, but I almost feel like I'm spying on something private, something I shouldn't disturb. Deciding I should just tiptoe away, I start to turn.

Nana's eyes flutter open. She squints. "Oh, Erin." Lifting her hand from Maxwell's belly, she places it on the sofa. "Come sit and talk with me."

Maxwell raises his head and whimpers until she touches him again. I understand. I remember the comfort of being cozied up to her. When I was little, we'd sit together in the rocker and she'd read to me. She smelled soapy clean.

Suzanna waits outside for me, three houses down the block. The excitement she offers tugs me one way at the same time Nana's warmth pulls me the other. I hesitate then cross the room, settling on the sofa beside where she sits on the floor. "I thought you might be asleep."

"No, just resting my eyes." She sits up straight, reaches for her glasses then slides them up the bridge of her nose. "How was your evening? Did you have a nice time with your friend?"

"We just talked and tried on clothes."

"Your mother said you rented a movie."

"I did, but we didn't watch it yet. Maybe tomorrow." I glance toward the door to the kitchen. The lights are off. "Where's Mom?"

"She turned in early to read." Nana covers her mouth and yawns. "I think I'll take a quick soak in the tub then do the same. I'm having some trouble settling down after all the day's excitement." She reaches up to me. "Would you give me a lift?"

I stand and face her. Nana's hands are dry and powder soft. As I pull her to her feet, I try to figure out what excitement she's talking about. "Did something happen while I was gone?"

"Happen?" Nana's brows pull together. "Your mother and I just ate pie and watched television. I couldn't have stood much more after all the unpacking and putting away. And then there was the trip to the grocery store. And the cooking." She pats my arm. "Mind you, I'm not complaining. It's a joy to be busy with my family."

I hug her, realizing the excitement she talked about was just the move. Shame tightens my throat. This day meant a lot to

Nana. I guess I should've known that, but until now, I didn't. I probably should've stuck around instead of going to the mall with Suzanna.

Ending the hug, I stand back and look at her. "I think I'll go to bed, too. I'm sort of tired." I almost choke on the lie. What started out smooth and clear is all twisted and cloudy now. I didn't expect my escape route would have ruts, guilty feelings to dodge along the way.

"I love you. Sleep tight," Nana says. "Stay warm."

"Love you, too." Heat creeps up the back of my neck. My heart beats too fast. "I'll put Maxwell out."

Max trots toward the front door, his bottom twisting in the prissy way that always used to earn him a rude comment from Dad. "Oh, no you don't." I hook a thumb in the direction of the backyard and lead him that way. Once outside, he squats to pee, then lifts his head and sniffs the air, as if he smells freedom beyond the fence and wants to explore. I watch him a minute, thinking of Suzanna waiting out front, of the night ahead. Then I go back inside.

I decide I better cover all my bases. A light shines under Mom's bedroom door so I knock and tell her I'm home. Usually, she tells me to come in and we talk for a while. By some miracle, this time she doesn't. She sounds sort of funny, like she's startled or something. We speak through her closed door for a few seconds then say good-night.

Twenty minutes later, after changing clothes and fixing my hair and makeup, I'm halfway out my bedroom window when the buckle of one spiked-heel boot catches on the inside latch. I have my free foot on the ground, the snared one raised high above the sill. I'm leaning forward, mooning the street. The temperature outside has dropped from comfortable to chilly. A breeze lifts the pleated hem of my miniskirt and scatters goose bumps across my butt. This is more than a rut, this is a major pothole.

Leave it to Suz and her great ideas.

I hear an engine and look over my shoulder. Her Honda Civic passes slowly by with the headlights turned off. She's supposed to wait down the street, but since I'm ten minutes late, I guess she got worried.

Before going through the window, I tossed my purse out. It's on the ground beside my foot. My cell phone's inside of it, ringing nonstop. It's a quiet muffled trill, but I panic anyway, sure Mom or Nana will hear it. My breath comes fast; I'm so scared I'm dizzy.

The second the phone goes quiet, I hear Nana humming on the other side of my door. I quit struggling with the boot buckle and stand still in spite of my cramped thigh. Her bedroom is next to mine; she probably finished her bath and she's headed there.

I'm shivering from coldness and fear when I finally hear Nana's bedroom door close. The humming stops. I twist my foot from side to side to work on the buckle again.

The bushes alongside the window rustle. I gasp, but see it's just Suzanna.

"Jeez!" I hiss. "You scared the crap out of me."

"Sorry," she whispers. "What are you doing?"

"Practicing to be a Dallas Cowboy cheerleader. What does it look like I'm doing? I'm stuck."

"Here." Suzanna squeezes in beside me. "Let me see." She leans in through the open window, reaches up, wiggles the latch with one hand while wiggling my boot buckle with the other. In no time, I'm free.

"I knew these boots would cause trouble," I mumble, pulling my leg from the sill, stumbling as I put my foot on the ground. "I feel like I'm playing dress-up."

"You are."

I reach for my purse as Suzanna slides the window closed.

She grabs my hand. "Let's get out of here."

Her car idles at the curb. Giggling, our ankles wobbling on our spiky heels, my silicone boobs bouncing like her real ones, we run across the dark lawn toward it.

Chapter 3

From The Desk of
Belle Lamont

Dear Harry,

Last night was my first at home with Cecilia and Erin. With remnants of our life together packed away in boxes around me, I dreamed of your roses. The dream was so vivid that, as I woke, their cloying scent filled the room and I felt the velvet petals brush my cheek.

I miss you so. Now, more than ever, I need your strong arms around me, your whisper of reassurance, your rational advice.

Just moments ago, I looked out my bedroom window and saw Erin sneaking out her window. She and another girl were dressed to kill — an appropriate cliché in this case since I know it would kill her mother to see her in a skirt so short and heels so high. Her father, too, if Bert even cares anymore. Sometimes I wonder.

The two girls made a beeline across the yard, climbed into a car and sped off, leaving me here wondering about my role in all this. My duty. Do I go to Cecilia and tell her? Or do I bite my tongue? Wait up for Erin, listen to what she has to say, then try to talk some sense into her? I'm leaning toward the latter. I have Erin's cell phone number, and I can always call her if she's not in by midnight. Besides, Cecilia's too strict with the girl. In this day and age, an eleven o'clock curfew on a Saturday night for a young woman of almost eighteen is going overboard if you ask me. Of course, Cecilia didn't.

I think our daughter lives in deadly fear that if Erin's allowed to be a normal teenager, the girl will put her through the same grief Cecilia put us through at that age. Which would serve CiCi right; I'm sure you'll agree. I say that with a smile on my face!

I don't think poor Erin has ever had a date. How could she when she's stuck beneath the weight of CiCi's expectations that she act like a middle-aged adult when it comes to everything except boys? With the opposite sex, she's supposed to stay ten years old and uninterested.

Being a man who raised a daughter, you'd probably be tempted to agree with Cecilia on that. But I'd have to remind you that at eighteen, I'd already received a marriage proposal. From you. You smooth-talked me into tying the knot, and I had already dated enough young men to know that you were the one for me.

So, there you have it. Only one day living under our daughter's roof and already I worry about overstepping my bounds. Though, to do whatever's best for Erin, I'll gladly suffer the wrath of both her and her mother. I only wish you were here to help me decide what is the best thing to do. Was this a mistake? My moving in with the two of them? Maybe I'm being selfish, but I need them. And they need me, though they don't know it. They need me, Harry. CiCi lives life in a blur. Because of it, she's missing out on so much, and so is Erin. Which is why it's a good thing I'm here.

But do they want me here? They act as if they do, but I'm not certain that isn't pretense to spare my feelings. Is their love for me sturdy enough to weather so much togetherness?

I realize something now that I didn't last week, or even yesterday. This won't be simple. For them or me. Maybe it goes against nature for parents and their adult children to live in the same house. Maybe Cecilia and I, maybe all mothers and daughters, are only meant to know one another as parent and child, not as grown women with more shared fears and desires than we care to admit. Which brings to mind a certain bread beater incident.

That blasted nasty Jane Binkley and her silly birthday gag gift! I swear, I thought I'd thrown the thing away, but CiCi found it in my things. I'll spare you the embarrassing details. Suffice it to say, I had to think fast to come up with a story. And even then, I didn't fool Cecilia.

Back to the subject at hand. After you left, I thought Parkview Manor was a good solution for me, the answer to CiCi's worries about me living alone and so far from her. I didn't mind moving there, really. Like I've said before, Parkview isn't a nursing home; good heavens, I'm not ready for that. It's simply a community of retirees, but they do have a nursing staff on the premises in case they're needed. Still, it wasn't what I'd hoped.

One day I may have to accept moving back to Parkview Manor or someplace like it. But for now, while I'm still able to care for myself and able to help CiCi with Erin, I couldn't bear to spend another day in the place. Gather that many old men and women together in one building and what do you get? A big ol' bunch of busybodies with too much time on their hands, that's what. Why, just last week, Ellen Miles tried to pry gossip out of me about Jane Binkley. I didn't waste a minute before setting her straight. I told her I don't make a habit of talking about other people's business. "Just because my apartment is next door to Jane's and I'm privy to most of the woman's coming and goings," I said, "doesn't mean I'll tell you or anybody else about the late hours men spend over there, or about all the giggling I often hear on the other side of my wall."

I swear, Harry, you should have seen Ellen's face! Her eyes bulged and she slapped a hand over her mouth like I had offended her, instead of the other way around.

Busybodies aside, Parkview just isn't for me. It doesn't seem natural to see only old, wrinkled faces day by day, to go out into the courtyard and never hear children laughing, to never see or speak to young families playing together or taking bike rides or walks around the neighborhood. A happy, healthy life requires a certain mix of ingredients. Babies and children. Teenagers. Middle-aged people and old folks. Most of those ingredients are missing at Parkview, and what remains is a very stale cake.

The only things I liked about the Village are a few dear friends I met and the reading group, which I formed and CiCi led. She's promised we can go on with it, that we'll keep meeting each week and she'll still read aloud for those of us with eyes too weak.

Speaking of my eyes, Cecilia would probably tell you a different story about my ability to take care of myself. Because my sight's getting worse, she's hired a baby-sitter to stay with me during the day. She won't listen when I tell her that, other than driving and reading and the like, I'm as self-sufficient today as I was five years ago and the five before that. My new glasses help with my vision. My only complaint is that the magnification is so strong my eyeballs look as if they might pop out of their sockets. I'm trying not to be vain, but sometimes I'm glad you can't see me like this.

I'll be thinking of you every moment next Saturday, the anniversary of our last day together. The truth is, I still think of you almost all the time on every day. I try to concentrate only on the good times, but often my mind drifts to the difficult times, too. Oh, how I wish we had had more patience with one another. Why did we spend even one precious moment on pettiness, jealousy or pointless blame? Because of your stubbornness and the resentments I collected like rare coins, we wasted minutes that could've been spent making joyful memories. If only we had it to do over.

That said, I must admit that sometimes I even miss our arguments. I miss your hard head, our standoffs. Without them, there'd have been no making up. And making up was the sweetest thing, wasn't it?

I'm asking Cecilia to drive me to Cleburne and by our old house next Saturday to check on your prize roses. If the weather held, they always lasted at least through mid-November. I hope that's true this year. I missed having you give me the first bloom this season. It was always my favorite gift from you, especially during our tough times. It seemed a promise that everything was all right between us. That you were sorry, or I was forgiven, or you'd given in and life would go on.

Saturday, when we turn the corner onto Bentwood Drive I will see your tender smile in the blooms. And I'll remember.

As always, your yellow rose,
Belle

Chapter 4

Cecilia Dupree
Day Planner
Wednesday, 11/5

1. 9:00 — Hoyt Couple — New patient appt.
2. 1:00 — Mom's Parkview reading group.
3. Call Bert. Remind him he has a daughter.

By nine-thirty-five, I'm wondering if Mr. Roger Hoyt will ever open his twitching mouth and start talking. He sits stiff and straight as a ruler beside his wife of twenty years, hands clutching the chair's arms like he's on a roller coaster that's about to take off. His expression tells me his tie is too tight. Only, he isn't wearing a tie.

"Mr. Hoyt . . . Roger. May I call you Roger?"

"Sure. Why not?"

Cut to the chase, I decide. Ask him point-blank. I lean forward. "Cindy has said that she feels you don't love her anymore. That you're bored with her." I catch his gaze, hold it. "How do you feel? Are you bored with your wife? Have you fallen out of love with her?"

Roger Hoyt reeks of fear, or it might be his aftershave; I'm not sure. He glances at the woman in question and clears his throat. "I still love my wife. It's just, well, I'm not *in* love with her. Not anymore."

Cindy's lower lip quivers.

I flash back to the moment Bert made the same admission to me, and I sympathize with Cindy Hoyt. "Okay, Roger. When did you realize this?"

He clears his throat again. "I can't put my finger on an exact moment. It just sort of happened over time. We stopped having fun together, stopped talking about anything except the kids and the bills. That sort of thing."

"So, you're saying you're more like brother and sister now?"

"Yeah, but we still . . . you know. We're more than brother and sister, but it's not enough." He shifts in the chair. "I want more."

"You've got commitment, the security of family, but no passion?"

He nods.

I turn to Cindy. "What's it like for you to hear all this?"

"It hurts." She blinks tear-bright eyes. "But he's right. We don't have fun anymore. We don't really talk. And our sex life has suffered. But I think we can work things out if we try."

I watch for Roger's reaction. Interesting. Cindy sees it, too, and looks down at her lap.

"Roger, when Cindy just said that, you cringed. Why?"

"I don't know. I, um, I guess I'm not sure if I want this anymore. I —"

Cindy sits straighter; her expression hardens. "That's just what I thought, Roger. Do you think I haven't noticed how much time you've been spending at work?" She turns to me. "I think he's starting something with his secretary."

"I am not!" Roger's face flames.

"Not an affair," Cindy adds quickly, anger replacing the hurt in her voice. "Not yet. But I saw the e-mails, Roger. I saw them. The woman couldn't be more than twenty-five." She crosses her arms and leans back.

A switch flips inside me. I stare at Roger and cross my arms, too. "Would you care to tell me about these e-mails between you and . . . ?"

"*Bitsy,*" Cindy hisses. Our eyes meet then

narrow in unison. In unity.

"So, Roger, you and Bootsy have been flirting with infidelity through e-mails, is that —"

"*Betsy.* Her name is Betsy. I — we're —" Roger scoots to the edge of the chair. Glares at Cindy. At me. "We're not . . . I . . ." He stands. "Fuck this! Fuck it! I won't sit here while a complete stranger and my wife gang up me."

Oh, no! No! Damn it! What's wrong with me? What am I doing? I reach my hand toward him. "Calm down, Mr. Hoyt. No one's ganging up on you."

"Oh, really?" He paces and tugs at his collar, at the tie that isn't there. "What would you call it then?"

"I didn't mean to upset you, I was simply asking a question. Perhaps I should rephrase."

"Perhaps you should." He flops down in the chair.

"It seems that the two of you are at a point of decision, would you agree?"

Roger's Adam's apple bobs. He and Cindy look at one another. The two of them nod.

I tap my index finger against my thigh and study the immature jerk, trying to see deeper. Will he choose some temporary, ego-boosting fun with little Miss Bootsy who, judging from the looks of Roger, is probably only after his money? Or will he decide to make an effort to revive what he once had with the mother of his children, this intelligent, attractive woman he chose to marry? This woman who has washed his dirty socks and underwear, stuck with him through the early, sparse-money years after he started his business, believed in him when he didn't believe in himself.

Realizing my thoughts pertain to my own marriage, not necessarily the Hoyts', I take a deep breath. This is about them, not me. "Both of you need to spend some time thinking about what you really want, what's really important to you." I zero in on Roger. "Do you want to preserve your commitment or move on to something else? Think hard about that. This affects not only your life, but also Cindy's. And your children's lives, too. It's not a decision to be made lightly."

I turn. "And you, Cindy." Her efforts to control her emotions trigger my own. My throat knots up; I tell myself to breathe. "If Roger stays, are you willing to work on the marriage? Can you put your suspicions and bitterness away and trust him again? And if he chooses to leave, what will you do? Your life will change dramatically. How will you deal with that? It's something to ask your-self."

We end the session. And while Roger doesn't promise to come back next week, he does say he'll consider it.

In the meantime, I have a lot to think about, too. It's clear I still have Bert issues. I thought I'd worked through the worst of them, buried the pain, cynicism and anger in a deep, dark grave. But judging from what just happened, they're all still alive. And thriving.

The paperback novel lies open in my lap. *A Room For Eleanor.* The current literary rage. Four hundred pages of angst and introspection.

Perching my funky new reading glasses on the bridge of my nose, I glance down at the page. The final chapter, thank God. If I have to spend one more week reading about the depressed and depressing Eleanor, I'll need a room, too. At the psychiatric pavilion.

I look up for a moment, scan the group of four women, all wearing glasses of some kind or another, and one man whose vision must be better than mine, since he's lens-free. Ten folding chairs sit empty behind them. We started the club a year ago with fifteen members. Fourteen women and Oliver something-or-other, the sharp-eyed old charmer who sits at the end of the first row beside my mother. The club has dwindled to these five people; I don't know why.

Lifting the novel, I begin to read aloud from chapter twenty-three.

"Eleanor locked the bathroom door, turned to the mirror then lifted the tweezers to her right eye. 'No more,' she whispered, plucking one lash then another and another, numb to the pain. 'No more . . .' "

As I read, my mind drifts to my session with the Hoyts this morning. I almost crossed the line, let my personal feelings affect my professional objectivity. I transferred my anger at Bert to Roger Hoyt. That scares me. I have no business counseling couples if I can't keep my own emotions out of the equation. I should've made every effort to connect with the man, prove myself to him, gain his trust, not put him on the defensive.

"She turned on the faucet and water spilled out, over her hand, into the tub, warm, soothing water to wash away the pain. And Eleanor whispered, 'No more . . .' "

It's just that, when I saw the Hoyts sitting across from me, middle-aged, miserable, together yet miles apart, I felt I was looking at a photo of Bert and myself from a year ago. Then Roger Hoyt finally started to talk, and I saw my own feelings reflected in his wife's eyes. Humiliation. Self-doubt. Fear. For a second . . . okay, maybe more like five minutes, I envisioned the two of us tackling the balding Don Juan, strapping him to the sofa, face-up, castrating him with a dull pair of fingernail scissors.

Not good. Not good at all.

"The water surrounded Eleanor; her legs, her body, her face, filling her with peace, with truth. All her life, she had tried to avoid what she knew in her heart. 'No more,' she thought now. 'No more.' "

I yawn. Okay, so maybe I do have an idea why the reading group has dwindled.

Halfway through the second scene, a loud snuffle brings my head up.

Mary Fran Hawkins and Frances Green, otherwise known as "The Frans" since they share not only similar names, but also an apartment, snore in rhythm, their chins on their chests. Mary Fran's book is on the floor. Frances still holds hers open, though it's migrating toward her knees.

I guessed the first second I met them that The Frans are lesbians, but Mother refuses to discuss it. According to her, it's an inappropriate assumption on my part and none of our business one way or another. But whether she'll admit it or not, I'm sure she knows it's true. Like she's always telling me, her eyesight's bad, but she's not blind.

Between The Frans and my mother, Doris Quinn files her nails and hums quietly to herself. Not a single silver hair on her head is out of place. She's a tiny, twittery, totally feminine woman. Always upbeat. Always ready to bat an eye at any man who happens to glance at her. Eager to sympathize with their hard luck stories. I can imagine Doris being the "other" woman in her younger days. The equivalent of Roger Hoyt's Bitsy or one of Bert's baby-faced . . .

There I go, doing it again. Transferring my anger at Bert to someone else. Comparing a sweet, romantic woman of eighty who loves people and life to one of Bert's bimbos.

At the end of the row of book lovers in front of me, jolly Oliver something-or-other, his book face-down in his lap, grins as he whispers something to Mother. She blushes, but pretends to ignore him, her gaze fixed on her copy of *A Room For Eleanor*, which she holds in both hands upside down.

"Eleanor opened her eyes, gazed up through the rippling water. Life shimmered above her, painful, chaotic, unpredictable life. She —"

"The End," I say five paragraphs before the final line. I slap the book closed. The noise snaps The Frans to attention.

"So, what did you think?"

Doris stops filing her nails and sighs. "Remarkable. A masterpiece." She presses a palm to her chest. "The ending . . ." She sighs. "It makes a person think, doesn't it? There was so much wisdom in it, so much hope, so much —"

"Bullshit," Mary Fran mutters, rubbing sleep from her eyes and eliciting a snicker from Frances.

Doris flinches. "I beg your pardon?"

"I thought it was an interesting selection, Cecilia," Mother cuts in before Mary Fran can elaborate. "Another fine choice on your part. Very thought-provoking, as Doris said."

Oliver smirks at her. "Come on now,

Belle. It was a real stinker, and you know it."

Doris points her fingernail file straight up. "Perhaps one person's odor is another's perfume."

The Frans snort.

"Thanks for the show of support, Mother. You, too, Doris. But I have to agree with the others." I tap a finger against the book's cover. "I don't get it. The book's been at the top of the bestseller lists for over a month."

Oliver winks at me. "There's no accountin' for taste, CiCi." He scans the room. "No offense, but we're gonna have to liven things up around here or pretty soon you'll be reading to a bunch of empty chairs."

I'm surprised by the look of distress that passes across Mother's face at his comment. Wondering about it, I reach down for my briefcase then place it in my lap. I pop the latches, open the lid, pull another *Oprah*-esque book from inside. "I'd planned this for our next selection." I hold the book up so the group can see the bland cover.

Everyone groans. Even Doris and my mother.

"Okay. I'm open for suggestions."

As they debate whether the next title should be a mystery, a family saga or an action adventure, I return both books to my briefcase. That's when *Penelope's Passion* catches my eye. The story has become my new addiction; I can't get enough of it. Or, to be honest, I can't get enough of the captain. I've been trying to squeeze in a paragraph or two between patients whenever possible. I tell myself it's a healthy diversion from reality. What's the harm in a little fun?

Well, I'll tell you.

Yesterday I met with two of my regulars, a sixty-year-old shoe salesman and his wife of thirty-five years. They blame his mother's penchant for going barefoot and wearing red toenail polish when he was a boy for his obsession with women's footwear and feet. Toes specifically. He's partial to sucking them and struggles to restrain the urge at work. While they talked, I caught myself thinking about a scene in *Penelope's Passion* where the captain and Penelope make love for the first time. In my daydream, though, I was Penelope.

Pathetic, I know. My mind should be on my patient's abnormal preoccupation with Jimmy Choo shoes, not on being seduced by some make-believe macho man. Still, the toe-sucker left my office happy, so I suppose it didn't hurt that my mind wandered a bit while he talked.

Studying the wrinkled faces before me, I remember Mother's bread beater, which

I've nicknamed "BOB," as in battery-oper-ated-boyfriend. Maybe she isn't the only one here, me included, who misses inti-macy. These senior citizens would probably appreciate a healthy diversion, too. The next best thing to sex I've found. Some relatively harmless fun. I'm betting even The Frans' relationship could use a shot in the arm.

"Ladies," I say in a raised voice to be heard over the chatter. I stand, put my open briefcase on the stool and clap my hands. "Ladies! You, too, Oliver."

The talking stops. They all look up at me.

"What do you think about this?" I pick up Erin's book, turn it over, read the blurb on back. . . .

"When Lady Penelope Waterford
     stowed away on *The Voyager*
She wanted only to escape an
     arranged marriage
To be carried away in the arms of a
     powerful ship
Toward a fresh start in a new,
     untamed land.

When Captain Damian Stonewall set
     sail
He wanted only to deliver his cargo on
     time,

66

To see his crew safely to the opposite
    shore
And collect the money owed him.

The captain never suspected he
    harbored a passenger
Or that one glimpse of her creamy skin,
    flaming hair
And flashing blue eyes would force him
    to question
His priorities and tempt him to break
    his own rules.

The lady never expected she might be
    forced to marry
The hot-tempered captain who found
    her hiding, soaked
And exhausted, below deck. Or that his
    touch would
Make her tremble with lust as well as
    with anger.

But as land disappears from sight
And the wind rages around them
Penelope and the captain discover their
    biggest
Surprise of all:

A passion more vast and powerful than
    the sea. . . ."

I lower the book to my lap and look up.

Doris whispers, "Oh, my."

The Frans snort, then smile at each other.

Oliver chuckles. "Now you're talkin'."

Mother looks from my briefcase, to the book, to me. She lifts an eyebrow.

Shrugging, I smirk at her. "Ladies and gentleman, I believe we just found our next selection." I turn the book around to show the group the sexy cover. "I give you, *Penelope's Passion*."

A hush falls over the room, but is broken seconds later by the sound of an ear-piercing alarm.

I hope it isn't someone's pacemaker going off.

Chapter 5

My kitchen smells like chicken and dumplings tonight. I think Mother's trying to fatten up Erin, but I'm sure it'll be me who ends up waddling, not my teenaged daughter. She can exist on a diet of French fries without gaining a pound.

We've fallen into a routine. One instigated by Mother. She cooks. We eat as a family at the table. Erin and I clean up. I'm amazed it's lasted an entire five nights; I don't know how she managed to recruit Erin in the first place, much less keep her coming back. But, though I enjoy the family time, I'm also a tiny bit jealous that my mother pulled off what I couldn't. Since this school year began, my offers of a home-cooked meal have been turned down. Erin's either had other plans for dinner or says she'd rather get takeout. I realize I'm not Julia Child or even my mother when it comes to the kitchen. But I whip up a decent omelet, and my spaghetti's not bad. I add spices to the Ragu.

"Did you talk to your dad today?" I scrape chicken into the disposal, then hand the plate to Erin.

"Yeah. He called right after school."

Right after I called and gave him an earful. If that's what it takes for Erin to receive some attention from her father, so be it. I'll bug that man from now until he drops dead.

Erin places the plate into the dishwasher. "Did someone straighten up my room?"

I laugh. "If so, they didn't do a very good job."

"I'm missing a book."

"*Penelope's Passion*?"

A blush stains Erin's cheeks as she reaches for another plate. "Yeah."

"I borrowed it and forgot to put it back. Sorry. When we finish up here I'll get it for you. I'm planning to read it at Nana's group so I'll be buying my own copy and copies for all the members."

Pausing with the plate in her hand, Erin's eyes widen. *"Mo-ther!"*

"What?"

"You're joking, right?"

"No. Why?"

"You *can't* read that to people their age."

I wet a dishcloth, turn off the faucet and wipe down the counter. "Why not?"

"There's *stuff* in it."

70

"You think your generation invented *stuff?*"

Erin lowers the plate she's holding. "But, they're *old.*"

Mother enters the kitchen, headed for the breakfast nook and the hutch where she keeps her knitting basket. "Listen here, smarty-pants," she says to Erin in a teasing voice. "We old people could teach you youngsters a thing or two about romance. There's a lot to be said for wooing."

"Wooing?" Erin scowls.

"That's right, wooing." Mother tucks the basket under her arm and smiles. "Candy and flowers. A walk in the moonlight. Stolen kisses on a front porch swing."

I want to sigh. It sounds so old-fashioned. And wonderful. In my dating days, an evening was considered romantic if the guy paid for the movie without trying to cop a feel afterward. How did my generation miss the boat? The one with champagne, candlelight and a string quartet?

"When I was young," Mother continues, "the boys pursued the girls, not vice versa. At least not in such an obvious way like I see today. We didn't call them on the phone or chase after them. A young man came to a girl's house and met her family before any dating went on." She pauses to give us The

Look. "And I might add that he came to the front door."

Erin tucks her lower lip between her teeth, and for a second, I sense a silent message passing between my mother and my daughter. But then a memory hits me full force, and I realize the message is for me, not Erin.

"Oh, I get it." I lean against the counter and cross my arms. "You're taking up where Dad left off, is that it? You're not ever going to let me forget about that time when I was seventeen and he caught Dave Baldwin outside my bedroom window."

"According to your father, the boy reeked of beer." Mother chuckles. "Harry was fit to be tied."

"You can say that again." Shaking my head, I look sideways at Erin. My laugh sounds nervous even to me; I hope she doesn't notice. "And after your grandpop put the fear of God into poor Dave, he tore into me like I was the one who'd been drinking beer. Which, by the way, Dave hadn't been drinking, either." *It was strawberry wine.* "I never convinced your granddad of that, though."

Mother joins us at the sink. "He thought —"

"I know, I know, he thought I was going

out the window." I glance at my daughter again. She's reading the instructions on the dishwashing detergent, which strikes me as odd, but lately everything she does strikes me as odd, so I blow it off. "Just so you know, Erin, I wasn't about to sneak out." *Not that night, anyway.* "Dave and I were just talking. But your granddad never believed that, either. And for the rest of his life, he never tired of teasing me about it."

"Suzanna and I are going back to the mall to look for a concert dress tonight," Erin says, as if she hasn't heard a word of our story.

"What about *See Dick Run?*" Erin and I always watch the popular reality-TV program together on Wednesday nights. Without fail. The show is completely ridiculous. Twenty steroid-enhanced jocks compete in physical challenges to win a week in paradise with a life-sized, walking, talking, breathing blow-up doll. At least, *I'm* convinced her head is full of air. But Erin loves the show, so I pretend I do, too. It's one of the few routines we still share. And, okay, I'll come clean; I'm caught up in it, too. It's silly fun.

"Would you tape it for me?" Erin talks over her shoulder as she hurries out of the kitchen. "I don't have time to watch tonight."

"Sure." I try to sound unaffected. "Don't forget it's a school night. Be home by nine."

"Nine-thirty," she calls from the entry hall. "The mall doesn't even close until nine."

"You know the rules."

"Jeez!" The front door squeaks open; I hear the rustle of her jacket as she slips it on. *"Whatever."*

The door slams, and I feel the distance growing between us in more than just a physical way.

At the sink, I rinse the dishcloth, avoiding my mother's gaze.

"About that incident with Dave at the window," she says.

"Good grief, are we back to that?" I wring out the cloth, then gather a stack of mail from the counter and shuffle through it. "It happened twenty-some-odd years ago. Could we just forget it?"

"Maybe you *shouldn't* forget such things. What's that you always say? What goes around comes around?"

"If you're implying what I think you are, Mother, don't worry about it. Erin's a hundred times smarter and more levelheaded than I was at seventeen. She isn't the least bit boy crazy."

Hoping to escape a lecture, I take the mail

and head for the backyard.

The patio light provides enough of a glow that I'm able to read.

Max looks up from his bowl and blinks at me, then returns his attention to his food.

I settle into a wicker chair, flip through the mail again, then place all but one piece on the patio table. The evening is cool, but not uncomfortable. It's already dark out, but I don't care; I'm numb and blind to everything except the texture of the expensive envelope beneath my fingertips and the return address in the upper left corner. *Gosset, Dusseldorf and Klein.*

Shooing away a fly, I turn the envelope over to open it, but can't bring myself to lift the flap. "This is it, Max," I say, eliciting a tiny moan from him. He stops munching and trots over. "The end of life as I knew it. No more Bert. Hurray!" My throat tightens. Erin might as well be gone, too. From now on, it'll just be Mother and me.

It won't be so bad, I tell myself. Who needs men anyway? Who can trust 'em? I'll learn to knit. That's something Mother and I can do together. Night after night. In front of the television. *Wheel of Fortune.* Mother will cook delicious meals for me. What better way to fill the emptiness than with smothered steak and buttermilk biscuits? Blackberry cobbler? She might even make my favorite chocolate éclairs. I'll gain so much weight that I have to buy my clothing at the tent and awning store. Which won't be an issue anymore since I won't be trying to impress a man. Think how comfy I'll be. How content. Fat and happy.

And alone. With Mother.

Max yelps. I look down at him. He tilts his head to one side. His brown eyes appear sympathetic.

"I'm sorry Max." I sniff. "It won't be just Mother and me. I'll have you, too. Since Dad's gone, you're the only male in my life worth bothering with, anyway. At least you don't leave dirty underwear on the bedroom floor."

His butt wiggles, like he's trying to wag his nubby tail.

"Your ass is cute, too. And you never expect me to kiss it."

He nuzzles his cold nose against my hand. "In fact, you're the best-looking guy I've seen in a long time." As I size him up, I have to admit, he is. His coat is smooth and shiny, his body looks strong, his eyes are sad, but clear. He comes from a long line of prize-winning English bulldogs, and it shows.

"I think you've got potential, Max," I say,

perking up a bit. "A good-looking stud like you? I bet if your services were for sale, every bulldog hussy this side of the Mississippi would be panting at your doghouse door. Someone in this family besides Bert might as well get some action." At least I'd get paid for Maxwell's philandering.

Max prisses over to the grass.

"Another point in your favor. You don't leave the toilet seat up when you pee."

He hunkers down.

"Really though, Max." I swat at a fly. "You might want to start lifting your leg. I don't know what the hussies would think of a squatting stud."

When Max finishes his business and comes back over, I scratch between his ears. "I might even enter you in one of those stuffy shows. I bet you'd take home the blue ribbon."

With one final scratch to Max's head, I return my focus to the envelope. I open it, pull the paperwork out, unfold it, then set it aside, facedown. Why not see what else came in the mail and put off the inevitable? I make my way through bills, flyers, an invitation to a party to celebrate an associate's twenty-fifth wedding anniversary. Good for her. Thanks for rubbing it in. I reach for an envelope from Erin's school. The letter inside is for parents of seniors. A meeting's planned next week to discuss graduation plans; announcements, caps and gowns, the class party. Already.

A wave of sadness sweeps over me.

Erin. She's not a little girl anymore. But she's not as grown up as she thinks she is, either. She's pulling away from me, but still requires my guidance. More than ever. But I need a different approach now that she's older.

With a sigh, I return to the legal papers. Can't put them off forever. Maybe I've been looking at this divorce all wrong. Maybe it's a new beginning rather than an ending. A chance to discover new interests. To rediscover old ones. To do something for *me,* for a change. I should redefine my relationship with Erin, focus more on my career, spend more time with Mother. Can't all that be enough?

When I flip to the last page, Bert's signature jumps out at me. Then mine. I suck in a breath of cool air.

My tears taste salty and bittersweet as I stare at the document that ends my old life and launches a new one.

New and improved.

Chapter 6

To: Suz@friendmail.com
From: Erin@friendmail.com
Date: 11/6 Thursday
Subject: Judd

Hang up your phone! I've been trying to call you! I'm hyperventilating! He's coming over again! Right now! If you get this message, call me on my cell at midnight in case I need an escape. ~ Erin

Stuffing my phone into my jean pocket, I hurry to the closet and look inside. What was I after? I scan the shoes on the floor, the clothes on hangers. My mind whirls, my heartbeat's skipping. I am seriously having a panic attack.

I tug off my girly pajamas, the ones Nana gave me for Christmas last year, and wiggle into my newest pair of hip-hugger jeans, the skintight T-shirt I bought yesterday, and a pair of pink rubber flip-flop thongs.

After hurrying into my bathroom, I get

started on my face. Blush on my cheeks. A little red lipstick, then a whole lot more. I blot my lips on a square of toilet tissue then apply mascara. Several coats. My hand shakes so much that the wand bumps my cheek, smearing black across it. "Not now!" I snarl, as I reach for the toilet paper roll again and knock over a perfume bottle. It clatters as it falls, making my heart thump all the harder. The last thing I need is to wake up Mom or Nana.

When my cheek is finally clean, I bend over at the waist and ruffle my hair, then straighten again and spray it. I step back and take another long look at myself in the mirror. Something's not right . . . something . . . I glance down at my chest. The jellyfish!

I return to the closet and put on a bra, then find the silicone inserts I borrowed from Suz's sister. When they're in place, I check my reflection again.

A girl I don't recognize stares back at me. A girl with wild hair, too much makeup and a big set of *ta-tas,* as Suz always calls them. A phony. A fake. A Britney Spears clone with brown hair instead of blond. Exactly the kind of girl I can't stand. So why am I doing this?

I cross my arms, turn away from my reflection. Because I'm sick of being boring, straight-laced Erin. Because I'm tired of sitting home with Mom while everyone else is out having fun. Because Judd wouldn't give the real me a second look.

Judd. Judd Henderson.

I met him Saturday night at The Beat. He's twenty, about to be twenty-one, a junior at North Texas. He thinks I'm also twenty, and that I'm a junior at S.M.U. At the club, he didn't look twice at Suz, though she stood right beside me. He walked straight over and asked me to dance.

We danced all night. Then, when his ride was leaving and he had to go, he kissed me. Nothing major, just brushed his mouth against mine and said he'd call.

He did. Night before last at ten. I almost died. He wanted to come over so I had to come up with an excuse really fast. I said I was sick. Strep throat.

He said he was sorry and promised not to kiss me. Not on the lips, anyway.

Just the thought of him kissing me again anywhere, especially with Mom and Nana close by, almost gave me explosive diarrhea, so I said that, according to the doctor, the strep throat was highly contagious and he shouldn't even come in the house.

So what did he do? He came to my window.

Like, how romantic is that? *Totally* romantic, if you ask me, no matter what Nana says. I'm pretty sure she hinted about Judd yesterday in front of Mom. She must've seen him at my window. At least she didn't come right out and say it. Which I can hardly believe.

Anyway, for maybe the best forty-five minutes of my life, Judd smoked cigarettes and talked to me in a low voice through the window screen. He told me he likes how I act all quiet and shy, but my look says something different. I didn't tell him that my "look" is the act, and that quiet and shy is the real me.

Before he left, Judd laughed and said hanging outside my bedroom window made him feel like he was back in high school. I said it did me, too. Then I remembered that I *am* in high school, and I felt even phonier than I do now.

Judd promised to call again to check on me and, a half hour ago, he did. Since I can't pretend to be sick forever, and he'd probably think it weird that a twenty-year-old woman would have to sneak out of the house to meet a guy, I told him Mom caught my strep throat and that the house is still pretty much off-limits. So, I'm meeting him out front at eleven-thirty.

Except for the strip of light beneath Mom's bedroom door, the hallway outside my room is quiet and dark. I decide it might be safer to go out my window again instead of risking her hearing the front door open and close. That way, I won't have to worry about the security alarm, either. I duck back into my room and lock myself in. What I'm really doing, though, is locking Mom and Nana out.

Ten minutes later I'm beside Judd inside his pickup truck, which is parked at the curb in front of my house with the engine and headlights off.

Judd turns down the music. "You sure you don't want to go somewhere?"

I shake my head. "I still have homework to do. I can't stay out long."

He pulls a pack of cigarettes off the dash and offers me one.

"No, thanks." I point at my neck. "The strep. I mean, I'm well and everything, but I don't want to push it yet."

"Oh, yeah. I forgot. I won't smoke, either, I guess." He tosses the pack back where he found it. "Sorry I didn't call yesterday. School and work have been kicking my ass."

"Where'd you say you work?"

"At the convenience store on campus." Judd reaches across the seat, tucks my hair behind my ear. "Just part-time. Until I graduate."

"Oh." I nibble my lower lip. *Oh? Oh?* Why can't I think of anything else to say? It's like my mind erased the second he touched me. "I don't work."

"Maybe you should." He smiles. "Then you could rent a place with some friends and we wouldn't have to sit out in front of your mom's like a couple of teenagers." He looks out the window at the house then shifts back to me, tracing the curve of my ear with a fingertip. "Let's go for a ride. I passed by a park on the way here."

My heart does a backflip. "I can't. Really."

I have the strangest feeling. Like there's this hum of energy between us, a current of electricity stretching from Judd to me, connecting us. Being this close to him makes me excited and freaked at the same time, though I don't know what I'm freaked about. It's not like we weren't even closer on the dance floor Saturday night. But this feels different. Tonight, we're alone.

Judd takes my hand and jerks his head, nodding me over. "Come here."

I scoot across the seat, closer to him. He puts his arm around me, and I tilt my head back and gaze up at him. No guy has ever looked at me the way he is, like he's seeing me inside out and naked and memorizing every detail. I could fall right into his dark, narrowed eyes, but something tells me I'd never find my way out again. I don't want to turn away, but I'm afraid not to, afraid I'll lose myself, as weird as that sounds. So I move my focus to his lips. They're not too thin, not too full, nicely shaped, parted a little. Beneath the lower one, there's a soft shadow of beard stubble.

When I got into the car, I was sort of cold, but I'm not cold now; that's not why I shiver. His fingers stroke my arm, right beneath my shoulder, scattering goose bumps across my skin and making the muscles in my stomach pull tight.

"Erin," he says, and then his mouth is on mine, soft and firm at the same time, warm, drawing me in, tasting of cinnamon gum and menthol as our breaths mix. It's not like I've never been kissed before; I have. But never like this, like I've stepped onto a roller coaster and there's no stopping it, no turning back. My control is whisked away on a rush of air while another part of me comes alive. The world outside blurs until the only things vivid are Judd and me; the texture of his hair between my fingers, the pull of his cinnamon lips and musky male scent, a soft scrape of beard against my cheek.

Quiet, insistent sounds come from deep in his throat. He shifts our positions so that I slide down some, my head pressed into the seat back, and he is centered between the dash and me. I feel surrounded, enclosed, cocooned by his hard body, his arms. His warm, dry hand cups my chin then skims my face, across my collarbone, my shoulder, down the side of my breast. Before I realize what he has in mind, his fingers inch beneath my T-shirt and he's touching my stomach, making my body hum and vibrate . . . *vibrate.* . . .

I jerk back, away from Judd, into reality. I reach for my buzzing jean pocket. Talk about good timing.

Judd frowns and leans back. "What's that?"

"My phone. I . . . um . . . turned off the ringer." My hands shake as I pull it from my pocket and push the talk button. "Hello?"

"Erin?" *Suz. Thank you, thank you, thank you.* I cringe when I think what might've happened if she hadn't called.

I understand now what it means to be swept away, like they always say in the romance novels I've started reading. When Judd kissed me, I felt I could only hold on tight and hope to land safely, like he pushed all the buttons, controlled the speed, decided if my heart beat faster or slower. While I was caught up in his taste and scent, in the magic his hands made, losing my self-control felt like a rush. But now that I'm able to think again, it scares me, too.

I slide closer to the door. "Oh, hi Mom. What's wrong?"

"Are you okay? You sound — Ohmigod! He's with you right now, isn't he? Were you —"

"No, that's okay." I glance at Judd. He stares at me and rakes a hand through his hair. "I'll be right in."

"Call me back," Suz whispers.

"I will. It'll just be a minute." I break the connection.

Judd lifts his hand to the back of my neck. "What's up?" Grinning, he glances at his lap. "Besides the obvious, I mean."

I can't help myself; I look down, too, then up again. Quick. I'm glad it's dark in the car so Judd can't see my face, which I'm sure is bright red. Or maybe he can. He laughs quietly, and I wonder if I'll ever breathe right again, if my heartbeat will ever slow down. "It's my mom. She . . . um . . . she's running a fever. She needs me to bring her some medicine."

Each new lie is easier than the one before. It's as if I've had this hidden talent for deception all my life, but didn't figure out how to use it until this year. I'm not sure how I feel about that, proud that I have something in common with Dad, or ashamed.

"Man, your mom must really be sick if she can't even get her own medicine."

"She is."

He moves closer, leans over me, presses me into the back of the seat again, his chest against mine, crushing the jellyfish his fingers crept toward only moments ago. I'm dizzy with dread at the thought of Judd's reaction if he finds out the truth. I'll die from humiliation.

"Come back out," Judd whispers. His mouth brushes across my lips, soft as butterfly wings, making me even dizzier, confused. How can you crave something and dread it, too?

"I need to study."

"Please." His tongue feels warm and wet against my lips, soft and irresistible.

I force myself to reach for the door handle. "Not tonight."

He grasps my arm. "Tomorrow night, then. I'll pick you up."

"No!" I catch my breath as his brows pull together. "I mean, I'll meet you. At The

Beat. I'll go with Suzanna."

Judd's fingers press into my flesh, not enough to hurt, but enough to get my attention. "I want you to go with me."

I turn to the window, look out at the house. Maybe it's time I stood up to Mom for once. Show her I'm not her baby, anymore. What can she say? It's not like I've never been on a date; I have. Before we moved here. School dances. Once with two other couples to a movie. She and Judd will meet, then we'll leave before either one of them can say too much. Before she figures out how old he is, or he figures out how young I am.

I turn to Judd. "Okay. Be here at seven. I warn you, though, my mother still thinks I'm seventeen."

He grins and gives me another kiss before I open the door. "See you tomorrow night."

"I'll be ready."

My knees shake as I step from the car and, when I stand, I feel a weight drop from my chest. Seriously. I press my forearm across my waist just in time to catch the silicone insert before it slips free of my shirt and falls to the ground.

"Suz?"
"Tell me everything!"

89

I kick off my pink flip-flops. "We made out in his car in front of the house."

"Shut up!"

"I'm serious." Pulling the phone from my ear for a second, I tug my T-shirt over my head. "I don't know what I was thinking. Everything got completely crazy. I mean, he had his hand under my shirt and I was wearing Katie's stupid fake boobs and —"

"Ohmigod! What did he say?"

I toss the silicone blobs onto the bed. "Thanks to your phone call, he didn't make it far enough north to discover that what he thinks are the Grand Tetons are really the Great Plains."

Suz giggles. "What do you mean, thanks to my call? Fake boobs or not, you would've stopped him." When I stay quiet for a few seconds, she says, "You would've stopped him. Right, Erin? You hardly know the guy."

I puff out my cheeks, let the air seep slowly from between my lips. "I don't know, Suz. I mean, everything was happening so fast, and I wasn't thinking about anything but . . ."

Dropping to the edge of the bed, I close my eyes and clutch the phone tighter. "Oh, God. What am I going to do? I said I'd go out with him tomorrow night. He thinks I'm something I'm not. *Someone* I'm not. And when I'm with him, I am. I don't even know myself. I wish I'd never let you talk me into dressing up like some hoochie and going to The Beat."

"He's not picking you up at the house, is he?"

"That's the plan. I'm taking your advice and standing up to Mom." I imagine Mom's expression when she sees Judd, and my stomach clenches. He looks his age. I'll have to get him in and out of here fast.

"She might surprise you. Your mom seems pretty cool and laid-back about most things."

"She is. Except when it comes to me. Since she and Dad split, her friends have been meeting over here about once a month for dinner. You should hear what they laugh about when they think I'm not listening. Sex . . . men. You wouldn't believe some of the jokes they tell after a couple of pitchers of margaritas."

Suz laughs. "Maybe you should get her drunk before Judd shows up."

"That's not a bad idea."

"It'll be okay, Erin. Just stay firm with your mom and keep your head on straight with Judd."

"Easy for you to say. You haven't kissed him."

"Wow." Suz sighs. "That good, huh?"

"Better." I sigh, too. "Maybe I should just tell him I want to slow down. That I just want to have some fun and not get so serious."

"Erin . . . I forget how little you know about guys. They don't see things like we do. I promise you that in Judd's mind y'all *were* just having some fun."

I hear a *click click click* at her end of the line, like her fingernail taps against the phone. "If you're really worried about what might happen," she continues, "then maybe you should just end it now. Call Judd and tell him you can't go. From what I saw of him the other night, I *figured* he might be a player. I just didn't want to say anything until I was sure since I could tell you liked him so much."

"But I don't want to end it." I fall back onto the pillows. "That's what's so crazy. I mean, I'm afraid of what's happening, but I like it, too."

For a few seconds, all I hear is Suzanna's breathing, then, "Tell me when and where you're going tomorrow night. I'll show up and watch out for you. You know," her voice changes to a teasing tone, "in case I have to step in and slap some sense into you."

I sit up. "Would you really show up? I'd

feel so much better if you were there."

"Are you kidding? You know me. I live to snoop in other people's business."

Chapter 7

At seven the next night, I'm watching out my window when Judd pulls up. I throw on my jean jacket to hide my inflated chest then wobble on my spiked heels toward the entry hall.

In the den, Nana sits on the sofa with Mom, teaching her how to knit. "Is he here?" My grandmother sounds more excited than me. Which is no big surprise, since I'm mostly terrified.

"Yeah." I don't stop to look at them. "Stay there. I'll get the door."

From the corner of my eye, I see Mom stand and start toward me.

Nana squeals like a twelve-year-old girl at a slumber party. "I can't wait to meet him."

"I can't, either," Mom says from behind me.

The bell rings. I reach for the doorknob.

"I can't . . . *Wait!*"

The change in Mom's voice stops me.

"Erin Dupree, don't you dare open that door. Turn around. What are you wearing?"

I look at her over my shoulder. "*Mom,* don't do this to me. Not in front of Judd."

Her expression looks the same as the day Dad moved out. My heart twists. I don't want to be anything like him, but maybe it's in my genes to hurt the people who love me, to lie and deceive. Did Dad feel trapped by her expectations like I do? Is that why he left?

"Where did you get those boots?"

I glance down at the red leather.

"Your hair . . . your face . . . you look —"

"My age, for once, instead of like a little girl."

She makes a strangled sound. "Not unless you're a teenaged hooker."

I turn my back to her and throw open the door. "Oh, hi, Judd!" His grin falls and his eyes widen when I grab his arm and pull him inside. "Meet my mom."

"Hello." He nods at her then gives me a sideward glance when she doesn't answer.

"And there's my grandma." I point. "See? Peeking around the corner?"

Nana steps out. "Hello, Judd. I'm Belle Lamont, Erin's grandmother." She smiles. "It's so nice to meet you."

Judd clears his throat. "You, too, Mrs. Lamont."

Nana adjusts her glasses. "So you're a

classmate of Erin's?"

"No, I go to —"

"We met through Suzanna." I nudge Judd toward the open door. "Don't wait up for me!"

Mom snaps out of her zombielike state. "Just a minute."

I sigh. I guess her developing a sudden case of laryngitis was too much to hope for. "What?"

"We need to talk." Her eyes narrow to slits. "Now."

My insides quiver like Jell-O, but there's no way I'm backing down. I narrow my eyes, too, and stare right back at her. "Wait for me in the car, Judd, I'll be right out."

"Sure." He glances from Mom to Nana and says, "Nice to meet you."

I close the door behind him.

"You're not going out looking like that." Mom's voice rumbles, like she's about to erupt. "You're not going out period. Not with him. He smells like an ashtray. He must be twenty years old."

I cross my arms. "Almost twenty-one. And I *am* going out."

Mom stares at me like I'm a stranger. One she doesn't trust. But behind her disapproval, I see more. Fear and confusion. For once, my smart mom the therapist, the woman with all the answers, doesn't know what to do.

For a second, I feel myself waver. We've always been close, *too* close, maybe. She's always been so proud of me, but there's no way I can ever live up to her dreams. I've made myself crazy trying, and what did it get me? Nothing but a bunch of perfect grades that don't mean much to anyone but her.

Well, no more. I'm finally doing something just for me. I open the door again. "See ya."

She grabs my arm. "Erin . . . you are not leaving this house."

I jerk away. "Watch me."

"Now, Cecilia . . . Erin . . ." Nana steps between us. "Arguing won't accomplish anything. You two talk this over rationally like the grown women you are."

"Erin is not a grown woman, Mother. She's —"

"Almost eighteen," Nana interrupts. "The age I was when your father and I became engaged."

Mom jabs a finger at Nana. "Don't you dare take her side!"

"I'm not taking anyone's side, Sugar." Nana blinks worried eyes at Mom, then smiles at me, but looks all nervous and twitchy, like it's up to her to smooth things over and she's not sure she can. "Erin, why don't you run and wash your face and change into something more appropriate. I'll go tell Judd you'll be a while."

I shake my head. "Sorry, Nana." Then I close the door and walk toward Judd's idling car as fast as my spiked-heel boots will carry me.

The second I slip in beside him, my cell phone rings. I pull it from my purse, look at the display, see that the call's from our home number. Mom or Nana. I turn off the sound.

Judd pulls away from the curb. "What was that all about?" He offers me a cigarette.

Music blares from the stereo speakers. I shake my head "no" and stare out the window. "My mom." I huff a laugh. "She's certifiable."

"She really does act like you're still in high school."

"More like middle school."

The scent of burning tobacco drifts to me, followed by a swirl of smoke. Trying not to cough, I look across at Judd. Now's the first time I've seen him when it's not pitch dark. The cigarette's propped in one corner of his mouth. A tiny white scar slices his tan forehead, right above his right brow.

His eyes look a little sleepy. Steering the car with one broad hand, he taps the wheel with the other. He looks sort of dangerous, like everything forbidden but tempting wrapped up in one hot package. For me.

Judd takes the cigarette from his mouth and grins. I melt inside.

Tonight will be worth any torment Mom puts me through as punishment. I refuse to worry about her or anything else.

Judd reaches across and unbuckles my seat belt. "Come here."

I smile and slide closer to him.

No worries. None at all.

Twenty minutes later, we're inside The Beat, standing in line to pay our cover, and I don't see Suzanna anywhere. What if she doesn't show up? What if Mom followed us? What if I see someone I know and Judd finds out I'm a fake?

What if . . . what if . . . what if? So much for no worries.

The club throbs with sound. "Judd . . . that's not Suz's cousin checking —"

"Don't worry about it. I've got you covered." He pulls an ID from his pocket and hands it to me.

The name and address on the laminated driver's license aren't mine. The photo, either, but the girl and I look enough alike that anyone glancing at the picture would think I've just changed my hair. The year of her birthday makes her twenty-one.

Judd leans down to my ear. "Memorize it." He nods toward the guy at the front of the line who's checking IDs and collecting money. "In case he drills you."

I don't want to do this, but what can I say? He thinks I'm as wild as my outfit. Admitting to him that I'm afraid of getting caught, that I don't drink anyway, would pretty much clue Judd in that I'm not the girl I've pretended to be. He'd dump me right here.

Taking a deep breath, I repeat my alias name, address and birth date over and over again in my mind, telling myself I'm only queasy because of the loud music and the thick smoke blanketing the room. I was nervous last week when I came here with Suz, but tonight's worse. Tonight I'm Judd's date. I'm breaking a law so that I can drink. And Suzanna's not beside me, giving me courage and keeping an eye on me.

When we reach the front of the line, the guy doesn't ask any questions. He glances at the ID, at me, then does the same with Judd and takes our money. I drop the license into my purse.

A wire cage decorated with colored twinkle lights hangs suspended above the center of the dance floor. Identical cages dangle from every corner of the room. Girls dance inside of them, dressed in retro clothes; shiny white patent leather boots, skintight neon pink hip-hugging short shorts, fishnet stockings, bikini tops. Glow-in-the-dark paint covers every inch of exposed flesh; peace signs, flowers and other symbols, reminding me of the *Austin Powers* movies.

Judd holds my hand and leads me through the crowd toward an empty table. I scan every face we pass, looking for Suz, my pulse pumping along with the music. I recognize a couple of guys from school. A football player whose name I don't know. A blond guy from my English class last year. They wouldn't know me. We never talked, but I remember the blonde being sort of a cutup. Funny and cute, but out of my league. What guy isn't? At least when I'm the real me, the other half of my newly split personality.

Judd pulls out a chair. "How's this?" When I nod and sit, he settles in across from me, waves a waitress over and orders a beer, then asks what I want.

I blurt the first thing that pops into my mind. "A lemon-drop martini." Once, I saw a movie where the main character drank them. They sounded good. Besides, maybe the lemon will disguise the taste of the alcohol. And the glasses seemed small compared to a beer can. Surely I can down a couple without getting wasted.

When the waitress leaves, Judd leans across the table and smiles at me. "You look hot tonight."

"Thanks." It's hard to breathe for reasons other than the smoke. I am hot, but not the way he means. His eyes make my skin burn. And the room *is* stuffy.

"Why don't you take off your jacket?"

I feel like I'm losing my last link to safety as I slip out of the denim and drape it over the back of my chair.

When I look up, Judd's eyeing my chest. The corner of his mouth spasms. He pulls a cigarette from his pocket and lights up.

For some reason, I don't know what to do with my hands. I cross my arms, uncross them. Lace my fingers together on the tabletop then lower them to my lap. I nod at the pack that Judd tossed center table. "I think I will have one of those."

"Help yourself."

My hand shakes as I pull out a cigarette and stick it between my lips. I don't think Judd notices. He lifts his lighter and strikes a flame. I've watched other people smoke, so I know what to do. Suck on the filter until the tip glows orange, draw smoke into my mouth. I stop short of inhaling. Still, I cough on the exhale. "The strep," I rasp, squinting through the haze at Judd. "My throat's still raw."

He laughs then looks past me, raising a hand. "Hey!" He pushes back his chair and stands. "I see some friends. Be right back."

My coughing fit starts the second he's out of earshot. I hold the cigarette to my side and gulp in gasps of air not much clearer than what I sucked through the filter. After another practice hit, then another and another, I'm finally able to pretend-smoke without the cough.

As the waitress delivers our drinks, Judd heads back to the table with two guys trailing behind him. He introduces us and they start to sit, but we're one chair short. "No problem, dude," Judd says to the guy left standing. "Erin can sit with me." He scoots my drink in front of him.

The two guys stare as I push out of my chair, walk around the table and lower myself onto Judd's lap. It's like I'm the main character in a play, or something. *Suz, where are you?* Finally I know how she must feel all the time. It's not like I thought, all this male attention. I feel divided; the new, wild, carefree me loves it, while the old, sensible, careful me wants to escape to someplace safe and hide. It's just like when Judd kisses me; I'm excited and uneasy at the same time. I feel powerful in a weird sort of way, but uncomfortable, too. I mean, a little attention is nice. But this is too much. How do I act? I feel exposed.

I feel something else, too. Pressing against the underside of my thigh. I look back at Judd. His mouth quirks up. I want to die.

While the guys talk around me, I take a drag off the cigarette and focus on the martini glass. They don't include me in the conversation. In fact, the only part of Judd that seems aware I'm around is the part I'm sitting on.

White granules ring the martini glass rim. I touch them, bring my finger to my lips. Sugar. Lifting the glass, I drink half of the contents in two big gulps. It's good, both tart and sweet. Just like a lemon drop. Just like Judd.

I take a sip. One more. Two.

After a while, Judd pulls me closer against him. His arm's around me, just above my waist. He nuzzles the side of my neck. "You're thirsty tonight. How about another?"

"Sure. Thanks."

When the waitress comes over, he orders then continues talking with his friends while I scan the club for any sight of Suzanna. The colored lights around the dance cages seem brighter than before; the music sounds better.

My martini arrives; it's yummier than the first. I don't just hear the music now, it pulses inside me. I move my shoulders to the beat, feel the press of Judd's forearm against my rib cage, cradling what's above. His thumb strokes lightly back and forth across the space between my armpit and my breast.

One of the guys at our table nudges the other. They sneak glances at my chest and grin at Judd like he won the lottery. That might have bothered me fifteen minutes ago, but now it seems funny. Hilarious. They think they're so smart, and I'm a total dumb ass. Too bad, they've got it backward. I want to find Suz so we can have a good laugh.

"Excuse me." I stand and smile down at Judd. "I'm going to the restroom. I'll be right back."

"I'll have another drink waiting for you." He's trying not to laugh at me, I can tell. I don't know why, since the joke's on him, not me.

On my way through the club, I get caught

in the tangle of people by the bar. The blond guy from English class stands among them. Just like all the other guys, he checks me out. But his expression shifts to surprise when he reaches my eyes. His brows pull together, like he thinks he might recognize me, but he's not sure. I turn away and push through the crowd.

Inside the restroom, it's quieter. I go into a stall, put the toilet lid down and sit. I dig through my purse, looking for my phone. I'll just call Suz and ask where she is. The phone's vibrating when I finally find it. The display tells me it's her. I push the talk button. "Where are you?"

"Erin! Finally! I've been trying to call you all night. Mom and I had a fight. She took my car keys. I'm sorry. Are you okay?"

My head feels disconnected from my body. My stomach's woozy. Leaning forward, I hug my knees and giggle. "He has a *stiffy,*" I whisper into the phone.

"What?"

"Judd." I snort. "*You know.* He has —"

"Ohmi — Erin! You are messed up! What have you been drinking?"

"Martinis. Only two so far. Judd's ordering me another one."

"*Two martinis?* Those are strong. And expensive!"

"Judd's paying." I lower my voice. "He got me a fake ID."

"I am not believing this guy. He's just trying to get you drunk! Ohmigod, you are so naive. I knew you shouldn't go there with him. You hardly know him, Erin. Call a cab and get out of there."

"That's stupid. Nothing's going to happen. I'm okay. We haven't even danced yet."

"Last night when you *hadn't* been drinking you weren't sure you could say 'no' to him."

She's right. "Okay . . . a couple of dances. Then I'll tell him to take me home. I'll say I'm sick or something." I do feel sort of sick. The toilet's spinning like a merry-go-round.

"No more drinks," Suz adds. "And don't let him kiss you. Promise?"

"I promise." And I mean it, too. About the drink part, anyway.

"I'm calling you in thirty minutes. If you're not out of there, I'm stealing the car keys and coming after you. Mom will just have to get over it."

When I leave the restroom, Judd's waiting outside the door. "Did you fall in?"

"I shouldn't have downed those drinks so fast."

He laughs. "You wanna dance? Cade and

Sean will watch your purse."

"Sure." He takes my hand, gives me that sleepy-eyed smile I can't resist. Suz couldn't be more wrong about him. Away from his friends, Judd's different. As sweet as he was when we talked through the window earlier this week. As nice to me as he was last night.

The first dance is fast. I move with the music, feeling more free than I ever have, less self-conscious, like the girl in the cage above my head. Maybe it's still the martinis, or maybe it's because of the way Judd looks at me, I don't know. What I do know is, I like the feeling.

A slow dance plays next. I love the feel of Judd's arms around my waist. I close my eyes, my head against his shoulder. He kisses the side of my neck. His hands slide down, press against my butt, skim up my sides. North to the Tetons.

I open my eyes. Woozy again. Unsure. I'm starting to think his hands are metal and these boobs I'm wearing are magnets.

I lift my head, see the guy from English class, staring at us.

"Don't." I look up at Judd, pull away some. "Don't touch me like that. People are watching."

"So, what?" He pulls me to him again, lowers his mouth to kiss me. "Nobody cares."

I turn away. "I care. Take me home. I feel sick."

Irritation flickers in Judd's eyes. "It's just because you drank too fast. It'll wear off."

"I'm serious. I want to leave."

His arms drop away from me. He steps back. "Fine then. Go. I'm staying." He walks off, leaving me alone on the dance floor.

I feel like I'm lost in a foreign country, surrounded by people I don't know. The table where I left my purse seems miles away. Since I don't want to face the guy from English class, I weave through dancers to exit the dance floor at the side. Judd's not at the table. Nobody is. My purse sits on the floor by a chair, available for anyone to steal. How stupid could I be? As if a couple of guys are really going to baby-sit my stuff.

Grabbing it, I bolt for the door. I don't know how I'll get home. Right now, I don't care. I just want out of here.

The second I'm outside, I burst into tears. I take deep breaths of cool, clean air, hoping it will clear out my head, my lungs, this dirty feeling inside me. In the parking lot, I find a car beneath a streetlight and lean against it. I'll call Suz. She'll tell me what to do. Not that her bright ideas didn't help get me into this mess in the first place. I open my purse and dig through all the clutter for my phone. "Erin."

I glance up. Judd walks toward me. He doesn't look mad anymore, just bummed, like I've been nothing but a pain, not the good time he expected. Poor him.

Returning my attention to my purse, I keep on digging.

"Come back inside. I'm sorry I yelled at you." He stops in front of me. "You drank too much, too fast. I figured you could handle it or I wouldn't have kept buying them for you."

As if. He really does think I'm stupid. My fingers push aside a pack of gum, my sunglasses. Where is that phone?

Judd touches my chin. My eyes stay on the purse. "I said I'm sorry."

Is he? He sounds sincere. I meet his gaze. And I'm confused all over again. One second I think he's the biggest, scheming jerk on the planet, the next second I want him to kiss me.

Which he does.

His lips whisper across the sides of my closed mouth, whisking away my doubts. My purse slides to the pavement as I wrap my arms around his neck and start kissing him back.

That's when everything changes.

Judd backs me against the car, and his mouth presses harder against mine, bruising my lips. I try to turn my head, but he moves with me. "Stop," I mumble against his lips. The word sounds muffled, but I know he hears.

Just like last night, his hand slips beneath my shirt.

I manage to wedge my palms between us, to push against his chest. "No." He doesn't budge. "Don't!"

Keeping me trapped against the car, Judd leans back. "Now what?" His face is hard and impatient.

Panic shoots through me. Then my temper kicks in. I push him again, and he steps away. "Now *nothing,* that's what. I asked you not to touch me like that."

"As if you're some sweet little virgin." He barks a laugh. "You wanted it. You've given me every signal."

"That's not true!"

Or is it? Nothing's clear to me anymore. I just wish he'd leave so I can puke. Or maybe I should just puke on him. "Is that the only reason you asked me out? So you could get your hands on these?" I point at my chest. "Well here, I'll make it easy for you." Reaching into my shirt, I grab a jellyfish and sling it at him. It smacks his forehead.

111

Judd flinches, stares at me a second, then stoops and picks up the silicone blob. "You've gotta be shittin' me!"

"Have a great time!" I yell at him, then pull out the other one and throw it at him, too. He ducks and it lands on his foot. "Enjoy yourself. That's what you wanted. They're all yours."

I'll buy Katie another pair.

Judd picks up the other one. "What did you expect, wearing these?" He tosses them back at me. "And look at the way you dress. You're nothing but a tease."

I will not cry. I won't. Not in front of him. What *did* I expect? Maybe I am a tease. Maybe that's what I've turned into.

Judd laughs under his breath then jerks his head to the side. "Come on. I'll take you home."

"Don't worry about it."

He stares at me a minute before turning and starting toward the building. "Whatever." His laughter trails behind him as he walks away.

I pick up the inserts and my purse then sit on the car's hood. Let the owner come gripe me out and call me names. Who cares? I'm used to it. I mean, supposedly I'm a naive, teenaged hooker tease. What could be any worse?

When I finally find my phone, I'm crying so hard I can't see to punch in Suz's number.

"Hey."

I look up. The guy from my last year's English class stands in front of the car, holding my jacket. "You forgot this."

Wiping my face with the back of my hand, I take it from him. "Thanks."

"You okay?"

"No." I'm sobbing again, sobbing and totally humiliating myself. As if I haven't already. "How long have you been out here?"

"A while. I know that guy. I thought you might need some backup."

I squeeze one of the jellyfish in my lap and wish for a quick death. Right here, right now. "I guess you saw the whole thing, then. You probably think I'm a tease, too."

He shakes his head. "What you did . . . you were amazing. So was the look on his face." He grins. "You didn't need me or anyone." Offering his hand, he helps me down off the car. "I'm Noah Sherwood."

My nose runs. I sniff. "I'm —"

"Erin. I know. We had senior English together last year."

I blink at him, surprised he even noticed me, much less knew my name.

"You were just a junior, though, right?" he asks.

"Yeah." He knew that, too? I put the blobs in my jacket pocket then slip it on. "I took the class a year early."

"Must be nice to be so smart."

"I'm not so smart, really. Just motivated. By my mom, mostly."

He has a great laugh, the kind that makes me want to laugh with him.

Noah nods at the building. "I'm surprised to see you here."

"Not half as surprised as I am to be here."

The tears start again. Noah must think I'm a total geek. "I don't know why I came here with him," I sob. Which isn't completely true. I just wanted to have some fun. To have a guy notice me for once and want to be with me. "I'm not even sure who I am anymore . . . or what I want."

"I know what you mean." He pulls a wadded up napkin from his pocket and gives it to me. "Sometimes I feel that way, too."

"You do?"

"Yeah."

I'm not sure about the napkin. It's stuck together in the center.

"It's clean," Noah says. "Other than the dried up chewing gum, I mean."

I laugh. He does, too. I blow my nose then cry some more.

"Hey, if you don't stop that, they'll have to put flood warnings out on the area lakes."

He's funny. And cute. He doesn't look the least bit dangerous. Which is okay with me. I've had enough danger to last me a while.

"You need a lift?"

Before I can answer, my phone buzzes inside my pocket. When I answer it, Suz says, "Are you on your way home?"

"Not yet."

"I'll come get you."

"That's okay." I smile through watery eyes at Noah. "I have a ride."

Chapter 8

From The Desk of
Belle Lamont

Dear Harry,

So much has happened since my last letter.

I fired my baby-sitter. Cecilia was fit to be tied, and we had words, I'm sorry to say. I held my ground, Harry. That woman (the sitter, not CiCi) refused to stay out of my kitchen. I swear, you'd think I'm ten years old the way she hovered over me whenever I cooked. Yes, my vision's bad, but I can whip up a meal with my eyes closed, and I told her so. I've convinced CiCi to give me a two-week trial run at home by myself. If I don't burn down the house, maybe her mind will be eased.

In happier news, twelve new people called to order a book for Wednesday's meeting. Twelve! Can you imagine? And four of them men. You know how I abhor rumors, Harry, but one is circulating that Doris Quinn delivered homemade cookies to the Parkview pool hall, made a few suggestive comments about the book, batted an eyelash or two, and that was that. Mind you, Doris isn't a floozy like Jane Binkley. Just a hopeless romantic and a brazen flirt. Or that's what I've always thought. When I told The Frans about the pool hall, though, they said they've heard stories about Doris's past that would make a sailor blush. You never can tell about a person, can you?

Enough about Doris. It's Cecilia who concerns me. I hope this less highbrow book is a sign she's going to stop being so serious about everything. Since Bert left, the only time I've seen her let down her hair, so to speak, is when her girlfriends, whom I've come to think of as the Margarita Martyrs, came to dinner Friday night. But that was little more than a man-bashing session that started with my shrimp nacho appetizers, iced tea and commiseration, and ended with sopapillas, margaritas and dirty jokes.

At least the get-together took Cecilia's mind off Erin for a while. That is, until the girl came home as tipsy as her mother. And on a motorcycle driven by a different young man than the one with whom she left the house. That's right, our Erin had a date. And of course, Cecilia didn't approve, primarily because the boy's an old geezer of twenty. I'm not making light of Cecilia's concerns. I simply wish our daughter didn't jump to conclusions so fast. Shouldn't Erin have a chance to explain herself before CiCi passes judgment? Of course she should.

After a tense yelling session — threats and punishment issued by CiCi, tears and door-slamming from Erin — the two have hardly spoken to one another. Erin hasn't ventured from her room this weekend except to have lunch and a tense, quiet drive with us to Cleburne yesterday.

Cecilia is on a painting frenzy. Her beige bedroom's fast becoming Grape Nehi purple. Tacky beyond words, but I'm taking a cue from Maxwell and keeping my mouth shut.

Oh, Harry. I'm twisted up inside. All this conflict takes me back to CiCi's senior year in high school. I lost my way for a while back then. You didn't know that, did you? I lost my way, my self, and didn't come back until months after she'd left for college.

Jack was already a senior at the university and hundreds of miles from home. CiCi was so busy with school and friends that we rarely saw her, remember? When we did, it seemed we were always at odds over something. Cecilia felt she didn't need us anymore. You handled it better than me. I knew it was normal for her to pull away, but I couldn't stand that she didn't want to spend time with me. Oh, I was proud of our kids, proud of us for raising them to be self-sufficient and independent and ready to take on the world. But I often felt like a penny in a parking lot. Forgotten and worthless.

I wanted to tell you what I was going through, but I couldn't bring myself to. My emotions seemed so self-indulgent, too silly for me to mention. So I kept them to myself until the day we left Cecilia at school.

Do you remember how I cried for weeks after? How the tears would start at the oddest moments? The first time, you cried, too, though you tried to hide it. Well, you didn't fool me, Harry. Not for a second. I can still see us driving away from her dormitory, pulling over when we were out of sight of it, holding each other while the traffic sped past.

When we dried our eyes and took off again, you moved on in other ways, too. But I couldn't. Not for months. I'd see your smile and hear it in your voice when I'd burst into tears. You thought I only missed Cecilia and Jack. I did, but more than that churned inside me.

Sometimes I'd jerk awake in the middle of the night with a feeling of such urgency, such helplessness and worry, with an ache as heavy and full as my breasts once felt when the children were babies and would cry in the night to be fed and held. But there was no release for this ache. No sense of being needed. Only need. Mine.

For more than twenty years I'd poured every ounce of myself into a task so important, so all-consuming, and it was over. I had given all I had and was drained dry of everything except a love so full it seeped from my pores. I wondered sometimes if it would just evaporate, go to waste somewhere up there in the atmosphere, or could Jack and Cecilia feel it across the miles? Did it drift from me to them, wrap around them in an invisible embrace when they needed reassurance?

During those moments in the middle of the night, I'd reach out across the darkness and there you were, next to me. In your arms, I found safety, comfort and more. I found my way back. I know you didn't fully understand my grief, but you were there, as steady and reliable as the change of seasons. And that meant everything.

But what about Cecilia? Her divorce from Bert has been finalized. The papers are signed. Sometimes I hear her crying in the night. Who can she reach out to for comfort as Erin pulls away?

A year has passed since you left. Can you believe it? Sometimes it seems so much longer, other times, as if you left only last week. Months ago, I stopped being angry with you for leaving me all alone. Now I'm only sad and lonely. Missing you.

Yesterday, we drove to Cleburne and by our house. Your roses are gone. The neighbors, those nice young newlyweds the Langleys who moved in three years ago, said that the new owners plan to build a room onto the house soon and most of the bushes had to go. They only left one at the side of the house, and it was barren, almost dead from neglect.

CiCi, Erin and I stood at the curb and cried, holding each other. We didn't care if the Langleys saw. The truth is, they cried, too.

You're not coming back. I know that now. Somehow over the past twelve months, I tricked myself into believing you'd show up some evening, suitcase in hand, and tell me you were home for good. Or that I'd wake up one morning and discover this has all been a terrible dream. But none of that's true.

Your roses are gone, and so are you.

Regardless, letting go is hard, so I'll continue to reach out to you through these letters. They keep you near to me somehow, and I don't know what else to do.

As usual, I've gone on too long. I love you, Harry.

As always, your yellow rose,
Belle

Chapter 9

Cecilia Dupree
Day Planner
Wednesday, 11/19

1. Check paper for Max's ad.
2. 1:00 — Mom's Parkview reading group.
3. Decline blind date with Mrs. Stein's second cousin's great-nephew.
4. Buy new bedspread to match purple walls.
5. Unground Erin.

The second week the Parkview group meets to read *Penelope's Passion*, there's an expectant energy in the room, a charged silence similar to the moment the curtain parts on opening night at a sold-out play. I glance up. Not an empty chair. Books are open and right side up. I turn the page. . . .

"How dare you lock me in here!" Penelope refused to let him see her tremble, though her wet dress clung to her, molding every curve and raising goose bumps on her skin. She met his dark gaze, saw amused sympathy glittering within it.

"Dear Lady." The captain chuckled, a deep sound she felt more than heard. "I'm not locking you in, I'm locking the men out. For your protection. Besides, you should thank me that you have quarters at all. And the finest quarters on this ship, at that. Mine. You'll find the bed to be quite comfortable." He strode past her, slow and sure as a tiger. Then he sat on the bed and patted the mattress. "It's large enough for two."

Penelope raised a hand to slap him.

The captain caught her wrist mid-swing and laughed. . . .

A tiny gasp brings my head up. Doris Quinn, who listens rather than reads, sits at the edge of her chair with her eyes closed. Perfectly manicured fingers press against her lips. Beside her, Jane Binkley, the Parkview Manor Mae West according to Mother, fans her cleavage with a bookmark. Two new male recruits, one a silver-haired Paul Newman type, the other a wiry, sunken-cheeked Don Knotts look-alike, nudge one another and grin.

I return my attention to the page. . . .

"Such poor manners, Lady Waterford. Have you so little appreciation for your host?" The captain drew her to him.

Penelope held her breath. His eyes no longer contained sympathy, amused or otherwise. Anger simmered within their depths. Anger . . . and something else. Something that had her softening against him until she was nothing more than clay in his hands, pliant, helplessly available for him to mold to his will.

Captain Stonewall pulled her closer still, and she felt the hard length of his manhood press against her midsection. . . .

A snort is answered with a snicker. I don't look up. I know The Frans when I hear them. . . .

"Since you've taken it upon yourself to stow away on my ship," the captain murmured, "I intend to make your voyage as enjoyable as possible." He traced the shell of her ear with a fingertip, skimmed the line of her jaw, paused at the pulsing hollow beneath her throat. "Nothing but pure pleasure until the day we dock."

A sigh sifts through the room, a giggle follows, a whisper then a chuckle or two.

I close *Penelope's Passion* and look up. "Okay, that's it for today. Next week we'll continue with chapters ten through twelve. The floor's open for discussion."

As the back-and-forth banter begins, I look at Mother. She looks back at me, shaking her head. A smile twitches her lips as she slips off her glasses to polish the lenses with the hem of her blouse. Her cream-colored silk. When I picked her up at lunchtime, I didn't notice she'd worn it. Strange. The blouse is a bit dressy for reading group. Oh, well. I have to give her credit. She's doing okay on her own at home during the day. Really, why should we pay someone to stay with Mother when we have Mrs. Stein next door, who checks on her daily, whether I ask her to or not?

"Captain Stonewall is such a strong, dashing hero." Doris's voice flutters with dreamy admiration. "He's a man who knows what he wants."

"And knows how to get it," Jane adds with a sultry laugh.

Doris nods her agreement. "If he lived in our world today, I wonder what he'd do?"

"Time." Mary Fran's voice is as bemused as it is cynical. "For rape, most likely."

A heated discussion ensues as to whether or not the captain's behavior is forceful or merely seductive.

I shift my focus to jolly Oliver who sits in his usual place beside Mother. Today his arm stretches across the back of her chair as if it belongs there. I stare a minute, but he doesn't budge. He doesn't even squirm. Instead, he looks directly at me, winks, then smiles.

So. What's that all about? Now I'm the one squirming.

"Excuse me, Miz Dupree?"

"Hi, Mr. O'Dell. What's up?" I ask the paunchy, red-faced man who is suddenly standing beside me.

He cuts a glance over his shoulder at the group, then blinks puppy dog eyes at me. They're always as sad as Maxwell's, even when he smiles. "While they debate, I wondered if I might ask you a personal question?"

"Of course you can."

"If you'd rather I make an appointment, I understand."

"No, that's all right. If we need more time later, we can schedule it."

He coughs. "I've been wondering how soon is too soon for a person to start dating after losing a spouse?"

"That depends on the person. How long has it been since Mrs. O'Dell passed away?"

"Six years."

I want to hug him. "Is there someone you're interested in seeing socially?"

His face flushes scarlet. "Iris Shelby." Turning, he gives a discreet nod in the direction of a heavyset woman I've come to know well.

Iris has steel-gray scouring pad hair, a double chin, lumpy knees and elbows. And she's the epitome of all that's missing in Herbert's life. Happiness bubbles out of her like fizz from a shaken soda can. Her eyes are as lively as a young girl's, and when she laughs, which is often, she throws back her head and gives it her all.

"I can't find my nerve to ask her out," Herbert whispers. "I'm eighty-two years old. It's been sixty years since I dated a gal. I don't remember how. And even if I did there's the problem of me not driving anymore. Doesn't seem proper to ask a woman on a date, then make her do the driving."

Screw professional propriety. This man needs a hug, and I'm going to give it.

Before I can, a knock sounds at the door, and Bill Burdette, the Parkview Manor Retirement Village manager, pokes his head into the room. "Sorry to interrupt, everybody. CiCi, could I have a word with you in my office if you have a minute?"

"Sure, Bill." I tell Herbert I'll call him tonight, then stand and look out at the small crowd. "Keep on keeping on. If I don't make it back before time's up, I'll see you all next week." I meet Bill at the door and we start down the hallway. "What's up?"

He fingers his jacket lapel. "We have a bit of a problem, I'm afraid. Mrs. Quinn's son and Mr. Rayburn's daughter are here with a complaint about your current book selection."

"What?" I make a face. "I'm reading to adults, not a class of ten-year-olds."

Pausing at his closed office door, Bill says, "Grown children of elderly parents often treat them like they're in elementary school." He shakes his head. "Just listen to their concerns, CiCi. I'm sure when they meet you and hear what you have to say, they'll calm down."

"They aren't calm?"

Bill's eyebrows lift.

My stomach falls. "Refresh my memory. Which one is Mr. Rayburn?"

"Good-looking guy. Silver fox. Sharp blue eyes."

I nod. "Paul Newman."

"Right." He puts on his happy face and

opens the door. "Mr. Quinn, Mrs. Kiley . . . I'd like you to meet Cecilia Dupree."

I smile. They don't. We shake hands.

"Cecilia's been kind enough to take time away from her busy counseling practice this past year to volunteer as hostess for Park-view's weekly reading group."

"It was my mother's idea." I sit in a chair next to Doris Quinn's scowling son, then explain how the group started and why we've continued it even after Mother moved out. I try another smile, without effect. "I read aloud because several of the members have problems with their eyesight. It's seemed to work well for everyone so far."

Mr. Rayburn's daughter crosses one crisp khaki-covered leg over the other. "Who chooses the books?"

"When we started, the members planned to choose, but no one could agree, so they decided to let me. Of course, I'm always open to their suggestions."

Mr. Quinn lifts a copy of *Penelope's Passion* from his lap and waves it in the air. "And *this* is the sort of trash you deem fit for a group of seniors?"

Oh, shit. I sit up straighter. "Actually *Penelope's Passion* is the first romance novel we've read, Mr. Quinn. Normally, I select a title from the *Literary Pen*'s bestseller list, but the members were bored with such angsty reads. A lot of them dropped out. I thought they could use a change of pace, and they agreed."

Mrs. Kiley taps her foot against the floor and turns to Bill Burdette. "And do you approve of pornography being read to your residents on facility property?"

Bill clears his throat. "I only approved their use of one of our meeting rooms. I'm not involved in any other capacity with the group or their selection of reading material."

That a'boy, Bill. Dump this all on me. I scoot forward to the edge of my chair. "I assure you, the book we're reading is not pornography. It's a *romance* novel. There's nothing remotely degrading about it."

"Label it what you will, Ms. Dupree. Romance, soft porn, erotica. A spade is still a spade." With a jerk of his wrist, Mr. Quinn opens the novel to a book-marked page and reads in a dramatic voice, *"Penelope laced her fingers through his hair and pulled his head toward hers. Her lips parted, welcomed the warm velvet touch of his clever tongue, the feverish heat his kisses spread across her flesh. 'So soft,' he murmured."*

He pauses, looks across at me, narrows his eyes, then continues, *"The captain touched*

Penelope's throat, causing a shiver to ripple through her. His fingers fanned over one pale breast, circled her nipple in maddening strokes that made her breath catch, trailed down her bare stomach. And then he dipped —"

Mrs. Kiley coughs. Loudly.

"Enough said." Quinn closes the book. "I believe that passage vividly portrays my point. It only becomes more explicit farther into the scene." He looks at Bill, whose face flames.

"Yes. Well." Bill glances at me, a plea for help in his eyes.

"Mr. Quinn . . ." I huff a laugh. "Tongue, breast, nipple and stomach are not dirty words. Besides, you read the scene out of context without knowing a thing about the story that led up to it."

His jaw muscle jumps. He crosses his arms.

"Haven't you ever watched any of the old swashbuckling movies of the forties and fifties? Errol Flynn?" I open my hands, palms up. "That's exactly what this is. A larger than life story. Melodrama. Adventure. Romance."

"Sex," he spits.

Okay. I've had enough of this prudish, pompous jerk and his uptight sidekick. Nobody here is paying me to act like a professional, so why should I? These people need to hear what I *really* think. Such as, maybe they should follow their parents' lead, since I've never met a couple in more obvious need of some spice in their lives.

I open my mouth to tell them, then come to my senses, square my shoulders, take a breath to calm my temper. "So the book has a sex scene or two. Studies support the importance of sexuality in people's later years. This novel might act as a substitute for the lack of intimacy in their lives or improve what they already have. Or it might just be good, fun entertainment." Leaning back, I smile.

Mr. Quinn continues to twitch and glare.

Mrs. Kiley appears horrified at the mention of elderly people and intimacy in the same sentence.

Bill's chair squeaks. "Maybe if the two of you explained the situation that brought the book to your attention. Mrs. Kiley?"

"It's Sue." She uncrosses her legs, crosses them again, blinks in rapid succession. "Yesterday afternoon I came by to visit Dad at the usual time. I always come on Tuesdays. But he wasn't in his apartment. I couldn't find him anywhere and he didn't answer his cell phone." She glances at the

133

man next to her. "That's when I ran into Mr. Quinn in the hallway."

He gives her a halfhearted smile of support. "It's Donald."

She nods and smiles back at him. "Donald had just left his mother's apartment. She —" Sue studies her lap and starts blinking again.

"Mother didn't answer the doorbell," Donald continues, coming to her rescue. "I had a package for her, so I let myself in with my key. Music was playing in her bedroom and . . ." He squirms in the chair. "I heard laughter. Mother's and a man's. As you can imagine, I was stunned. I just stood there. I didn't know what to do. And then . . ."

"And then Mrs. Quinn and my father walked out of her bedroom and into the living room where Donald was," Sue finishes for him.

"*Danced* out. They were dancing. And wearing *robes,*" he adds, his voice low and appalled. "In the middle of the day. Their *feet* were bare."

I chew the inside of my cheek. Bare feet and dancing! Oh, the scandal of it.

Sue glares at me as if she hears my thoughts. "Dad said they met at your reading group last week. The day you started that book. His friend Oliver had in-

134

vited him to attend and he didn't have anything on his agenda so . . ."

Donald stares down at his knees. "They met *last week* and already they're . . ." He scrubs a palm over his face. *"Jesus."*

I cover my mouth to hide a smile. *Way to go, Doris. Paul Newman. What a catch.* When I regain some composure, I say, "I'm sorry. I don't see what any of this has to do with the reading group."

"It's this book," Donald snaps, tossing *Penelope's Passion* onto Bill's desk.

"They're lonely and vulnerable." Sue appears on the verge of tears. "And the book . . . well . . . it's titillating, to say the least. It might've put ideas in their heads."

"Good grief." I stand. For the third time today, I throw professionalism out the window. "They're human beings. Intelligent adults! Just because they're in their seventies doesn't mean they're brain-dead. They don't need a book in order to get *ideas.*"

Sue folds her hands in her lap. "They're in their *eighties,* not their seventies."

"Good for them. I hope they're having the time of their lives. And if I had anything to do with them getting together, good for me, too."

Donald Quinn bolts from his chair, turning his anger on Bill. "I don't care if this woman's a licensed therapist or not. You either ban this reading group from Parkview Manor, or form a committee to approve the books she chooses before they're read. If you don't, Mrs. Kiley and I are going over your head to file a formal complaint against this facility. I'm sure some of your other residents' family members would be happy to join us."

Donald Quinn and Sue Kiley leave the room together.

Sighing, I fold back into the chair and meet Bill's stare. His slackened face is pale. "Well . . . I guess he told you."

"CiCi . . ." He puffs out his cheeks.

"I know. I'll choose another book."

"And —"

"I'll bring it by so you and whatever committee you form can give it your blessing before we read it."

Bill drums his fingertips on the desktop. "I'll have to check into that. Forming that type of committee might raise liability issues for the Village."

"Are you saying you want us to disband?"

He nods. "For the time being, anyway."

"Fine." I stand up again. "I'll go tell the kids they're being censored by their children."

At six-fifteen, I step back to admire the

new bedspread I bought after work. Plum and pale yellow. Bert would hate it, just like he'd hate the color I painted the walls. Nothing but neutrals for that man. Except when it comes to women, I guess. The flashier the floozy the better. Next week I might paint his beloved den sea-foam green or fire-engine red.

Erin pokes her head into the room and eyes the spread without comment. "I'm home." She turns to leave. The routine's been the same every day since I grounded her. She lets me know she's home from orchestra practice, goes to her room, comes out for dinner, then returns to her room for the rest of the night.

"Erin?"

She faces me again, crossing her arms.

"How was practice?"

"Okay."

"I've decided to let you off the hook a few days early. Just promise me no more drinking, okay? And no more dates with twenty-one-year-olds."

"He was twenty." When I scowl, she says, "Fine."

I toss a throw pillow onto the bed, then start from the room, pausing at the door to give her a hug. I'm surprised and pleased when she hugs me back.

Erin follows me into the backyard. It's cool out. The sky's a pearly gray. Twilight gray, I tell myself, though it's probably smog. I grab a dog brush off the patio table, whistle Max over, then sit in a chair and start to work on his coat. He sniffs the air, growls low in his throat when the poodle next door barks.

Leaning against the side of the house, Erin watches the movement of my hand across Max's back. "What are we doing for Thanksgiving?"

"The usual. Nana has a feast planned."

"Do you care if I have a friend over? Nana always makes too much anyway."

"Suzanna?"

"No, someone I just met. They don't celebrate Thanksgiving at their house. The parents are from Scotland."

I'm all for getting to know Erin's friends. "Okay. As long as Nana's fine with it. She's the cook."

After one final stroke of the brush, I lean back and inspect Max head to toe. His glossy coat gleams. His muscles ripple. He looks proud and strong, as dashing as Penelope's captain. I pat his rump. The hussies will swoon.

This morning, I called to tell my veterinarian Max is available if he knows of anyone looking to breed a female. I also called an ad in to the newspaper and sent one off to *English Bulldog* magazine.

I ask Erin to run get the newspaper so I can check to make sure the ad ran. When she comes back out with it, I scan the classifieds, locate my ad and then look up to find her watching me. Her nervous expression fills me with dread. "Something on your mind, sweetie?"

"Sort of." She nibbles the cuticle on her index finger. "Suz and I have been thinking."

Uh-oh. Suzanna and thinking are a dangerous combination.

"You know we both want to go to UT in the fall and, well, Suz is going to live in a dorm on campus, and the applications for housing are due soon, and I *really really* want to live on campus, too. With Suz."

I shake my head. "We already decided you'd live at home."

"*You* decided. You didn't ask me."

"You're not living in a dorm, Erin. It doesn't make sense. We live close enough to the university that it isn't necessary for you to move away."

"*Please,* Mom! We're not *that* close."

I fold the paper, lay it aside, push away from the patio table and stand. "I'm not going to discuss this right now." Maxwell's water bowl's empty. I walk to the faucet, twist the lever and pick up the hose.

"But early applications are due *next week.* We'll miss out on the best dorms if we don't get ours in. Suz —"

"I said I'm not going to discuss this." Water streams into Max's bowl.

"Why not?"

"Because . . ." My throat closes. Because I don't think she's ready. Because she's not prepared to face the world on her own. Because dorms are havens for sex, alcohol and every other sin on the planet. I should know; I sampled them all when I lived on campus.

I draw a breath to finish my sentence, but I can't speak.

Because I'm not ready to let you go.

The truth hits me square in the nose. Is this about what I need or what Erin needs?

I swallow. "It's a waste of my money when you can just live here."

"Fine." She stomps to the back door, opens it just in time for my mother to stick her head out.

"Dinner's ready," Mother says in a sing-song voice.

Ignoring her, Erin and I scowl at each other.

"I'll just ask Dad for the money then," Erin yells.

Mother blinks at her, at me, and then backs out of sight. Erin follows, slamming the door.

"Damn! Damn! Damn!" I shout kicking Max's bowl with each curse and slopping water over the edges.

Mrs. Stein, my neighbor, peeks over the fence, holding her poodle, Pom Pom. "CiCi? I thought I heard you out here."

"Hello, Mrs. Stein."

"Your shoes are getting wet."

I glance down. The running hose points at my feet, drenching them. "So they are."

Her eyes frown; her face doesn't, thanks to a recent round of Botox, I guess. "You never returned Jerry's call. My second cousin's great-nephew? The Bar Mitzvah?"

"I'm sorry. I can't make it."

"But he's a very successful man. And handsome. He still has most of his hair."

"Thanks, but I have other plans." I shrug. "Sorry."

She glares at me, then down at Max. Pom Pom yaps, sending Max behind a bush to tremble. Mrs. Stein and her dog disappear.

I kick the water bowl again. If Bert goes against me on this dorm thing with Erin, I *will* bury his body underneath the willow tree. Piece by piece. Except for *that* piece. His manhood, as Penelope would say.

Maxwell comes out from the bushes and nudges my leg with his nose. I lean down and scratch his head. "Max, old pal, by next fall you may have one very special chew toy."

Chapter 10

After dinner the next night, I'm at the table reading a dog-show training manual and eating a piece of Mother's cinnamon devil's food cake when the phone rings. The man at the other end saw the newspaper ad. He wants more information. We have a lengthy conversation, then agree to get together over the weekend so he and his dog Gertie can size up Max.

Mother walks into the kitchen to get her knitting bag from the hutch as I'm hanging up. Before we can speak, the phone rings again. It's Bert, returning my call from last night. I tell him what's up with Erin.

"I don't mind giving her the money, CiCi."

"*I* mind." I lick icing off my fork. "I don't want Erin living in the dorm."

"It might be good for her."

"Who are you to say what's good for our daughter, Bert? I can count on one hand the number of times you've seen her in the past six months." I start to shake, inside and out.

Mother pretends to be preoccupied with searching inside her bag for who-knows-what, but I'm sure she listens.

"I'm just trying to give Erin some space," Bert says in his oh-so-calm and practical tone. "You know, to sort things out."

"She doesn't need space, she needs to know that her father cares about her, that when you walked out on me you didn't walk out on her, too."

"You *asked* me to leave, CiCi. Remember?"

I stab the cake with my fork. He's right. Because I was angry. Because I thought he'd fight for our marriage, that he'd insist we at least try to work things out. Instead he acted defensive and all-too-eager to pack his bags. "You're embarrassed, aren't you, Bert? That's why you avoid her. You're embarrassed because you know Erin's on to you and what you did."

"And why is that, CiCi?" An undercurrent of rage buzzes in my ex's voice. "Did you tell her things to turn her against me?"

Good. Let him lose his temper for once. Let him be the one who goes off on a rant, not me. "I didn't tell her anything. Erin has eyes. She's not stupid. And if you're thinking of making up to her by giving her whatever she wants, that's a mistake. Erin needs you to be her father, not her best friend. She needs you to do what's best for her, not what's easiest for you." I ignore the nagging feeling that I should take my own advice.

Several tense, silent seconds later Bert says, "Okay, I'll tell her she has to wait a year before she can move out. That's fair, isn't it?"

The shaking subsides. I scrape a finger across the cake's icing. "I can live with that."

"And I'll spend more time with her. Call her more. I want to. I miss her. It's just . . . I can't stand the thought of her hating me."

"She doesn't hate you."

"Maybe. You're right, though. I haven't been there for her. Not enough. Even before we split. You've done a great job with her, CiCi. She's a good girl."

I hate it when he's nice, when he admits fault, when he compliments me. I don't want to remember Bert's few good qualities, only his many bad ones. "Thanks," I say and then we hang up.

"Where is that needle?" Mom continues to dig in her knitting bag. "Why, here it is." She holds it up for me to see.

I lick my finger. "How did you do it, Mother?"

"Do what, Sugar?"

"Hold everything together so well? Do everything right?"

She places the bag and needle on the table and crosses over to give me a hug. "I didn't do everything right. Far from it."

"You had a perfect marriage. I never once heard you and Dad have a real roof-raising fight. And I know as well as anyone that he could be hardheaded and stubborn as a jackass. Didn't you ever just want to strangle him?"

"Well, I wouldn't go that far, but we did have our squabbles now and then."

"But you always ended up letting him have his way. You always gave into him. You wanted to go to Hawaii on vacation but y'all never did. You went to Colorado. Every year."

She shrugs. "Your father loved to fish. He hated sand."

"Remember that bed you fell in love with? The brass one? How come you never bought it?"

"Harry thought all those curlicues on the headboard were silly." Mother laughs. "He said it was too feminine."

"So you just gave up. And you never complained about it. Weren't you the least bit resentful?"

"The bed wasn't important enough to

cause a stir over, Cecilia. Neither was Hawaii."

I bite my lip. What's wrong with me? I shouldn't be jealous, even a little bit, of my mother's easygoing nature, the fact that she could keep a marriage running smoothly when I couldn't. "See, that's where you and I are different. I wasn't as big of a pushover as you, but I let Bert have his way most of the time, too. Then I stewed about it."

Mother lifts her chin. "I wasn't always a pushover. There were times when Harry didn't get what he wanted."

"Name one."

Her mouth quirks up at the corner. "You'd probably rather not hear this from your mother, but I feigned a headache or two in my day."

"Oh, that." I laugh. "Only one or two? See, I'm right. You were the perfect wife."

We sit across from one another at the kitchen table.

"No wife is perfect, CiCi. No husband is, either."

"You're just being modest. You were a model wife and a model parent, too. You cooked nutritious meals, made sure we spent time together as a family."

"People weren't in as big of a hurry back then."

"You hardly ever lost your temper with Jack or me, either. And still, when I went off on my own, I messed up."

"Nonsense."

I blink back tears. "So, what's going to happen to Erin? Bert and I have screwed up her life."

"Cecilia . . ." Mother reaches across and touches my hand. "I wasn't the saint you make me out to be. And as for losing my temper, if your father were here he could set you straight about that." She laughs, pats my hand, then sobers. "You haven't screwed up anything. Bert's the one who strayed."

I sniff. "I know, and I can't forgive him for hurting Erin. But I made mistakes, too. I didn't love Bert when I married him, not in the right way. You knew, didn't you?"

She nods once. "I suspected."

"It must've been awful for him, sensing I wasn't happy and not knowing why. Then, when he found those letters I wrote to Craig and never mailed . . ." I close my eyes. "I said terrible things in them. I told Craig I wasn't over him."

The memory of Bert's hurt eyes stabs me, the questions he asked, my lame reassurances. "I married Bert on the rebound. To help me get over Craig. To get over the miscarriage."

"Bert adored you. You cared for him, I know you did."

"But I didn't love him. Not then. That wasn't fair to him. I don't know, maybe I even got pregnant with Erin on the rebound, to help me forget about losing Craig's baby."

"CiCi," Mother says when I try to look away. Pressing my lips together, I meet her gaze. "You loved Bert. It was clear as could be on your face whenever you watched him with Erin."

"Eventually, yes. But it came too late for him."

I return to my dog-training manual, though my heart isn't in it.

"This talk of letting husbands have their way," Mother says, bringing my head up. "Is that what your purple bedroom walls are all about?"

I grin. "What do you think about candy apple-red for the den? Bert would hate it." And, I know I sound shallow, but that makes me love it all the more.

Thirty minutes later, I'm still at the table reading the training manual when the doorbell rings. Mother sits across from me, knitting.

"I'll get it!" Erin yells from the hallway.

Seconds later she walks into the kitchen with her backpack over one shoulder. A blond-haired guy, also toting a backpack, is at her side. "Mom, Nana, this is Noah."

Dread rises up in me. It's the kid with the motorcycle. I only saw him from a distance the other night, but I recognize the blond hair. I stand as he approaches the table.

"Thanks for inviting me to Thanksgiving dinner, Mrs. Dupree." He shakes my hand. "I'm looking forward to it."

My eyes dart to Erin. So, her Scottish "friend" is male. She avoids my gaze.

"You're in for a treat," I say. "My mother's turkey and dressing will make your mouth water."

"Oh, such flattery, CiCi." Mother shakes Noah's hand and laughs. "Do go on."

Erin moves up beside biker-boy Scotty, hooks her arm through his, then gives me a look that dares me to comment. "Noah and I are going to do our homework together. You care if we use the kitchen table?"

Mother doesn't waste a second gathering her knitting so I follow the model parent's lead, grab my manual and step aside. "It's all yours. So . . . you go to school with Erin, Noah?"

"I graduated." He and Erin dump their backpacks onto the table and sit side by side. "I'm at Tarrant County Junior College. We had English together last year, though."

We talk a minute longer, then Mother and I start from the room. "We'll leave you two to study."

In the den, Mother and I settle in on opposite ends of the couch. I toss the manual on the coffee table. "I don't like the looks of him."

She hands me two needles and a spool of yarn. "Why don't we pick up where we left off yesterday?"

"He has an earring."

"I didn't see one." Mother looks at my fingers. "Your hands are too stiff. Loosen up."

"You didn't see that stud in his left ear? How could you miss it?"

"Pay attention, Cecilia. Like this. Over, under —"

"What's he trying to pull by saying he's Scottish? His accent's as Texan as calf fries."

Mother's hands go still. "For heaven's sake, Cecilia, give the boy a chance. Erin, too."

The doorbell rings again. "What is this? Grand Central Station?" I start for the entry hall. "If this is that Judd kid, I'll —" I swing open the door, look up into a pair of cheery blue eyes peering from beneath a felt forties-style newsboy cap.

"Howdy do, CiCi."

"Oliver?" In the flesh. All six feet and three or four inches of him.

He removes the cap. "Belle around?"

"Uh . . . yes." I frown. Smile. Frown again.

He leans to one side, looks past my shoulder. "Could I — ?"

I step back. "Um. Sure. Come on in."

I lead him into the den. "Look who's here, Mother."

Mother glances up from her knitting. "Oh." She lays her needles and yarn aside, stands, adjusts her glasses like she doesn't quite believe her eyes. "Oliver. How nice to see you."

He grins. "Why, Belle, you're looking fit as a fiddle tonight."

Mother blinks and flutters. "Don't be silly."

"No, I mean it. You're pretty as a peach."

I fold my arms. Good thing Mother's a gourmet cook. She hates baloney. She'll set the old fart straight in her tactful way.

"Oh, well that's so sweet of you to say." Tilting her head to one side, Mother smiles up at him. She looks flattered. Coy. Pretty. As a peach.

I frown at her as a memory plays through my mind. Daddy whistling *"The Yellow*

Rose of Texas," coming up behind Mother at the kitchen sink, her surprised laughter as he twirls her around. *You're my prettiest yellow rose, Belle.*

I step between Mother and Oliver. "Daddy always called you his yellow rose of Texas. Remember, Mother?"

"Of course I do, Sugar." Her voice is soft and as startled as her eyes.

Oliver looks around me, nods at the spot on the opposite end of the couch from Mother. My spot. The spot where Daddy always sat when he visited. "May I?"

I shake off an odd sense of panic, of defensiveness. "Sure. Have a seat."

He does. So does Mother. I stay put.

Oliver clears his throat. "I have an idea about the reading group. I want to offer my apartment as a meeting place. It may be on Parkview Manor's property, but I pay for it. Don't see as how anybody would have grounds to stop us from gathering there. And we could read whatever we choose."

Mother brightens. "That's a wonderful idea, Oliver."

From the direction of the kitchen, I hear Erin's and biker-boy Scotty's laughter, hers high-pitched, his deep. Studying? My foot.

"CiCi?" Mom's voice snags my attention again. "Isn't Oliver's idea wonderful?"

Nodding, I say, "I've been thinking, though. You don't really need me. You could get books on tape. I should've thought of that in the first place. It makes more sense."

"No!" they blurt in unison.

"I don't know about you, Belle," Oliver says. "But I get darned tired of conversing with machines these days. You make a phone call, you get a recorded message and are expected to leave one in return. You drive through at the bank, you get an electronic teller."

Mother nods her agreement. "People stay in touch by e-mail instead of by phone."

"And the list goes on and on," he says. "I like having you read to us, CiCi. Feels like the old days when we'd gather 'round the campfire and listen to someone tell a story."

I picture him in a flannel shirt, the sleeves rolled up, effortlessly splitting logs with a hatchet then tossing them into the flames. Mother admiring his flexing muscles.

"I agree," she says, a shy smile curving her lips. "It's more personal."

He winks at her. "More intimate."

She blushes and averts her eyes.

The sick feeling returns, the panic, the defensiveness. Don't fall for his good ol' boy charm, I want to tell her. Stick with "BOB."

Your battery-operated-boyfriend will never break your heart. He'll always be there when you need him, and when you don't, you won't have to feign a headache since "BOB" is perfectly content in his bathroom drawer. "BOB" doesn't fish; he won't mind going to Hawaii. And he won't feel emasculated by a curlicue brass bed. No slinky lingerie needed for "BOB." You can turn him on, or off, with the flick of a switch.

"All right." I tap my foot, wishing I had a switch right now to turn off that gleam in jolly Oliver's eyes. "Your place it is, then. Same day, same time?"

He chuckles, pleased with himself. "That works for me. I'll let the others know."

I wait for him to stand and go. He doesn't. He twiddles his thumbs, looking like an overgrown kid on prom night.

"Belle, I thought I'd see if you might like to take a little drive. Maybe go for some ice cream."

Mother folds and unfolds her hands in her lap. "Oh my, no. I couldn't."

He grins. "Of course you could."

"Not at this hour."

"It's only seven-thirty."

She avoids looking at me. At Oliver, too. "I just ate an enormous dinner."

He claps his big, rough hands together.

"Well, then. I'm right in time to buy you dessert."

Mother's eyes flash panic signals.

"We have devil's food cake," I say, helping her out with the pushy old coot. A burly, charming, lumberjack of an old coot, but a coot nonetheless.

"Yes!" Mother smiles her thanks and stands. "We have ice cream, too. I'll get it."

Oliver follows her. "I'll help you."

"No ice cream for me," I say, on his heels. "Just cake." If he thinks I don't know what he's up to, he's in for a big surprise. I'm keeping an eye on Oliver Winston. I'm not about to let him put ideas in Mother's head and take advantage of her loneliness, her vulnerability.

My pace slows when it occurs to me I heard those same words come out of Sue Kiley's mouth about her dad and Donald Quinn's mother. Lonely. Vulnerable. *Penelope's Passion* putting ideas in their heads. I made light of her concerns. In fact, I thought she was being ridiculous.

Erin and Noah don't even look up when we enter the kitchen. They sit, shoulder to shoulder, heads together, whispering and snickering over their open books. Funny, I don't remember the subject of math ever being so humorous.

Frustrated, though I'm not sure why, I go to the back door and let Maxwell in.

"Oh, Oliver . . ." Mother hands him the ice-cream carton, covers her mouth and laughs at something he says as I pass back through the kitchen with Max beside me.

Three slices of cake sit on the counter. "Which one's mine?"

They're too wrapped up in each other to hear me. All of them. Mother and Oliver. Erin and biker-boy Scotty. "Hey, did you hear we're supposed to get a cold front this weekend?" No response. "A possible ice storm." Nothing. "I'm moving in with Mrs. Stein's second cousin's nephew and we're opening a toupee shop." Nobody cares.

Good grief and pass the chocolate; I give up. As the saying goes, three's a crowd. Or in this case, five.

I take a plate and head for the bedroom. I'll just keep the door open and my hearing turned up. Hormones have gone haywire in my house tonight. I don't trust anyone.

When I reach my bedroom, I set the cake on the nightstand and grab the new romance novel I started last night. I read ahead of the group and finished *Penelope's Passion*.

Gazing into Maxwell's sad eyes I hook a thumb at the bed. He whines as if to ask, *you sure you're not gonna swat my butt?*

"You're in the clear," I say. "Come on."

He takes the leap, then snuggles up next to my leg as I settle against the pillows, the novel in my lap. "They can keep the lumberjack and biker boy. You're all I need to keep me warm, Max." I fork a bite of cake, then open the book's cover. "Just you and Daniel Cade Colton, Texas Ranger."

And maybe someday soon, a "BOB" of my very own.

Chapter 11

To: Erin@friendmail.com
From: Noah@friendmail.com
Date: 11/21, Friday
Subject: Stuff

did i tell you how awesome you looked today at lunch? i hope it works out for you to hear my band tonight at the beat. oh, and don't worry about that a-hole being there. he and his buds got kicked out last week for fighting and they're banned from the place. you sure about thanksgiving? i don't think your mom's too crazy about me. who is scotty? forgot to tell ya she called me that once last night. later, noah

To: Noah@friendmail.com
From: Erin@friendmail.com
Date: 11/21 Friday
Subject: re: Stuff

Did I tell you I think guys who play

guitar are seriously sexy? I'll be there to hear you tonight. Can't wait! Suz and I are going to a movie, I'll be home by my totally ridiculous curfew, then I'll go out the window, like always. Scotty? Who knows? My mom's having a midlife crisis or something. Ignore her. I do. And no way am I letting you get out of Thanksgiving! Thanks for picking me up at lunch. I know it's out of your way.
~Erin

I click Send then watch the message disappear into cyberspace. Seriously sexy? Guitar players are seriously sexy?

Leaning back in the chair, I close my eyes and groan. I am such a moron. Noah will think I'm making a move. I *am* making a move. But what if he doesn't feel that way about me? What if he just wants to be friends? I mean, we met two weeks ago, but we've never had a real date. And he hasn't kissed me yet, not really. Just a peck on the cheek sometimes, like today when he dropped me at school after lunch. Which, by the way, Mom doesn't know about. The times Noah's taken me to lunch, I mean.

Since day one, Noah and I have either seen each other or talked every night. He comes over a lot and we study or watch TV.

A couple of times I've climbed out the window after curfew and we've sat in the yard and talked since he doesn't have a car, only a cycle. He held my hand last time. We didn't stay out long, though. The weather's getting colder. Which is probably the only reason he held my hand. Because his fingers were freezing.

So why does Noah tease me and flirt if he just wants to be friends? Like in his e-mail, saying I looked amazing? That's flirting, isn't it? Maybe not. Maybe he's just being nice. Giving me a compliment because he feels sorry for me.

My cell phone rings as I'm logging off my e-mail. I see that it's Dad and don't answer. He took Mom's side when I asked him if he'd pay for me to live on campus next year. He said he'd rather I wait until I'm a sophomore.

I totally lost it. He's allowed to act my age, but I'm not? How fair is that?

Now Dad calls me all the time, like he's trying to make up for not helping me move out, not to mention everything else he's done. Sometimes he asks me to dinner or a movie. Sometimes he just wants to talk. Which is crazy since we don't have anything at all to talk about. Last week I caved and went with him to Pappadeaux's. Afterward, we stopped at this coffee shop for dessert and, surprise! His current girlfriend works there. Natalie. Or Nattie, as Dad calls her.

Puke.

Supposedly she's only working in the coffee shop part-time while she goes to college. Which tells me just how young she is. He's never introduced me to one of his girlfriends before. Maybe he thinks it's okay now since the divorce is final. Or maybe he's serious about this one.

Puke again.

All I need is a stepmom I run into every day on campus next year. Or to hook up with some guy and find out he used to go out with my stepmom.

Double puke.

I find Mom and Nana in the backyard. I sit beside Nana at the patio table. She's watching Mom trot Max around on a leash. Mom looks ridiculous running along beside him, her posture all stiff and straight, her steps perfectly spaced. She's been acting weird lately. Training and grooming Max all the time, painting the house wild colors. After her purple bedroom, she started on the den. It's so red it looks like someone got murdered with a chain saw in there. She makes me crazy, but still I feel bad for her, too. Dad really hurt her, and I know she's not over it. But what can I do?

"Oh, hi Erin," Mom calls out. "Watch this." She gives a short, shrill whistle, and Max stops trotting. Mom grins like he just did a cartwheel or something.

"That's impressive, Cecilia," Nana says. "You'd make your father proud."

Mom unleashes Max then walks toward us. "Erin, did I ever tell you that we always had a bulldog when Jack and I were kids, and that Grandpop used to enter them in competitions?"

"I don't think so."

Nana's laugh sounds light as air. "Up until your mother started high school and got too busy, she loved helping him train."

Mom's out of breath. She sits in a patio chair across from us. "Do you have plans for tonight? I thought we all might go out for Chinese."

"I'm going to a movie."

"With Noah?"

"Suz."

"Good. You're spending too much time with that kid."

I cross my arms. "Whatever, Mom. We've never even gone out. He just comes over."

"It's not a good idea to let one guy monopolize all your free time. Is he still coming for Thanksgiving?"

"Yes, is that a problem?"

"Of course not," Nana says. "The more the merrier. Less leftovers, too."

Mom gets all slit-eyed as she stares across the table at Nana. Her cheeks cave in, like she's biting the insides of them to keep from saying something. She turns to me. "When's the movie?"

"Seven-thirty."

"I guess it's just Nana and me for Chinese food then."

Nana coughs. "Sorry, Sugar, I forgot to tell you, Oliver is coming by tonight. He's singing a solo at Parkview's Christmas party this year, and he asked if I'd accompany him on piano. We're going to practice." She fans her face with one hand. "My goodness, it's hot out here."

"Hot?" Laughing and shivering, I turn to Mom. "You're not hot, are you? It's November."

I don't think she hears me. Her expression reminds me of Max's when we leave him in the backyard alone too long. For a minute, I forget I'm mad at her. "Hey, Mom," I say, trying to sound upbeat. "You should ask the Margarita Martyrs over."

She frowns. "The who?"

The surprised look on my grandmother's face makes me laugh. "Ever since y'all got together last time, Nana's called your friends that."

"I swear, Erin Dupree. Even as a little girl, you never could keep a secret," Nana says.

Our nosy neighbor pokes her head over the fence. Her dyed red hair is pulled back into a tight bun. Her lips are red, too, and her overtanned skin is stretched too tight across sharp cheekbones. I know she has to look in the mirror to draw on her eyebrows. What is she thinking? Is she blind?

"Hello you three."

Mom waves and wiggles her fingers. "Hello Mrs. Stein."

"I was in the yard and I couldn't help but overhear that you're footloose and fancy-free tonight, CiCi."

"Not necessarily," Mom says. "I haven't asked Max yet if he wants Chinese."

"You'll never guess who I ran into at the grocery store today," Mrs. Stein continues as if she didn't hear Mom's sarcastic comment. "The Calloways? Raymond and Lila? Used to live in the tan brick house at the end of the block? Well, I invited them to dinner and they asked if they could bring their son, Anthony. Remember him? He lived with his parents. Still does."

Mrs. Stein makes a tsking sound as she

stoops to pick up her barking poodle. "Such a shame. Forty-three years old and never married. Such a gorgeous man, too. Almost pretty he's so perfect. And what a wardrobe."

When I giggle, both Mom and Nana nudge me under the table with their feet.

Mrs. Stein's nostrils flare when she looks at me. "Well, I take it you've heard all the talk about him. Raymond and Lila assure me it's not true. So anyway, CiCi, I was thinking how nice it would be if you'd join us tonight."

"I'd have to bring Maxwell."

Mom's joking, but I can tell by Mrs. Stein's shocked eyes, that she doesn't know that. She wrinkles her nose and holds her poodle tighter. "Pom Pom would be too nervous with him there. She's delicate, you know. Surely he'd be okay alone for a couple of hours while you and Anthony get to know one another better. What do you say?"

At ten o'clock, Suz parks in our driveway. She nods at an old-timey car at the curb. "Whose is that?"

"I don't know. Nana's friend's, I guess."

"It looks like something out of a black-and-white movie."

"So does Nana's friend."

Suz laughs. "Erin!"

"I didn't mean it that way. He's just, well . . . what's the word? A gentleman, I guess. He treats Nana like a queen. And he . . ." I try to find the right word, one you'd read in a romance novel to describe a man like Nana's friend. "He swaggers. You know, like John Wayne."

Suz laughs again. "I'll wait down the street for you. How long will it be?"

"Give me thirty minutes."

"Okay. I'll have time to get a cherry-lime then."

Reaching for the door handle, I turn to her. "Maybe Noah's just nervous. Maybe that's why he hasn't kissed me yet."

"You are so naive. Guys don't get nervous about stuff like that."

"How do you know? Why wouldn't they? We do."

Suzanna taps her fingers against the steering wheel to the beat of Avril Lavigne. "He's just messing with you. Trying to keep you guessing. That way, when he *does* kiss you, you'll be so relieved who knows what you might give in and do." She wiggles her eyebrows.

"You are such a dork." I open the door and step out. "See you in thirty minutes."

Piano music plays in the living room.

White Christmas. I close the front door and head for the den.

Mom's watching the movie *When Harry Met Sally,* which she's seen a million and one times. "How was dinner at the Steins' with pretty Anthony?"

She lifts some sort of pastry from a plate on the coffee table. "I got a severe stomachache and had to call and beg off." Mom takes a bite and talks with her mouth full. "You're home early. You have another hour until curfew. Not that I'm complaining."

"We couldn't think of anything to do after the movie. Besides, I'm sort of tired."

"You've had a busy week. The Scot hasn't helped matters by coming over every night."

"Noah, Mom. His name is Noah. And he hasn't come over every night."

"Right. Sorry." She takes another bite. "Mmmm. Try one of these chocolate éclairs Nana made. They're so good they should be illegal."

"No, thanks." Mom finishes off hers then starts on another. If she doesn't watch it, she'll have to buy a whole new wardrobe. She's starting to look pudgy. "I think I'll go to bed."

The piano music stops.

"Wait," Mom says, her mouth stuffed with chocolate goo. She swallows. "Tell me about the movie first. Was it good?"

"It was okay."

"So, just you and Suzanna went?"

I should've known I wouldn't escape a pop quiz. "I already told you."

"Is that a 'yes' or a 'no'?"

"*Yes.*" I glance up at the ceiling. "Jeez."

Nana and her friend come into the room. She walks, he swaggers. "Oh, Erin, you're back. You remember Mr. Winston, don't you?"

"Oliver," the old man says. "How are you, young lady?"

I like him already. I like anybody who interrupts my mother, the interrogator. "Good. How are you?"

"Fine as silk thread."

Yawning, I look at my watch. "Well, see you later. I'm going to read in bed."

"Maybe we can help Nana with the Thanksgiving baking tomorrow," Mom says before I take two steps.

"I'm going shopping. Besides, you can't cook."

Mom looks all offended. "Says who?"

Nana and I burst out laughing.

"Uh-oh," Oliver says. "You ladies are treading on shaky ground."

"Okay, you two." Mom smiles. She has a dot of chocolate icing above her top lip.

"Then I'll go shopping with you. You and Suzanna haven't had any luck finding a concert dress without me."

"I found one. They did alterations. I'm picking it up."

Her smile falls. "Oh."

Why does she always have to make me feel so guilty?

As I head down the hallway I hear Nana say, "I changed my mind, Oliver. I think I would like to go for some hot tea."

"This late?" Mom blurts. "We have tea."

"In bags," Nana says. "For some reason, I'm craving the real thing, leaves brewed in a pot, with real cream."

I close and lock my bedroom door. No way am I living here when I start college. Mom's so needy all the sudden that even my seventy-five-year-old grandmother can't leave the house without her butting in. If I stay here, *Mom* will be seventy-five by the time she gets a date and *I'll* be the one on the couch stuffing my face with chocolate.

Memories of that last night with Judd twist my stomach when Suz and I walk into The Beat. I remind myself that everything's different this time. I'm dressed somewhere in between the old, boring me and the new, wild me, I'm not wearing so much makeup, and my hair doesn't look like I stuck my finger in a light socket, as Grandpop used to say. Oh, and no jellyfish tonight, either. They're back where they belong, on Katie's concave chest.

Suz's cousin isn't working the door tonight so I use the fake ID Judd gave me. Not that I plan to drink; I don't. Just the thought of a lemon-drop martini makes me woozy.

Music blares and pulses, but it's the piped-in kind, not Noah's band, Cateye. The three of them are on stage setting up. Noah wears jeans and a black T-shirt. The other two guys have on seventies-looking aviator-style sunglasses, even though it's dark in here.

As Suz and I weave our way through the crowd toward the band, I notice how thin and tall Noah is. Thin in a good way, all angles and wide shoulders, nothing soft about him.

When Noah spots me, he props his guitar against a speaker, says something to the bass player, hops down off the stage and comes over. He says hello to Suz as he takes my hand and eyes my hair and clothes. "Hey, I like the look." When he grins, I think I was wrong that nothing about him is soft; his eyes are. He gives me a quick kiss on the cheek. "You smell good, too. No cigarettes."

I laugh. "I decided to save my money and just breathe the secondhand smoke." It's like every ounce of energy in my body zooms in on the feel of his hand around mine. Warm. Dry. Strong. The tips of his long fingers are callused from playing guitar.

"Who's your drummer?" Suz asks him. She's had her eye on the guy since the second we walked in.

"Tonto." Noah grins at Suz when he sees her checking out his friend. "Come on up, I'll introduce you."

We follow Noah onto the stage and meet the other two guys in the band, Tonto and Reese and then Suz and I leave to find a table since it's time for them to start their set.

They play old rock and roll, but put their own sound to it. Some of the songs I recognize from Mom's collection of old vinyl albums and eight-track tapes I used to listen to when I was little.

"They're good," Suz shouts over the noise.

I think so, too. Noah not only plays lead guitar, he sings. He doesn't seem the least bit embarrassed up there on stage. Not that he should be. He has talent. He looks hot, too. Now I understand why all those girls at rock concerts way back in Mom's day, or maybe even before, used to scream and cry and faint.

I'm not the only one who notices, either. The way the hoochies at the next table look at Noah, I'm surprised there's not a big pool of drool on the floor at their feet.

Back off. He's with me, I want to say, but don't have the nerve. Besides, *is* he with me? I mean, yeah we're talking, but maybe that's all.

When the band takes a break, Reese heads for the bar and Noah and Tonto come over and sit with us. "You were incredible," I tell them.

Focused on Suz, Tonto drums the table-top with his palms. "I hope the manager thinks so."

Noah balances on the two back legs of his chair and scans the room. "He says if this works out tonight, we might get a standing Friday night gig."

"I could use the cash," Tonto adds, taking Suz's glass of Coke when she offers it to him. "The pay's good here."

"You'll get the job." Suz gives Tonto her flirty smile while he gulps down her Coke. "The crowd was into you."

"Yeah. Some really old dude in the back was even busting a move." Tonto gives Suz back her drink, resumes drumming the table, and shifts his attention to Noah. "We need to get Miner back. Something's missing without him."

"Our keyboard player," Noah explains to us. "He quit last month." He turns back to Tonto. "Miner's through. He doesn't have time to play anymore since he's working a full-time job."

"Erin could play keyboard, couldn't you, Erin?" Suz tosses her hair like an actress in a shampoo commercial. "She plays piano."

Noah leans forward. The front legs of his chair hit the floor. "I thought you played cello?"

"I do. But I've had piano lessons since I was six." I don't add that, unlike most kids, my mom never had to bug me to practice.

"You should hear her," Suz says. "She could play professionally."

I look away. "Whatever."

"She could." Suz offers Tonto another drink of her Coke and totally ignores me. "Trust me, she's a music genius. It's her thing."

The thing that's added to my loser status ever since I hit middle school. Face it, if you're in a rock band, you're cool. But join school band or orchestra and you can pretty much kiss any chance at prom queen goodbye. As if I'd want to be prom queen anyway.

Nodding his head and tapping his fingertips on the table, Tonto stares at me. "What do you think, Noah? We still have Miner's keyboard. She could practice with us on Sunday."

"I think that's a good idea." Noah smiles at me. "If you want to, I mean."

"Sure." I shrug. "Sounds like fun."

"Bring your cello, too." Noah stands. "We might come up with something."

At 2:00 a.m. when The Beat closes, Noah takes me home on his cycle, and Tonto follows Suz to her house in his truck, since it's late and she's alone.

I wear Noah's helmet and hold tight around his waist as the cool air rushes past us.

He parks at the curb at the end of my block and cuts the engine. Together, we walk six houses down to my yard and stand under the pear tree to the left of my bedroom window.

Noah sees me shiver. "Cold?"

"Sort of."

He opens his jacket. "I'll share."

I step closer and he wraps the jacket and his arms around me. He's five or six inches taller than me. I tilt my head back to look up at him.

"Thanks for coming tonight," he says, his breath warm against my face. It smells like peppermint. No cinnamon. No tobacco. No bad memories.

"I had fun." He looks into my eyes for what seems like forever, and I think *just do it,* but he doesn't. A story Nana told me about her and Grandpop's first kiss slips into my thoughts. Quick, before I can change my mind, I lift onto my tiptoes and kiss Noah, just touch my mouth to his and leave it there. Not long, but longer than the pecks he's given me.

When I pull away, my heart pounds so hard I hear it. Noah stares into my eyes again, and then his arms tighten around me. This time, *he* kisses *me,* so slow and gentle I feel like I'm floating. I lift my arms and encircle his neck, hold on to him. With Noah, I don't feel any fear or dread or pressure for more. I only feel his arms around me, his lips against mine, the beat of his heart keeping time with my own.

Chapter 12

From The Desk of
Belle Lamont

Dear Harry,

Happy Thanksgiving! What a wonderful day we had. I do so enjoy cooking for our family. We missed Jack and his family. And we missed you.

CiCi mentioned how much you loved my chestnut dressing. Erin said nobody would ever match your deviled eggs, then realized she'd insulted mine and got embarrassed about it.

Erin's friend, Noah, carved the turkey. While he did, I sensed that, like me, CiCi and Erin thought about Bert, since after he and Cecilia married, you turned the carving over to him. I know Erin wished her father was with us; I think during that moment, Cecilia did, too.

Erin's Noah is a friendly, outgoing young man. He seems to have his head on straight, and he holds his own with CiCi, which is the best thing of all and a hoot to behold. When she saw that I'd placed Bert's carving knife on the table, she took off for the kitchen mumbling something about Christmas rolling around before a kid Noah's age could slice a turkey without an electric knife. When she came back, he'd already served her the first slice, me the second and was filling Erin's plate. In Noah, our daughter has met her match, I'm afraid. One thing is obvious; he's crazy about Erin, and the feeling is mutual. When they look at one another, I'm reminded of us when we were their age and falling in love.

What a beautiful gift, our love, our years together. I never realized how quickly the time would pass. When I was young, my mother always told me that life waits for no one. I didn't understand then, but now I do. I can either live it, or watch it streak by and leave me behind.

A while back, Erin asked if I thought young men get nervous about first kisses like girls do. I told her about ours and the weeks leading up to it. Sometimes it seems like just yesterday, that summer we met. In my memories, the days are fringed in gold, the long walks and cold swims, the sunshine and the laughter. Nothing else mattered except the way you looked at me. Oh, how I loved that look.

I told Erin how, after my family moved to town and into your neighborhood, you drove by my house for days in your brother's '41 Ford sedan before "just dropping by" to meet me. How three more days passed before you found the nerve to call and ask me out on a date.

I still laugh when I think of how you stuttered and stammered and beat around the bush. We talked for at least an hour about everything from our families to Dizzy Gillespie to Jackie Robinson playing with the Dodgers. Finally, Mr. Dryden broke in on the party line and said, "Son, I need to make a call. Ask her out and get it over with." And so you did.

We went to *The Ghost and Mrs. Muir*, remember? The theatre was so crowded we had to sit in the balcony. Gene Tierney and Rex Harrison were incredibly romantic. So were you. You held my hand in the dark, and I just knew you'd kiss me before the night ended. But you didn't. Not then or on the next date or the one after that. I swear, Harry, you certainly knew how to make a girl suffer and doubt herself. You had me questioning everything from the scent of my perfume to the fit of my girdle.

Then at the end of date number four,

when you walked me to my parents' front porch, I took matters into my own hands.

Well, apparently either Erin followed my lead, or Noah found his nerve, because I saw them necking out front before he left tonight. So sweet. But it worries me, too. Can you imagine what CiCi would do if she found out about Erin sneaking out her window after curfew to meet that boy? Go into a tizzy, that's what.

Erin doesn't know I followed her to a nightclub where Noah's band played. I stood in the back and kept an eye on things. Not because I'm a busybody, but because I'm concerned for her safety. Blending in with a crowd of teens and twenty-somethings was no easy task, let me tell you. Don't worry. I didn't go alone. A friend took me. I know my limitations. I don't trust myself to drive anymore with these eyes.

Speaking of my friend, I've never lied to you, Harry, and I won't start now. His name is Oliver Winston. I hope you know I'd never betray your memory by allowing my relationship with him or any other man to become more than friendship. Still, I have to start living again. Watching Erin push her fears aside to dive headfirst into life, makes me realize I've been a coward, afraid of drowning. I refuse to piddle away any more of the time I have left. And I do so enjoy Oliver's company. I'm sure if the two of you met you'd hit it off in an instant.

Anyway, guess who Cecilia caught sneaking in after 2:00 a.m. on that night Erin went to the nightclub? No, not our granddaughter. Me. Unfortunately, my body isn't up to climbing in and out of windows these days, so I came through the front door. Not that I feel I need to sneak around. For heaven's sake, I'm a grown woman three-quarters of a century old! Still, Cecilia was beside herself. You always wondered if she heard anything you said all those times you got onto her as a teenager. She heard you, Harry. Loud and clear. Your words came out of her mouth. What a scolding she gave me! I half expected her to ground me and send me to my room.

As far as Cecilia knew, Erin was asleep through all this, and I didn't say otherwise. I'm still in a quandary about what to do about Erin's secret. Though I don't approve of her method of breaking away, I understand. Erin's ready to fly, but CiCi's determined to clip her wings.

Should I confront Erin and encourage her to stop breaking her mother's rules? To work things out with CiCi? I just wish she'd go to her and explain that she needs a bit more freedom. I'd like to believe that Cecilia would be reasonable, but I guess I'm being an idealistic fool. CiCi's anything but reasonable these days. Since separating from Bert, she's become so cynical it scares me. If she doesn't come to terms with what's bothering her soon, I shudder to think what color she'll paint the bathroom. Or my room, for that matter. The place is starting to look like a carnival fun house.

On a happier note, remember I told you the reading group was forced to disband? Well, we're meeting again in a different location. The Frans told Billie Jean Bilderback who told Ellen Miles who told me, that the problem had something to do with Doris Quinn and Frank Rayburn. When I mentioned that possibility to Jane Binkley, she said she'd heard rumors that the two of them are fooling around. Who knows if that's true? As I've said before, Jane has a bit of a dirty mind.

Then again, Doris is such an eyelash batter, I wouldn't put it past her. I'm not sure what her love life has to do with our reading group, but if I find out, I'll let you know. Until then, my love . . .

As always, your yellow rose,
Belle

Chapter 13

Cecilia Dupree
Day Planner
Wednesday, 12/5

1. 10:00 — new patient consultation.
2. 1:00 — P.V. reading group/finish Penelope.
3. Demand refund at dry cleaners for shrinking slacks.
4. 5:00 — drop Max at Gertie's.

Mother and I huddle in our coats on our way to Oliver's apartment and the final three chapters of *Penelope's Passion*. Tiny lights twist around the lampposts that line the walkway through Parkview Manor's courtyard. The multicolored glow adds a warm festive touch to this nose-numbing, gloomy afternoon. A short distance away, at the entrance to the park, the duck pond gazebo also twinkles and blinks.

I wonder how many of Parkview Manor's residents will spend the holidays alone? It's too sad to think about. I guess I understand why people do crazy, desperate things in search of another chance at love.

I understand, but it doesn't mean I'll follow that path to frustration. I'd rather shave my bikini line with a dull, rusty razor than go on a date. Will I feel the same way, though, years from now when Mother's gone? When Erin's grown and on her own? Or will I grasp at any opportunity, no matter how foolish, that might land me a little companionship?

Which brings me to my ten o'clock appointment and the biggest opportunity-grasper of all time. Henry "you-can-call-me-Hank" Bocock. Fifty-six and going through his third divorce. Ex-rodeo cowboy turned rancher. Lover of snakeskin boots, starched open-collared shirts and gold neck chains to accent his furry throat.

As it turns out, my neighbor, the ever-so-helpful Mrs. Stein, my very own Cupid in a caftan, referred Hank to me, certain I might help him "get over Gloria." Funny, I got the distinct impression that Gloria was the last thing on Hank's mind. He seemed more interested in my legs than my advice. A fact I found amusing since, beneath my opaque black stockings, my calves are almost as hairy as his chest; I haven't shaved in four days. No, make that five.

But back to my point. In order to meet a prospective companion, (me), Hank shelled out a good amount of change for a therapy session he didn't need. Pretty creative of Hank, I must admit. Or Mrs. Stein; I'm not sure who came up with the idea. What the incident tells me, though, is that competition in the middle-aged dating world is fierce. I don't want any part of it. I'll stick with the safety of the tried, true and loyal to keep me company; Max, movies, the King (of Hearts, not Elvis).

I glance across at Mother. She hums "Winter Wonderland," a smile on her face.

"So what sort of novel do you think we should start next week?" I ask.

The humming fades into a *hmmm.* "Jane, Mr. Gaines and The Frans all called this morning. They want another romantic adventure." White puffs drift from Mother's mouth with each word she speaks. She secures the top button of her coat. "Oh, look. There's Jane now."

We both call out a greeting to Jane Binkley, whose wild, bushy hair is a different shade of blond today, and the Don Knotts look-alike ahead of us. Jane's hips swing as, arm-in-arm, they round the corner of the walkway connecting Parkview's bungalows to the apartment building. They yell "hello" and go inside. Don's step is so springy I wouldn't be surprised if his head hits the ceiling when he walks down the hall.

Mom tucks her gloved hands into her coat pockets. "According to Jane, others in the group want another romance, too."

"And you?"

"I wouldn't mind. Look how much our membership has grown since we started *Penelope's Passion.* It's wonderful, isn't it?"

Her eyes are as sparkly as the twinkle lights, as happy as I've seen them in a very long time. I tell myself her perkiness is due to the spirit of the season, or possibly a result of coming to live with Erin and me. But then I glance up at the building and see Oliver Winston standing at his third-story window looking down at us, and the truth slides like an avalanche right down to the pit of my stomach.

They've spent a lot of time together lately. The past two Friday nights, Mother's tiptoed in after 2:00 a.m., reeking of cigarette smoke. *Dancing,* she tells me when I ask where they've been. *Just friends. No big deal. No need to get upset.*

Right. Sure thing. If you think I believe that, stand on your ear. First my daughter, now my mother. And here I am, sandwiched in the middle like a pickle in a bun, trying to keep them from ruining their lives.

And feeling like a hypocrite.

Intellectually, I understand Mother's need for companionship. Like I told Donald Quinn and Sue Kiley about their parents, Mother's a grown-up, and I have no business butting into her love life. But I'm finding it's not so simple to be reasonable when it's my own parent flirting with love. It's not so amusing. Or sweet. Or easy to accept.

Up at the window, the old fart smiles and waves. Mother smiles and waves back. "Oliver says the reading group is the buzz of the village. Everyone looks forward to it. I swear, I think if we met every day instead of just once a week we'd still have a full house."

As I reach for the door to the building, it swings open and Bill Burdette, the manager, steps out. Squinting, he glances over his shoulder before aiming his gaze at me. "We need to talk."

"Okay." His serious expression tells me he's not preparing to ask me to tap dance at the Parkview Christmas program. "Go on up, Mother. I'll be there in a minute."

Bill waits for Mother to leave then steps outside and closes the door.

"Are you having a hot flash, Bill?" I shiver and laugh. "How about we have this discussion inside where it's warm?"

"I don't want anyone to hear this." He glances around again, sees that we're alone then says, "Iris Shelby and Herbert O'Dell eloped last night."

"No kidding?"

He shakes his head. "They're eighty-something years old. Both of them."

I lower my voice to a whisper and lean toward him. "Iris isn't pregnant, is she?"

"That's not funny, CiCi. I thought we had an understanding that the reading group was on hold."

"We're meeting in a private residence."

"Within this facility."

"In Oliver Winston's home, which he pays for. I don't understand why you're so upset. As long as it's legal, he can hold any kind of meeting he wants, and Parkview Manor's in the clear. Besides, what does this have to do with Iris and Herbert getting married?"

"They attend your reading group, don't they?"

"Front row and center every Wednesday." The cold numbs my toes. I stomp my feet to jump-start my circulation. "So?"

"Iris Shelby's son has power of attorney over her money. He writes the checks for her to live here, and he's not the only one. Many of our residents receive financial assistance from their children or have turned over legal control of their funds. If we piss off the kids, the parents could be forced to move someplace else. Then the Village loses money and my job's at risk."

"Calm down, Bill. Iris is only one resident." I step around him, open the door and go inside. My panty hose feel like they're about to cut me in two. I must have accidentally bought a size smaller than my usual medium.

Bill follows me down the hallway to the elevator, walking fast until he's at my side. "There's more." The elevator dings. The doors slide open and three women step off. Bill straightens, flashes his too-white teeth. "Seasons greetings, ladies. Bundle up if you're going outside. Jack Frost is paying us a visit today." His chuckle is loud and hollow, like a shopping mall Santa's at the end of a very long day.

I step onto the elevator. Bill joins me. I push *Three*. Bill's smile falls as the elevator rises.

"Saturday when the maintenance guy went out to the duck pond, he heard voices in the gazebo. "When he checked it out, he found Jane Binkley and Stanley McDougal inside getting it on." He shudders.

An image flashes through my mind. The shriveled-up old prune of a guy I saw with Mrs. Binkley only moments ago. Naked. In the gazebo. On Jane. I shudder, too. The elevator dings. I burst out laughing.

"Shhhh!" Bill blinks terror at me as the doors slide open. He blows out a long breath when we find the hallway empty.

"I'm surprised at you, CiCi. What if your mother was in that gazebo instead of Jane?"

I sober. "I'd be horrified."

"Then how can you laugh?"

"I know. But, the thing is, it *wasn't* my mother." As I start off toward Oliver's apartment with Bill on my heels, I struggle to control my humor, but do a miserable job of it.

"Pardon me for saying so, but I expected a more mature reaction from you."

"I'm sorry. It's just . . . it was something like forty-eight degrees on Saturday. They didn't get frostbite, did they?"

I notice a twitch at one corner of Bill's mouth. "According to the maintenance guy they spread Jane's chinchilla coat on the bench underneath them and covered up with her full-length mink."

"I hope the animal rights people don't get wind of this."

Bill glares.

I laugh again. Nothing but the best for Jane. I've seen her apartment. Very classy, from the artwork on the walls right down to the fancy brass toilet paper holder in the bathroom. So I'm guessing there must be more to skinny little Stanley McDougal than meets the eye. What that "more" might be, I'd rather not contemplate.

When I reach Oliver's apartment, I stop and turn to face Bill. Behind him, Roy West, wearing a cowboy hat and swinging a cane, escorts Ellen Miles toward us. Her rubber-soled shoes squeak against the tiled floor.

"CiCi," Ellen calls out. "You were right on target about me needing to get up off the couch and become more involved. Roy and I have been bowling on Mondays, coming to reading group on Wednesdays, doing water aerobics on Thursday mornings and going to the Village dances on Saturday nights. I have so much energy now I can't believe it."

Roy winks. "I'm having to double up on my vitamins just to keep up with the woman."

When they stop alongside us, Ellen takes my hand. "Thank you. I owe you so much."

I'm overcome by the gratitude I see in her eyes, as well as by the change in her. Ellen was lethargic and depressed only a few weeks ago when we first met. "You're wel-

191

come, Ellen. But you made the changes, not me."

Roy knocks on Oliver's apartment door. Someone inside calls, "Come in!" He releases Ellen's arm. "We'll leave the door open for you, CiCi," he says, his dentures whistling.

I glance inside.

Bill looks over my shoulder. "Notice anything unusual?"

In the past when I've attended Parkview functions, the women tend to gather on one side of the room, the men on the other. That isn't the case today. The scene inside Oliver's apartment looks more like a crowded cocktail party than a reading group. Couples talk and laugh together. Some hold hands.

"They're paired off," Bill says. "Almost all of them."

"Is that such a bad thing?" I try to sound self-assured, but inside I'm as conflicted as I've ever been.

"For the most part, yes," Bill says defensively. "But there is one bright spot in all of this. Sales of flowers, candy and condoms are up more than forty percent in the gift shop and store."

"Condoms?" I glance back at him. "You're joking."

"Nope."

"See? What are you worried about? They're practicing safe sex."

His brows lift. "The maintenance man said that before he interrupted Mrs. Binkley and Mr. McDougal in the gazebo, he heard her call him 'Captain.' "

I chew the inside of my cheek and try to look clueless. "So maybe Mr. McDougal was in the service."

"I've read the book, CiCi. I know all about Penelope and the captain. It's pretty steamy stuff."

Yeah, and I bet Bill enjoyed every sweaty word, but before I can say so, commotion erupts inside the apartment, and someone yells, "Call 911!"

Bill and I push our way through the murmuring throng of people in the living room. They stare down at the center of the floor at something I can't see. I feel a hand on my arm and glance over to find Mother at my side.

"It's Frank Rayburn," she whispers, her face as white as the snowflakes dancing in the air outside Oliver's window.

"Everyone step aside, please," Bill yells.

The crowd parts, and I follow him to where Frank lies on the floor faceup. Mary Fran, a retired R.N., pumps Frank's chest and counts while Francis gives mouth-to-mouth.

Doris kneels at Frank's feet, her body trembling. "Not again. This can't happen to me twice." She looks up into my eyes. I take her hand and help her stand. "It isn't fair."

I ache for Doris. She should've guarded her heart after her husband died. But it's too late to tell her that now. Too late for Doris, but not for my mother.

Mother's eyes are closed, her palm pressed to her chest. I hope she learns a hard lesson from this terrifying moment. Nothing's worth the panic Doris feels right now.

In the distance, a siren's wail pierces the hushed winter day and suddenly, in my mind, I'm not holding Doris's hand, but Mother's, and instead of Frank on the floor, it's Dad. The past unfolds. Mother's desperate eyes, her cry, her body crumpling like a paper doll. And me completely helpless as something vital, something I'd convinced myself would last forever, slips through my fingers, and the world spirals out of control.

In the hospital Emergency waiting room, Mother and I sit on either side of Doris. Frank Rayburn's daughter, Sue Kiley, paces in front of us. Oozing dread from every pore, Bill Burdette sits in a corner and watches her.

It seems like hours before a young, female, frazzled-looking doctor walks in and takes Sue Kiley aside. They talk in quiet voices for a few minutes, then the doctor exits through the same door she came in while Sue gathers her purse and coat.

When Sue starts down the hallway after the doctor, Bill hurries behind her, calling her name. He catches up, stops her. I can't hear their conversation, only the sharp, angry tone of Sue Kiley's voice.

Doris excuses herself to join them and, after a bit of back and forth between her and Frank's daughter, she takes off with the woman.

I turn to Mother. "How are you doing?"

"One second you're laughing, the next your life changes. Just like that." She blinks at me. "I can't help thinking about your father. This brings it all back."

"I know."

"Poor Doris."

"She set herself up to get hurt again."

"By caring for Frank?" Mother frowns concern at me.

Tears burn the backs of my eyes; I don't know why I'm so emotional. Memories of Dad, I guess. "Frank Rayburn is close to eighty if he isn't already. Doris lost one man she loved. Why would she want to put herself through that again?"

"Oh, Sugar." She covers our joined hands with her free one. "That would be a miserable way to live. Not allowing yourself to care for anyone because you're afraid of getting hurt."

Bill saves me from a discussion I'd rather not begin by stopping in front of us and clearing his throat. I glance up at him, anxiety heavy in my chest. "Is Frank — ?"

"Mr. Rayburn will be fine. He's awake and answering questions. It wasn't a heart attack. He just passed out."

"Thank God," Mother murmurs. For Doris's sake, she's stayed strong and calm, but now she starts to shake.

I wrap an arm around her shoulders. "You okay?"

She leans into me. "I am now."

I look up at Bill. "Why did he faint?"

"Apparently Frank's been taking one of those new drugs for . . ." He clears his throat again. "For sexual dysfunction and —"

"Oh . . ." Mother lifts a hand to her cheek.

"He didn't suffer one of those four-hour erection side effects the commercials talk about, did he?"

Mother blushes. "CiCi! For heaven's sake."

Bill looks at the floor.

I shrug. "I'm just asking. I'm guessing

that could make a man pass out. You know, from lack of blood supply to the brain?"

"It wasn't that. Apparently he's on blood pressure meds, so he's not allowed to take anything for his . . ." Bill darts a glance at Mother. "His doctors won't prescribe anything for the dysfunction, so he borrowed some pills from a friend. The medication caused his blood pressure to drop. That's why he fainted."

I puff out my cheeks. "Wow. Not good."

"Sue Kiley is in full agreement with you on that point. She advised me to call Parkview's lawyer."

"As if you had anything to do with this." I shake my head. "Unbelievable."

Mother sighs. "Why is it people so often feel the need to cast blame?"

Bill scratches his head. "She advised that you call your attorney, too, CiCi."

"What?" I stand. "Why? What did I do?"

"She mentioned something about inciting irresponsible behavior among the members of the book group by exposing them to obscene reading material."

Mother gasps. "My word! *Penelope's Passion*?"

My head throbs. Lack of oxygen? From my waist-pinching control-top panty hose, perhaps? Maybe I'll pass out, too. Then I'll sue the panty hose manufacturer for inciting irresponsible flab constriction or something. Apparently a person can press charges for anything these days. "But I only have a divorce attorney. Robert Spinks. Ending marriages is all he does."

Mother pats my arm. "Don't worry, Sugar. This will blow over. You'll see."

"I wouldn't count on it," Bill says. "Sue Kiley's royally pissed." He sends Mother a sheepish glance. "Excuse my language, Mrs. Lamont."

"We'll ask your neighbor, Mrs. Stein." Mother talks fast, taking control of the situation since I can't seem to move or speak. "She'll know someone. She knows everybody."

I imagine my attorney-to-be, compliments of Mrs. Stein, in gold neck chains, snakeskin boots and skintight black leather pants, with an extreme comb-over that flaps open to the side like a hinged door as he pounds the table and bellows, "I object!" Just what I need. A lawyer who's a combination of you-can-call-me-Hank, mama's boy Anthony and the balding Bar Mitzvah guy all wrapped up into one scary package.

I draw a long breath, blow it out slowly. "No thanks, Mother. I'll ask Robert. He'll refer me to someone."

★ ★ ★

At a quarter past five o'clock, I pull into Rod and Sally Coker's graveled driveway. The small ranch-style house sits on ten acres of land just outside of the city. I'm proud of myself for being only fifteen minutes late and just making one wrong turn. Finding the place was no easy feat for a directionally challenged person like me. I need landmarks, lefts and rights. As in, you'll pass a tan brick house before crossing a railroad track. Take a left at the first street after the dump yard. Instead, Rod Coker gave me, exit north on farm-to-market something or other. Go about three miles, then take the southwest fork in the road for another five or so.

In the back seat of my minivan, Max snuffles as he shifts around in his kennel. Most likely he fears he's headed for the vet and some poking and prodding, possibly even a stick in the rump with a sharp needle.

"Calm down, Max," I say over my shoulder as I turn off the ignition. "What are you griping about?" He doesn't have to worry about a lawsuit, Mother's romance or Erin's biker-boy.

Max rattles the metal door with his nose.

"You should thank me. You've got two weeks ahead of nothing but sex and frolic in the country with the sinfully sumptuous Gertie, no strings attached."

He gives a plaintive cry.

"When it's over, you can just walk away. Never see her again. No child support. What a deal."

A blast of cold hits me as I step out of the car, open the back door, let Maxwell out of his kennel and leash him. Rod and Sally meet me in the yard. Both sixty-ish, he's as hard and callused and stone-faced as she is soft and round and animated.

"You're here!" Sally stoops to welcome Max with a scratch to the snout. "Gertie's been waiting for you, big guy," she says in a baby-talk voice. "You two are going to make me some grand-puppies. Yes you are!"

Max makes a pitiful sound and looks up at me with irritated eyes.

Rod Coker shakes his head, lights a cigarette and grumbles something unintelligible.

His wife stands. "Oh, hush." She gently slaps a mittened hand against her husband's arm, her eyes on me. "Rod thinks bulldogs are worthless because they don't hunt or point or retrieve. I say there's value in being cute and lovable."

I nod and laugh.

Mr. Coker huffs and takes a deep drag of tobacco.

He strikes me as a man who appreciates a dollar as well as a diesel truck and a well-oiled gun, so I say, "The puppies should make you some money. Gertie's from a good line. So is Maxwell."

He blows out a stream of smoke. "That's the only reason I agreed to this."

Sally climbs the steps to the porch again and opens the screen door. "Gertie! Gertie girl! Maxwell's here."

The little black and white dog wiggles out onto the porch, then she and Sally come down into the yard.

Sally claps her hands together. "Why don't you take Max off the leash, Mrs. Dupree? Let them get reacquainted."

When the Cokers came to my house to check out Max, the two dogs got along well enough for the few minutes they were together, though Max didn't make any amorous moves. Of course, Gertie wasn't in heat then. I expect more aggression from him now.

I take off his leash.

Gertie steps toward Max.

I hold my breath.

Max cowers.

Gertie sniffs.

Max looks back at me, tilts his head, yelps.

Good grief. Some Don Juan. I smile at the

Cokers and shrug. "It's his first time."

Sally giggles. "He's nervous."

Rod smirks and takes another drag. "What kind of stud dog gets performance anxiety?"

"*Rod!*" Sally cuts her gaze my direction. "Maybe he doesn't like an audience. Let's give them some space."

They follow me to the car. I get out Max's kennel, his water and food bowls, his favorite chew toy, which Rod eyes with undisguised scorn. Not a good idea, bringing the squeaky pink kitty, I realize, shooting a glance in Max's direction just in time to see him squat and water a sparse patch of snow.

Nice touch, Max. I hold my breath, hoping the Cokers won't turn around. Why can't he lift his leg? The big wuss. Doesn't he care that his reputation's at stake? Not to mention the stud fee?

I drop the kitty and the bowls, stalling for time. "Oops. Sorry to be so clumsy."

Sally picks up the toy. "How darling! Look, Rod."

He grunts, then pokes the half-smoked cig into the corner of his mouth and lifts the bowls from the ground. I take them from him, and Sally and I follow as he hauls the kennel onto the porch.

"Well, that's it, I guess." I whistle for Max.

He prisses up onto the porch and sits at my feet. I stoop to look at him. "Mind your manners. Be good to Gertie."

As Rod mumbles his way down the steps and Sally coos for Gertie, I lean forward and whisper into Max's ear. "Prove Bert wrong, would you? Don't be a girly-dog. Show the world you can be as macho as the next guy."

He blinks at me then looks out into the yard where Gertie's humping Rod Coker's leg.

"Good gawd," the man snaps, shaking the dog off him.

Max lifts his gaze to mine. *This is the girl you've chosen for me?* his eyes seem to ask.

Poor dog. He doesn't want a date any more than I do. I'd call the whole thing off, but unfortunately this breeding thing isn't just a diversion anymore. If Sue Kiley really goes forward with a lawsuit, who knows what kind of legal fees I'll wrack up? The extra money will ease my mind.

I give Max a little shove to the rump. "Where's your sense of adventure, buddy? Go get her. You can do it."

But as I drive away and see Max in the rearview mirror, lying in the yard, his head between his paws, I'm not so sure he can.

I tell myself he'll warm up to her eventually.

Or maybe not. Maybe he needs a boost.

I could go back to the hospital and ask Mr. Rayburn the name of his Viagra connection. Better yet, I could read Max a few choice chapters of *Penelope's Passion.* Maybe the book will have the same effect on animals that it does on people.

Chapter 14

The offices of Colby and Colby Attorneys are modest by Dallas standards. Robert Spinks, my divorce lawyer, assured me that the Colby brothers' lack of refinement in decor did not denote a lack of professional ability. According to Robert, Nathan Colby is the best, the one you want on your side if you end up in court. As I stand in the lobby staring at the empty chair behind the receptionist's desk and the dusty computer atop it, the big fish mounted on the wall, frozen midflop, I start to have serious doubts about Robert's judgment.

I slip out of my coat, fold it over one arm, then step closer to the entrance of the short adjoining hallway. There's an open door on the left. I see a long conference table inside surrounded by chairs. Farther down the hall is a second open door, across from it, a third.

"Hello?"

No answer. Rhythmic tapping drifts from door number two. Deep, throaty laughter from three, the squeak of a chair.

"Hello!" I call out, louder this time.

The laughter stops. A head pokes out of door number three. Salt-and-pepper crew cut, wire-framed glasses. "Hey, there. I'm sorry." Nice smile. Sincere. A touch of small-town Texas in his drawl. "Be with you in a second. Let me end this call." The talking head disappears.

I take another step into the hallway, tap the sole of my snazzy new pumps against the carpet. My shoe fetish patient sold them to me at a drastic discount. They're perfect with my suit. I dressed up for the occasion. Or down, depending on your perspective. Nice and conservative. Serious professional. Don't want to look like the sort of loose, lecherous woman who'd lure old folks down the pathway to sin.

After a minute, the salt-and-pepper crew cut strolls out of his office, tightening his tie. "Sorry about that. Could I help you?"

"Are you Nathan Colby?" I hope so. His eyes are a sharp blue. Alert and intelligent.

"I'm Everett. Nate's brother. You here to see him?"

I glance at my watch. "I have an appointment at ten."

"Ah." He nods at door number two, beyond which the tapping ensues. "Follow me."

A man sits behind the desk, his back to the door, his boots propped and crossed on the credenza beneath the window he faces. The boots are scuffed hikers, not buffed cowboys like You-Can-Call-Me-Hank's. He wears jeans that look new, a pale blue dress shirt with sleeves rolled up to the elbows . . . and earphones. His fingers drum the flat surface of the laptop that's perched on his thighs.

Everett walks into the office and across to the edge of the desk. "Nate."

The man turns slightly, but the movement has nothing to do with his brother's voice, which he obviously doesn't hear. I see his face in profile. His eyes are closed. His head moves along with the beat he drums on the laptop. Rubbernecking, my dad would've called it. *"I can't get . . ."* he sings under his breath, off-key.

"Nate!" Everett knocks on the desk. "Hello."

". . . sa-tis-fac-tion . . ." tap, tap, tap *"no sa—"*

Everett pulls one earphone aside. *"Nate!"*

I expect a startled shout, boots falling from the credenza, the laptop crashing to the floor. Instead, he simply opens one eye. "Hey there, brother." The earphones come off. He yawns and stretches then, easy and smooth, lowers his feet and twists his chair around. "Well, now . . ." He nods at me. "Hello there, ma'am."

A slow grin spreads across a long face carved in hard, jutting angles. Only the grin is soft, full of sheepish charm, a boy caught fishing when he should be in school.

Everett shakes his head and sighs as Nathan places the laptop on one of the many paper stacks that clutter his desk. "Your ten o'clock's here. Ms. — ?" He glances across at me.

"Dupree." I slip an arm from beneath my folded coat and shake Everett's hand. "Cecilia."

"Glad to meet you, Cecilia." Everett nods at his brother who walks around the desk to join us, tucking his shirt in. "Meet Nathan." He cups a hand around the corner of his mouth and whispers, "He thinks he's Mick Jagger. Humor him."

"Sorry I didn't hear you come in." Nathan Colby extends his hand. "The place goes to pot when Jo's not here. Our secretary. She's off on her honeymoon. Cancun."

I give the younger of the two men the once-over as I shake his hand. His hair is longer than his brother's, over the ears and minus the salt. His drawl is lazier, deeper. No grooves at the corners of his eyes or mouth yet, only the hint of their approach.

He doesn't wear glasses. No tie.

"I'll leave you to it," Everett says, heading for the door.

I want to yell, *Come back!* Robert made a mistake. He referred me to the wrong brother. He meant to say Everett, not Nathan. Middle-aged Everett of the professional attire and haircut. Fast-moving, professional Everett. Everett, whose appearance says "ambitious, savvy, mature." Everett of the wide gold band, third finger, left hand.

Nate's eyes are the same blue as Everett's and, surprisingly, as sharp, but the resemblance ends there.

He motions me into a chair then returns to his place behind the desk. "So . . . I read the papers Robert faxed over."

"I was served last week. Sue Kiley didn't waste any time. The media, either. There's already been a small article in the *Dallas Morning News.*" Uneasiness ruffles inside me, a premonition of danger ahead, an icy curve in the road. "At least my name wasn't mentioned." Yet.

He shuffles through a pile on the right corner of his desk, finds Robert's fax, glances over it. "Four plaintiffs. Looks like Miz Kiley isn't the only one who wants to sock it to you."

"Apparently there's no end to the number of people who want to blame me for their parents' resurrected hormones." I gesture at the paper. "I don't even know who two of them are."

Nate lays the fax on the desk. The chair squeaks as he leans back and laces his hands behind his head, elbows out. "You want to tell me what led up to this?"

I draw a deep breath and launch into the facts. Mother and the reading group, the fall-off of attendance, the introduction of *Penelope's Passion.* The sudden surge of amorous incidents among Parkview's residents, the warning from Doris Quinn's son and Frank Rayburn's daughter. Finally, I finish with the Viagra incident and Frank's close call.

When I finish, Nate whistles. "That's quite a story." He doesn't laugh, but his eyes do.

I sit straighter. "They don't have a case, right?"

"Of course they have a case." His expression becomes more serious. Good move on his part since I refuse to hire an attorney who considers my predicament a big joke. He leans back farther, so far I'm afraid he might fall backward through the window behind him. "Remember the restaurant chain that got sued years back over serving the coffee too hot?"

I nod. "McDonald's."

"They paid through the nose. It was all over the news."

"I remember."

"The right lawyer can make a case out of most anything. I figure you know that."

I feel sick. I'm not sure if it's the bad news or the blueberry doughnut I ate in the car on the way over. "I guess I was hoping you'd say it isn't so."

"It's so." The corner of his mouth curves up. "Sorry." He lowers his hands from behind his head, lets the chair drop. "The good news is, the right lawyer can also fight any case. And with a little luck, win."

"Are you the right lawyer, Mr. Colby?"

"Nate." He grins that grin again, full of little boy charm. "I think I am."

"And how are you in the luck department?"

"I get my fair share."

I bet you do.

He holds my gaze. "Of luck, that is."

Did the room just heat up by twenty degrees, or am I having my very first hot flash? The man's either flirting or trying to run me off. Must be the latter. What would a studly young lawyer like him want with a pastry-addicted, perimenopausal girl like me? A girl who, at the moment, desperately needs to burp?

I fold my hands in my lap and force myself not to glance away from Nate's eyes. "I realize this case is a crap shoot, Mr. Colby."

"Nate."

"If you don't think it's worth your time, I understand."

"On the phone, you said the reading group is unanimously on your side? Even the parents of the people filing suit?"

"That's right. They feel that I'm not only being victimized, they are, too. They're eager to testify or give depositions or whatever else is needed."

"And they're all of sound mind, in your opinion?"

I start to answer in the affirmative, but then I think of our new member Paulie Perkins who blurts out his own lines of dialogue in response to Penelope's questions. And Nita Mae Newsome, who once in casual conversation, mentioned that she hadn't slept all night because she'd been worrying about what would happen to Penelope if the captain deserted her after the ship docked. I wince. "*Most* of the members are mentally sharp, yes."

"Well, I'd like to give it a go, then. It'll be a

nice change from medical malpractice and car wrecks."

After a short discussion about fees and a payment plan, an awkward moment of silence follows. Awkward for me, anyway; Nate doesn't seem fazed. We stare across at each other. He smiles. I smile back and try to digest the doughnut in a quiet, ladylike manner. His eyes lower to my calves, and suddenly I wish I'd worn slimming, concealing black slacks instead of a beige skirt. I cross my legs, then wish I hadn't. Don't get me wrong, I'm flattered by his interest, but I feel like Sharon Stone in that infamous *Basic Instinct* scene where she's being interrogated. Not that the man would be turned on by my granny panties if he did see up my skirt, but still. . . . At least my shoes are good. Young shoes, not dowdy, not middle-aged like the panties.

Uncrossing my legs, I press my ankles together. Why does it matter what he thinks about the shoes? About my legs? The panties? My age? I lift my chin, glad there's no pimple on it today, mad at myself that I'm glad, that I even care. "So, what's next?"

"I have some documents to file. Lawsuits usually take their sweet time. I'll stay in touch, though. Let you know what's happening each step of the way."

He takes down my phone number, my address, a few other facts.

Sensing we're finished, I stand and slip on my coat, then reach beside the chair for my purse.

"Just out of curiosity," he asks, "what do you think about all these old folks getting cozy? From a therapist's viewpoint?"

"Seniors who engage in healthy sexual relationships tend to be happier and more active. They maintain better social skills. But I never encouraged their actions. I just read a novel to them. They made their own choices about their romantic relationships."

"And from a daughter's point of view? What if it were your mother involved in a relationship at this stage of her life?"

The question catches me off guard. "My mother's not alone." The words sound snappish, even to me. Opening my purse and avoiding his eyes, I dig inside for my keys. "She lives with my daughter and me. She has plenty of companionship, plenty to keep her busy."

I glance up, find humor again in his blue, blue eyes. I don't appreciate his amusement, don't like what it seems to imply. That I'm not fooling him. That he sees right through me. But what does he see? That I know what's best for my own mother? That I don't want her hurt again? That I can't stand seeing her with a man who isn't my dad?

I return my attention to my purse. *Where are those damn keys?* And where did that last thought come from? It's not that way at all. I'm not like the people suing me. I'm not thinking about me, I'm thinking about Mother. What if she begins to care too much for Oliver and ends up like Doris? Shattered, emotionally fragile, worried to death over the health of some old man? Or worse, what if she marries him?

From the corner of my eye I see Mr. Colby unfold his tall, rangy body from the chair. "Here they are," I say. The keys jingle as I reach across the desk to shake his hand. "Keep me informed."

"Sure thing. And don't worry."

"I'm not worried."

He tilts his head to the side, cocks a brow. "If that look on your face isn't worried I don't know what is." He glances at his watch. "We could grab an early lunch. You could ask me more questions. Ease your mind."

"It's eased, I assure you." He sees too much. If he didn't have Robert's endorsement, I'd change my mind about hiring him. I muster my most confident smile. To prove I'm not worried. To prove him wrong.

Crazy, I know, since Nathan Colby's on my side. "Goodbye."

"Sure you won't join me for lunch?"

The burp escapes. *Classy, Cecilia. That'a way to make an impression.* Heat creeps up my face. "Thanks, but I'm not hungry."

"Obviously not." I can tell he's wrestling with a grin as he escorts me down the hallway. "I'll call you soon. In the meantime, don't you be putting ideas in any old geezers' minds. You might want to check out the Christian bookstore down on the next corner."

I open the door, then turn to glance back at him.

"I bet they sell romances." He loses the wrestling match. The grin wins. "The safe-sex kind. Kisses only."

Saturday morning, Erin, Mother and I head for the Galleria to finish our Christmas shopping. The mall is crammed with other procrastinators, all in a wild-eyed rush. Ah, the spirit of the season.

We agree to meet at one-thirty for lunch at a café on the upper floor of the mall, then Erin heads off in one direction, and Mother and I in another.

It's almost two before Erin, arms loaded with packages, makes it to the café and goes through the line. Mother and I are already finished eating and are watching the mass of shoppers below.

"I found shoes to go with my concert dress." Taking another bite of roasted chicken, Erin pulls a box from beneath the table and removes the lid.

The shoes look painful, the heels high and spiked, the toes narrow. I'm crazy about them. For me, not her. I keep my mouth shut. I'm learning. It isn't easy.

"Very funky," I say, sipping my tea. "They're perfect."

Mother winces. "I'd hate to have to walk in them. There was a time I would've, though."

The concert's tomorrow afternoon. Erin's been in a good mood all day and yesterday, too. It's great to see her so enthused about something besides biker-boy. Not that I can complain too much about him. They don't really date much, he usually just comes over. A couple of times they've left with Suzanna and another kid in Suz's car. But they're always back early, before Erin's curfew.

"I can't wait to hear your solo," I say.

Erin picks at her food. "It's not really a solo. Just a short part of one piece where only I'm playing."

Mother takes off her glasses. "Hmmm. I

thought that's what a solo was." She polishes the lenses with a handkerchief she pulls from her purse.

Erin shrugs. "Sort of, I guess."

I smile at her. "Well, I bet you'll do great. You've been practicing hard these past weeks."

Erin blushes and looks away.

"Well you *have* worked hard!" I've never known my daughter to be so modest about her music. "Two and three nights a week is a lot. I feel like I've hardly seen you this month."

A kid with mohawked blue hair walks by. Nose ring. Tattoos by the dozen. He wears a T-shirt sporting a picture of some strung-out looking rocker on the front. "Thank God you're into orchestra instead of some punk band or something," I mutter under my breath. "I'm really proud of the choices you've made, honey."

I wait for Mother to back me up. She doesn't.

Erin picks at her chicken and doesn't look up.

Baffled, I set down my glass and lean back in my chair. "Are you excited about the concert or just ready to get it over with?"

She looks up and smiles. "I'm excited."

Good. Maybe she's through with the boy-crazy phase and ready to focus again on what's important. Her music. Her school-work. Scholarship applications.

"Noah's coming."

"What?"

"To the concert tomorrow. Noah's coming to hear me play."

"Oh." I sigh. So much for what's important.

"That's nice, Erin," Mother says. "I like him."

"You see too much of him," I say. Which isn't exactly true, but I can't help worrying about her having a steady boyfriend so young. "You should spend more time with girlfriends. Maybe see other boys from time to time."

Erin makes a face. "Don't start. A minute ago you said I was spending all my time practicing."

"It's just. . . ." I fidget, desperate for the right words, words she'll hear. "You can't be too cautious when it comes to guys. How well do you even know him?"

"Well enough."

"What's his college major?"

She lifts her chin. "General Studies."

"General Studies isn't a major, it's a cop-out for someone with no direction, no ambition."

"He has ambition! He just took this year to decide what he wants to do."

"Which is?"

"Go to film school. He's applied for scholarships all over. He's waiting to hear."

She folds her arms and fidgets, as if she's upset, which makes me suspect that the scholarships are not to schools around here. I remind myself how it felt to be young and to care for someone, then watch them leave, and I feel a twinge of sympathy for her. But relief outweighs it.

Mother tucks her hanky back into her purse. "Noah seems to be a nice enough young man, Cecilia. He's very polite."

"So was Eddie Haskell and look at all he did when the grown-ups' backs were turned."

"Who is Eddie Haskell?" Erin asks.

"*Leave It To Beaver* Eddie? *'Good morning, Mrs. Cleaver.'*" I mimic in a sarcastic voice.

Mother laughs. "Oh, CiCi. You've become such a cynic. Why don't *you* spend some time with Noah when he comes over? Get to know him better. Maybe he'll surprise you. Maybe you'll like the boy."

My daughter beams at her Nana. "I bought him a Christmas present."

I cross my arms. "You didn't put it on my

220

credit card, did you?"

She gives me the same irritated look that Maxwell did when I left him at Gertie's. "I paid for it."

"Where are you getting so much money all the sudden?"

Erin blushes again.

Outside the door of the café, a girl calls her name.

Erin waves.

"You were awesome the other night!" the girl yells. "I can't wait —"

Erin knocks her soft drink to the floor as she pushes back her chair. Mother and I gasp, but the lid stays on. Erin leaves the cup where it fell and rushes over to the girl.

Watching the two of them talk, I pick up the cup. Erin keeps glancing over her shoulder at me. "Wonder what that's all about?"

"I wonder," Mother echoes. Something in her tone raises my suspicions that she just might know the answer, but isn't telling.

Erin's face is flushed when she returns to her chair.

"Who was she?" I ask.

"A girl from orchestra."

"I don't recognize her."

"She, um, plays violin. For some reason, she can't wait to hear my solo, either."

She picks up her fork, and pushes the food around on her plate.

"Okay, what's up?"

"Nothing's up." Erin pushes her plate to the center of the table.

Shifting my gaze, I say, "Mother? Do you know something?"

"Leave me out of this, Sugar. It's none of my business."

I narrow my eyes. Since when did she start butting out? "So . . . what were we talking about? Oh, the money for Noah's gift."

"You give me an allowance." Erin pulls the straw from her drink and starts chewing the end of it.

"And you always complain that it isn't enough to get by."

"So maybe I'm learning to budget. Just like you said I should."

Why am I so tense? She's old enough to be interested in a boy, to buy him a present. If I don't lighten up, I'll push her farther away from me. She's a normal teenaged girl.

Which answers my question of why I'm so tense.

Counting to ten, I relax my shoulders. "Well, that's good that you're budgeting. So, what did you get him?"

"I'd rather not say." She tosses the straw on her plate.

I can't help it; I scowl at her, make a noise of frustration.

Erin scowls right back at me. "You'll find out soon enough. I'd just rather Noah see it first, if it's okay with you."

And even if it isn't okay with me, her tone of voice implies.

"I wish you could come to the Parkview Christmas Pageant this evening and hear Oliver sing," Mother says. I know her well enough to recognize that she's trying to ease the tension by changing the subject.

"I wish I could too, Mother, but if Sue Kiley or any of the others suing me are there, it would be too awkward."

"I doubt they'll attend. I'm sure they feel the same way."

Erin looks at me slit-eyed, then shifts and smiles at her grandmother. "I'll be there, Nana."

Mother pats her hand. "That's sweet of you, Erin."

"Noah's going, too. He's taking me."

"Not on that cycle, he isn't." My shoulders tense up again. I push back my chair, gather the packages.

"*Whatever.* We'll take my car."

I stand. "I've had enough shopping for today. Let's go home. I need to call a plumber to come fix the disposal."

"Oliver said he'd fix it," Mother says as we start off in the direction of the mall's parking garage. "The leaky bathroom faucet, too." Without missing a beat, she changes the subject again. "If the two of you don't mind, I was considering inviting him to spend Christmas with us. Since Jack and Lydia and the kids will be here I'd like them to meet him."

My stomach dips. She wants the rest of the family to meet him? Not a good sign. I stop walking so abruptly that Erin and Mother almost run into me. People swarm around us. "Aren't you moving a little fast? Daddy's barely been gone a year."

Mother looks stricken, and I want to kick myself. Still, now that I've started, I can't seem to stop. "Where are *his* kids? Doesn't he want to spend the holiday with them?"

"His daughter lives in Colorado. She's an animal rights activist and a vegan. His son is a cattle rancher up in the Panhandle. As you might guess, they don't see eye-to-eye. The two haven't spoken in years. They rarely spend holidays with Oliver for fear the other will show up and make a scene."

"Sounds like a lovely family." One I have no desire to make part of mine.

"I like Oliver," Erin says. "I think we should invite him."

They stare at me. Mother's eyes look hopeful, Erin's, rebellious. I'm outnumbered. "Whatever you want to do. The more the merrier, right Mother?"

Ho, ho, ho.

The Parkview pageant starts at six. Oliver picks Mother up early so they can practice. He tells her she's "as pretty as a Christmas package," then looks at her as if he'd like to unwrap her.

Just a friend? My foot. She's only fooling herself.

At five-twenty, Noah arrives on his cycle. Erin suggests they take her car, then rolls her eyes toward me. He acts as if he thinks the car is a good idea, which only irritates me more. I know an Eddie Haskell clone when I see one. Why can't he be difficult so Erin would understand why I don't trust him?

By five forty-five, I'm alone. Again. No Mother, no Erin, no Max. This isn't exactly the new beginning I envisioned when I received the divorce papers.

It's already dark out. I call every one of the Margarita Martyrs but only get machines. My friends have probably given up on me. I've been so preoccupied with work, Mother, Erin and now the lawsuit, that I haven't been in touch in a while.

I slip into my flannel pajama pants and a long-sleeved T-shirt, put a pair of wool socks on my feet. In the refrigerator I find leftover pasta salad, ham for sandwiches, nothing that appeals to me. I close the door and open the freezer. No more frozen dinners since Mom moved in. I reach for the carton of ice cream.

Out of nowhere, a vision of Nate Colby flashes before me. Amused blue eyes, one-sided smile, lazy drawl asking, *Finally hungry, ma'am? Or just using fat and sugar as a substitute for the good ol' roll in the hay you really need?*

Heat slaps my cheeks. I draw back my hand. Stupid of me to be irritated at the man. He's not even here. I only imagined him. It's me I should be mad at, for letting him get to me. Grabbing the carton, then a spoon from the drawer, I head for the den and my movie video collection.

Fifteen minutes into *Chocolat* and a quarter of the way through the carton of chocolate praline pecan, guilt gets the best of me. I should be at the pageant. When did I turn into such a wimp? I don't *want* to face any of the people who filed suit on me, but why should I hide? They're the ones being foolish, the ones who should lay low, not me.

I'm supposed to be spending more time with Mother. And, honestly, I'd like to hear her on the piano accompanying Oliver's solo. And do I really want to miss The Frans' tap dance to "*Jingle Bell Rock*"? Jane Binkley's bell solo? Don Knotts as a reindeer, or Frank as Mr. Claus with Doris as his missus?

Tonight will probably be my last chance to see all the members of the reading group together. Unless, of course, the Parkview case goes to trial and they show up. Frank and Doris are moving out after the first of the year, thanks to their children. Frank's moving in with his daughter. Doris will lease an apartment at a new facility in Fort Worth, closer to her son. A few of the others are being forced to leave, too. And all because of a romance novel.

I sigh. No, not because of the novel; because of their kids' attitudes, their expectations about how people their age should behave.

I'll miss them. All of them. They've grown on me, become my friends. Something I never counted on when I started the reading group. Truth is, I considered them more of an imposition, a duty, than anything else.

Nathan Colby's question to me about Mother plays through my mind. I dig the spoon deeper into the carton, scooping out another bite of creamy, gooey comfort and denial.

I'm a therapist. I recognize my own shortcomings. Sure, I'd like to ignore or deny them, but right now I can't. When it comes to my mother and Oliver, my attitude and expectations are no different than those of the people suing me. I admit it. I also admit that their interest in one another is normal, natural, even healthy.

But she's *my mother.*

I allow myself one last bite. Dad could be a real pain in the butt sometimes, but I miss him. I want Mother to miss him, too. She was his yellow rose of Texas. The love of his life. He's not here to stand up for himself. Maybe that's why I feel that's my job now. Silly, I know.

Placing the lid on the carton, I check my watch. I'm missing the dinner, but the entertainment doesn't start until seven. If I hurry, I can make it.

Luckily I haven't taken off my makeup yet. I put on the black pantsuit I wished I'd worn to the law office, run a brush through my hair, grab a coat and head for the door.

Before I reach it, the phone rings.

"Ms. Dupree, it's Sally Coker."

"Oh, hi, Mrs. Coker." It's been a couple of

days since we last talked. "Is Maxwell okay?"

"He —" She titters. "This is embarrassing, just a minute."

I hear muffled talking, like she has her hand over the mouthpiece, then, "This is Rod Coker." Gruff. Annoyed. "We're through with your dog. He can't get it up."

"Oh, I —"

"Or won't. I don't think he's interested."

"Maybe he —"

"Face it, lady. If your dog wore clothes, he'd be prancing around in purple sequins."

Chapter 15

To: Erin@friendmail.com
From: Noah@friendmail.com
Date: 12/18 Tuesday
Subject: news and other stuff

My Dearest Erin Elizabeth Dupree,
(i started out that way because it sounds more romantic.) i got the pics developed that i took at your grandmother's Christmas pageant and at your concert. there's this one, and when i saw it, it was love at first sight. she has long brown hair, big brown eyes, a killer bod. you just wouldn't believe her. who would guess I'd fall in love with someone in the parlor of an old folks' home?

i finished my last final today. it went all right, I'm just glad to be done. when i got home a few minutes ago, there was a letter in the mail for me from Montana State University. they're giving me a scholarship if i transfer there in the fall. have I told you about that school? i visited last summer and it's awesome. you probably wouldn't think a state like Montana would have a great film school, but they do. a lot of celebrities have vacation homes around there. I heard Peter Fonda is an adjunct professor, or was at one time. anyway, they've filmed some great movies around there, too, like *A River Runs Through It.*

now for what I really want to say. the thing is, Erin, I'm excited and I'm not. i mean, this is my dream, but I don't want to leave you. MSU is something like almost 2000 miles from here. I'll miss you so much. but, I don't want to talk about this in an e-mail. i just wanted to tell you first, even before my parents. and the truth is, I was afraid to look in your eyes and say it in person.

change of subject. i wish you'd tell your mom about the band. you have to play with us at the beat on new year's eve, even if the gig isn't over until 3:00 a.m. we're only half-ass without you. Tonto and Reese feel the same. the crowd thinks you rock and so do we. but that's not the only reason i wish you'd tell your mom. I'm just afraid you're gonna get caught and then things will be really bad for you with her. and she'll like me even less. I'll talk to her with you. I'll tell her how I'd never let anything happen to you, that i don't let you out of my sight when we're at the club, and that i never would. if anything bad happened to you, I'd die.

call me after you eat dinner tonight, and I'll come bye. later, love noah

(p.s. don't worry — the girl in the picture was you, not that old lady who played the elf!)

I stare at the screen, too numb to move. Why? That's what I want to know. Why does life hand you something good, let it become important, then snatch it away?

A little zing of music announces an instant message. Suz's ID pops up on the screen.

Suzicue: you there?

Pinkflipflop: just got on.

Suzicue: what u doin?

Pinkflipflop: crying. noah e-mailed. said he fell in love with me at nana's pageant.

Suzicue: that's so sweet! why r u crying?

Pinkflipflop: he got a scholarship to msu. montana

Suzicue: ohmigod!

Pinkflipflop: yeah. he'll find someone else.

Suzicue: no worries. montana girls don't shave their legs or pits. they have to be hairy to stay warm.

Pinkflipflop: hahaha. now I'm laughing and crying.

Suzicue: they all have ugly toenails. can't reach to paint em cuz of bulky fur parkas.

Pinkflipflop: whatever!

Suzicue: have the lowest teenage pregnancy rate in nation. guys don't want to do it in back seat of car for fear they'll freeze off u know whats.

Pinkflipflop: stop! stomach hurts!

Suzicue: k. I'll stop if u stop crying. he won't last a semester he'll miss you so much

Pinkflipflop: it's wrong for me to hope that. should be happy for him.

Suzicue: maybe you should go to msu 2.

Pinkflipflop: ha! mom won't let me move across town.

Suzicue: can't imagine u with hairy pits anyway.

Pinkflipflop: i should just break up with him.

Suzicue: wow, you'd do that?

Pinkflipflop: it'll be easier to get it over with.

Suzicue: maybe. so what about the band?

Pinkflipflop: don't know. guess I'll have to quit.

Suzicue: not before new year's! u have to play.

Pinkflipflop: beat wants us too late. noah says come clean with mom. she'll never go for it. don't know how I lasted this long.

Suzicue: spend night at my house on new year's.

Pinkflipflop: what if she calls your mom?

Suzicue: parents will be at party till wee hours.

Pinkflipflop: what if she calls and nobody answers?

Suzicue: we'll think of something. cateye should dress retro with u in body paint and outfit we bought including katie's fake ta-tas. think of them as part of costume.

Pinkflipflop: whatever.

Somehow or another, Suz got the idea that she's the band's manager. We all play along. It makes her happy.

Suzicue: I'll do your makeup and hair. it'll be fun.

I seriously doubt it. Nothing sounds fun anymore. Makeup, hair and ta-tas are the least of my worries. Who cares? After New Year's Eve, I won't have Noah anymore. Nothing else matters.

Pinkflipflop: gotta feed max.

Suzicue: thought he was away making puppies?

Pinkflipflop: he couldn't do it.

Suzicue: do what?

Pinkflipflop: you know, *IT.*

Suzicue: shut up!

Pinkflipflop: seriously. dad cracked up when i told. said max is light in the loafers.

Suzicue: omigod! hehehehe. light on his paws u mean.

Pinkflipflop: hahaha. mom took max to vet. he's depressed not gay. mom thinks he's upset about family stuff. u know dad leaving, nana moving in.

Suzicue: your mom's a therapist, can't she help him?

Pinkflipflop: says she didn't take doggie depression course. I think she's depressed 2. she's gorging on dessert like we're having a sugar shortage. some family, huh? dog needs therapy and so does mom the therapist. she only hangs out with old people, my dad only hangs with young bimbos. nana's lovesick and

Suzicue: nana's in luv?

Pinkflipflop: she's all flirty whenever Oliver's around moody when he leaves. weird seeing her with some 1 besides grandpop.

The truth is, though, I'm glad she's not hiding out anymore. Before she moved in with us, whenever Mom or I would talk to Nana and ask what she'd been up to, it was always reading, or watching TV or trying a new recipe. She never spent time with friends or went anywhere. Which must've been totally boring, if you ask me. Even for an old person.

Now it's Mom who's hiding. She's closed the door on life outside of our house or her office. Like she's afraid of what might happen if she ventures out. Not that I want her to start dating or anything. As weird as it is to see Nana with someone besides Grandpop, it would be even weirder to see Mom with someone besides Dad. That's not really fair, though. Dad has a girlfriend. I guess Mom's allowed, too. She could at least do stuff with her friends. The Mar- garita Martyrs haven't even been around lately.

Suzicue: b glad your family's not boring like mine.

Pinkflipflop: nope they aren't that. max is howling now.

Suzicue: see u and sorry about noah.

Pinkflipflop: me 2.

Chapter 16

From The Desk of
Belle Lamont

Dear Harry,

Merry Christmas! Though I missed you, we had a wonderful day. Jack and Lydia and the kids are here. It's so good to see them. We don't do so nearly enough since they moved. The children have grown. Except for the earrings, nose stud and tattoo, Jack junior looks just like you.

You won't believe the news! Cecilia's being sued over that book I told you about. Can you imagine? What a big ol' silly mess. She doesn't know it, but the entire reading group has been meeting here during the day while she's at work. We're putting our heads together to come up with ideas to help her case, or at least help pay her legal fees. Doris and Frank, whose children are lead plaintiffs in the suit, suggested everyone finagle money from their kids in the name of charity, then give it to CiCi for her defense. That would serve them right. Ellen Miles suggested a bake sale, as well. And The Frans are getting together a petition. More ideas are in the works. I'll keep you informed.

Oh, Harry . . . another year over, a new one ahead. That and a dear friend's near-death Viagra accident have me thinking about my life. If I could've stopped time in one place and lived there forever, when would I choose? The summers of my childhood? How good it would be to see Momma and Daddy again. To run through the fields on our farm with my Callie, Will and Claire, my legs lean and strong, baked brown by the sun. No worries to speak of. I'd always feel safe, knowing my parents were there to take care of me.

But then there'd be no you, no Jack or Cecilia. So maybe I'd choose when our children were little, before they started school, when we lived in our tiny white house on the corner of Tenth and Vine. The one with the faulty plumbing that always made the bathroom smell like rotten eggs, and that clanky furnace we decided only worked on odd-numbered days of the month.

I often recall the winter it snowed past the windows and you made that sled out of an apple crate and old skis. We bundled the kids up and took them to the steepest hill in the park, then all piled on and rode it down, again and again, until one ski fell off and everyone toppled over. Cecilia got a mouthful of snow and cried so hard her eyes swelled. You and Jack teased her so mercilessly that she rode it again just to prove she wasn't afraid.

I could've clobbered you, Harry. Sometimes you were too hard on her. Trying to toughen her up, you'd tell me. Well, she's tough now, Harry. You succeeded. She's tough on herself and everyone around her at times. She won't admit that she's hurting or reach out to me or anyone else for a shoulder to cry on. I tell myself that she'll get over this and show her soft side again. She always forgave you, didn't she?

I'm sorry. I don't mean to cast blame. You were a good father, you just expected so much. Still, despite your mule headedness, rotten egg smells and a clanky furnace, our children's early years were a happy part of my life. I was content. We'd waited an eternity, it seemed, to finally be blessed with children, and after it happened, I never took that blessing for granted. Even with the stress of more bills than money, hectic days of stubbed toes and runny noses and no social life, I could stay in that time forever and be satisfied.

But then I'd miss seeing our children grow up, all the times they'd struggle over something and succeed, the fun of having teenagers in and out of the house at all hours of the day and night, all of them laughing and so full of life. Of course, I haven't forgotten that it wasn't always fun and excitement. We had plenty of sleepless nights. Worry. Tears. Even disaster. But I wouldn't have traded it. Just as I wouldn't trade our years together after we'd raised them. Alone again, just the two of us. Rediscovering each other. Traveling. Grandchildren.

So I suppose it wouldn't do to stop time. Each stage had joy and heartache and so many surprises. I love every memory, though I admit that, while we were making those memories, there were moments I wanted to run away and leave no forwarding address.

When you died, Harry, I thought that time had stopped for me, too. Stopped in a place I didn't want to be. A place of no joy, no more surprises, only heartache. But I was wrong. Tonight I discovered that, if I allow it to be so, even this stage of my life can be rich and full.

Oliver kissed me. Remember, I told you about him? Oliver the old fart, as CiCi calls him? Well, the old fart kissed me, and it was wonderful.

So, there you have it. Maybe I'm wrong to tell you, but that's that.

I'm so torn. Happy and ashamed. Thrilled and guilt-ridden. Most of all, angry. Angry at you for making me feel so confused. I tell myself that if our destinies were reversed, if I were gone and you were here, I'd want you to keep making memories, not just exist on the ones from the past. Just because a person is old and widowed, why should they be expected to sit on the sidelines, only existing, not living. Why, Harry? Tell me. Is that what you want for me? If not, then why do I feel I am betraying you by caring for Oliver?

I want one last gift from you. A sign. Something to assure me you understand and accept whatever I decide to do with the rest of my life.

I love you, my husband. Ornery as you sometimes were, I always did, and I always will. Caring for someone else, too, will not change that.

As always, your yellow rose,
Belle

Chapter 17

Cecilia Dupree
Day Planner
Friday, 01/5

1. 9:00 a.m. — First Weight Wackers meeting.
2. 10:30 — patient follow-up/Roger & Cindy Hoyt.
3. 1:30 — 1st meeting w/Smythes' teenaged daughter, Halee (drug problem).

At noon, I close the Hoyts' file, remove my reading glasses, and head for the fridge in the office kitchen for my fat-free, sugar-free, carb-free, taste-free shake, compliments of my new Weight Wackers diet plan. I'm popping the top on the can when Willa, my secretary, steps in, her purse over her shoulder.

"Sure you don't want to grab a burger with me?"

"Why would I want juicy beef, hot melted swiss and crispy fried potatoes when I can have this?" I lift the can.

"Bless your heart. Tried that one. Lost five pounds, gained back eight." Willa, who I would swear purposely gains weight so she can test each new fad diet that comes along, eyes me with sympathy. "New Year's resolution?"

I nod and point at my butt. "I'm tired of looking like a pear."

She scowls. "Girl, don't give me that. You're tiny."

"Okay, so I'm a tiny pear. A pear's still a pear. Small at the top, bigger at the bottom."

She shakes her head. "All right, then. Enjoy."

I take a sip. "Yum."

Back at my desk, the Hoyt file beckons. They're making progress. Roger fired his secretary, Bitsy or Bootsy or Betsy, whatever her name is. Cindy takes classes to sell real estate now, so her entire world no longer revolves around her husband. They claim I've helped them save their marriage. If that's true, I'm glad. Still, I wonder why I couldn't save my own marriage.

The phone rings. Since Willa's gone to lunch, I pick it up. "Cecilia Dupree."

"CiCi, it's Bill Burdette over at Parkview. Do you have a television in your office?"

"A TV? Sure. Why?"

"Turn it on to *The Scoop*."

"What's up?"

"Just do it."

I start to inform him that I don't take orders from anyone, least of all him, but curiosity gets the best of me. With the cordless phone pressed to my ear, I walk to the entertainment center across from my desk. "You don't strike me as someone who'd watch tabloid TV, Bill."

"I don't. My secretary does. She said they mentioned something about the case."

"Our case?" Opening the cabinet doors, I flip the television on.

"Yep. After the commercial they're supposed to — shhh. Here . . . it's on again."

A perky blonde wearing too much makeup appears on screen. "And now the stories our reporters are hard at work on to bring to you in the weeks ahead. First, from deep in the heart of Texas, we have reporter Steven Motley with news of a retirement village sex scandal. Steve —"

The scene shifts. Dread sucks the air from my lungs. A shivering man holds a microphone. He stands beside the sign at the entrance to the Parkview Manor grounds. Cars whiz past on the highway beside him.

"Son of a bitch," Bill hisses.

"Hi, Mary Ann," the reporter says into

the microphone, "Recently I spoke with Dale Renfro, a prior Parkview Manor employee . . ."

"*Son of a bitch!*" Bill explodes. "That asshole."

"Who is he?"

"Our maintenance guy. He quit two weeks ago."

". . . an eighty-year-old gentleman ended up in the hospital," the reporter continues. "According to Mr. Renfro, this Dallas retirement community became a haven for hanky-panky after the facility brought in Dallas therapist Cecilia Dupree to host group readings of sexually explicit material to the senior citizens residing here."

"We'll definitely look forward to more on that," the blonde says with a wink, a chuckle and a rise of her brows. "And now over to Lyle Peters in Minnesota who's covering —"

I switch off the TV, close my eyes, clasp one hand over my mouth.

"No wonder that slimy weasel quit." Bill has murder in his voice. "I'd bet my last dollar he's selling this story. There's no telling who the bastard's talked to."

I lower my hand. "What do we do?"

"Watch our backs and screen calls. The media will be after us next. Get ready."

In the pit of my stomach, the diet shake

247

starts to gurgle. I sit on the edge of my desk. "You really think so?"

"Count on it. I've already had one call. The guy wanted to film a seniors-gone-wild video here at the Village."

Not so long ago, I might've laughed at the prospect of such a movie. Not today.

Bill and I promise to keep one another informed if the vultures start circling, then say our goodbyes.

I decide to call Nathan Colby about all this. It's been more than a couple of weeks since we've spoken. Before I can look up his number, the phone rings again.

"Cecilia Dupree."

"Hey."

"Bert?"

"Yeah. I was afraid you might be at lunch."

I glance at my half-finished shake. "I am."

"Sorry to interrupt. I wanted to talk to you before I call Erin."

"Is something wrong?"

"No, everything's great. Fantastic, actually. I'm getting married."

"Oh." I deflate like a punctured bicycle tire. Lovestruck. That's how he sounds. Like a man who's head over heels. I remember when he sounded that way about me. About us. I remember how sweet he looked and the guilt I felt because I didn't share his feelings, and because he didn't even realize it yet. "Wow. Congratulations."

His laugh is self-conscious. "Thanks. Her name is Natalie."

The college coed and coffee-shop counter girl. "The redhead."

Irritation creeps into his voice. "No, not the redhead. Erin's met Natalie. They seemed to get along."

Right. Like a cat and a canary. "Erin told me about her." How old did she say? Twenty-four? Twenty-five? How nice. The older sister our daughter's always wanted. They can have pillow fights. Trade clothes. Paint each other's toenails. "I hope you're both very happy. I wish you the best." And I should, I guess. Wish him the best, that is. I really do hope this time his bride marries him for the right reasons and will love him from the start, not wait until it's too late.

"We'll be moving to Amarillo."

"Oh." Another puncture. "Why Amarillo?"

"The coffee shop where Natalie works? They're branching out. They've offered her the management position. And since I can work anywhere . . ."

"I see."

Silence. Then, "CiCi, I just, well, I want

you to know —"

"You don't have to explain —"

"I regret a lot of things."

A sigh seeps past my lips. "I know that, Bert. So do I."

"I made mistakes, and I wish . . . I want you to know that I did love you."

"Don't, Bert. Please."

He coughs. "I just wonder . . ." Another cough. "How do you think Erin will take the news?"

"I guess you'll find out soon enough."

"I don't want to upset her."

Since when did our daughter's feelings become a priority to him? Not when he came on to our cute, young neighbor. Not when he so easily gave up on our family and marriage, or when he stopped calling Erin more than every other week or so. "She's dealt with worse and survived, Bert. She'll survive this, too."

And so will I.

I continue to try to reach my attorney, but only get a machine.

Work is my salvation, a fact my one-thirty appointment backs up. Sixteen-year-old Halee Smythe's drug experimentation takes my mind off the *Scoop* segment and makes all my other problems seem insignificant in comparison. At least for a while.

At four-thirty, I show up at the attorney's office unannounced, hoping Nate can work me in. I want to hear his take on the television segment. Surely the negative publicity will hurt the case. Or maybe I'm just the pessimist Bert often accused me of being.

Inside Colby and Colby, I go through the same routine as before.

"Hello?"

This time, Nate comes out into the hallway instead of his brother. He wears a suit, and wears it well. Hormones that have been missing in action for so long I'd thought them dead, show up waving flags.

"Well, hi there," Nate says. His eyes are tired, his smile is anything but. Lazy, yes, but in a flirtatious way. Could that be true? Could it be possible he's flirting with me? That he really was the last time I was here, too? Silly or not, I'm flattered to think it might be possible.

He blows out a work-weary breath as he runs a hand through his hair.

I catch myself wanting to do the same thing; run my fingers through his too long, wavy brown hair, to feel the heat of his scalp on my skin. To just touch him, period. How long has it been since I've touched a man? Since a man touched me? Going without has caught up to me, I guess. Here's this virtual stranger, and just because he's all male, just because his eyes seem filled with promises of forbidden fun, because his arms look strong and inviting, I have this overwhelming urge to throw myself into them.

Shocked, I step back. "I hope you don't mind, I, um . . ." Oh, God. I burst into tears.

He frowns, then moves toward me.

Turning my head away, I raise a hand to stop him. "I'm sorry. I don't even know why I'm crying." Which is true. The lawsuit and sudden publicity? Bert's engagement to a blushing debutante? Mother and Erin moving on without me? That I haven't had sex in so long I could probably classify as a virgin again? Maybe all of the above. I should be ashamed, I know. At least I don't have a child in crisis. At least I have work I love. A good book to curl up with at night.

I cry harder.

Finally, I shudder and sniff. "I'll quit. I promise. Just give me a second."

"Don't worry about it. I'm used to tears. I have three sisters. When I was growing up, we had more crying jags around our house than a hospital nursery."

Sputtering a laugh, I look up at him.

He nods toward his office and I follow him in. From a CD player on Nate's credenza, Led Zeppelin sings about climbing a stairway to Heaven. I imagine that's what sex with him would be like. Climbing straight to Heaven.

Oh, help. My knees are shaking.

Nate turns off the music then hands a box of tissues to me as I slink into a chair. I take one and blow so hard into it my nose honks, which should probably embarrass me, but the man's already heard me burp, so what the heck? Miss Manners I'm not, and he knows it.

Facing me, he leans against the desk, crosses one ankle over the other, loosens his tie, then takes it off. "Tough day?"

Shaking my head "yes," I honk again into the tissue.

"I can relate." His eyes are kind. No more mocking glint, no hint of salacious thoughts. Damn, I blew it. Probably a good thing.

"You too, huh?" I dab my wet cheeks.

Nate lets out a long breath. "Missed my morning racquetball game 'cause I had to be in court."

"Wow, that is tough." I don't even attempt to keep the sarcasm out of my voice.

He points over his shoulder at his desk, which is even messier than the last time I saw it. "Jo's gonna have my hide when she gets back from maternity leave and sees all this."

"Maternity leave? I thought she was on her honeymoon just before Christmas?"

"She was. The baby came early."

"I'll say."

"The kid couldn't have had worse timing. Everett and I are swamped."

I tilt my head. "*You're* not about to start bawling, are you?"

"Not unless it'd make you feel better."

I laugh, and my tension melts like wax beneath a flame.

For a minute, he doesn't say anything, just squints and studies me. "So, you wanna tell me what stirred up those tears?"

"The part you can help me with, yes. The rest I'll have to work out myself."

As I fill him in on the *Scoop* segment, he reaches for a fishing fly rod that's propped against his computer and winds the reel, listening. "Sure didn't take 'em as long as I thought."

"You expected this?"

"I figured the national media might catch wind of the story. A sex scandal in an old folks' home is too good to pass up."

"Please. It isn't a sex scandal."

"They'll make it into one, I can pretty much promise you that." He starts to work on a knot in the fishing line. "Sex stories make for good ratings, and this one has an interesting twist."

"The publicity's going to hurt the case, isn't it?"

"Maybe, maybe not. Guess we'll just have to wait and see about that. Either way, we'll deal with it."

"How? Bill seems to think reporters will be breaking down our doors soon."

"Well, ma'am . . ." Nate props the fishing pole against the wall. "You just give 'em your best smile and say your attorney advised you not to talk about the case. I'll be the bad boy."

I'd *love* him to be the bad boy. Bad with me. Very, very bad. Pathetic? Maybe, but that's what I think when I look into his eyes and his mouth quirks up at one corner. I just wish he wouldn't call me ma'am. Ma'am is a middle-aged woman, which to him I guess I am. I peg him at thirty-one, thirty-two at the most. A decade behind me. Who do I think I am? Demi Moore? Obviously I'm reading too much into the way he looks at me. He could be my younger brother. My very sexy, very much younger brother. Problem is, my body's reacting to him in a way that's not the least bit sisterly.

My cell phone rings, fizzling all fantasies. I see that it's mother, and excuse myself to answer the call.

"Hi, Sugar. Oliver called this morning and said everyone's worried about you. So I invited some of the reading group members to dinner tonight. Can you make it home by six-thirty?"

I glance at my watch. "Sure. I'm just about to leave the attorney's office."

"Oh, good. Invite Mr. Colby. It would be the perfect time for him to meet us and us him."

I cut my gaze toward Nate. "I don't know if that's a good idea," I say, my voice low.

"Why not? I made my special pot roast."

I chew my lip a moment, then lower the phone. "How do you feel about pot roast?" I ask Nate.

Nate's crazy about pot roast. Carrots, too. And potatoes and brown gravy and home-made rolls. All of which Mother spent the afternoon preparing and none of which is allowed on my Weight Wackers diet plan. Since, with this group, anything's up for discussion, and I don't especially want my extra pounds to end up the topic of the night, I nibble Mother's meal rather than eat the prepackaged food I bought this morning.

Erin nibbles, too. Pushes her food around with her fork and offers a polite response whenever someone addresses her. After about fifteen minutes, she excuses herself, takes her plate to the kitchen, lets Max in, then heads off with him toward her bedroom. Which isn't unusual. What worries me are her downcast eyes, her pinched voice and drawn-in posture. Bert must've called and told her his news. I'll talk to her after everyone leaves.

Iris Shelby, now Mrs. Herbert O'Dell, refills her plate for the second time. Her generously padded physique reminds me of my own grandmother, her cushiony hugs, how good it felt to snuggle against the pillow of her bosom and listen to her read to me when I was a kid. Food obviously isn't Iris's only passion. After a month of marriage, she still looks at Herbert with moon eyes.

Nate lifts the breadbasket and offers it to her. "What brought you to Parkview Manor, Iris?"

She takes the basket from him. "I lost my first husband four years ago. We owned a home, and I had a mind to stay in it since the mortgage was paid up." With great care, Iris butters a roll. "For close to a year, I puttered around in that big ol' house. I wasn't scared by myself, just lonely."

Nate nods his understanding. "So you moved."

"It took a peeping Tom to get me to budge."

Jane Binkley's eyes light up, then narrow. *"Really..."* She leans forward. "Why don't I ever get the good calls?"

Mother flattens a palm to her chest. "My heavens, Iris, you must've been scared out of your wits."

"Scared and shocked silly." Iris dips her roll into her potatoes and gravy. "I was climbing into bed one night when the phone rings and this deep quiet voice says, 'I've been watching you. I've seen you naked in the shower.'"

"Bastard," Mary Fran mutters.

Francis snorts and nods.

"Mercy," Stan McDougal says, his eyes lighting up as he exchanges a suggestive look with Jane.

"Wow, Iris," I say. "I can't imagine."

"Neither could I." Iris's brows arch. "He saw me naked and he still wanted to call? When I asked him that, the sucker hung right up."

Silence drapes the table. Then I snicker and Nate starts laughing.

When Iris tilts her head back and joins us, the veil lifts and everyone else laughs, too.

Iris looks pleased with herself. "Well, I got a little spooked, I guess. The very next day I started looking for a retirement community. A place where I'd be surrounded by people in my same situation. A place without a window in the bathroom." She turns to her new husband. "And then I met Herbert."

As he lifts her hand and kisses it, Herbert's puppy dog eyes smile back at his wife. I notice they don't look so sad anymore. "Took me a while to get up my nerve to ask Iris out. CiCi's reading group helped break the ice."

Nate leans back and squints at Herbert. "How so?"

"See, I'd never thought to join because it just seemed so high-brow and boring, folks sitting around shooting the breeze about made-up stories. Then that old boy over there," he nods and grins at Oliver, "he tells me about this new book the group's ready to start. *Penelope's Passion.*" Herbert slaps his thigh and wiggles his brow. "Hey, now! This sounds more up my alley. A little adventure, a little hoochie-koochie. When I find out Iris is in the group, that cinches it for me. I talked to CiCi one afternoon after we adjourned. Told her about my worries. She called me later that night to continue the conversation and set my mind right. The rest is history."

Recalling that conversation, I feel proud,

despite myself. Herbert was so nervous, so insecure and unsure, so lonely. Look at him now. Happy. In love. Confident. If I had a part in making that happen, I'm thrilled. And confused. Why wouldn't I want those same things for my mother?

Smiling at me, Nate lifts his glass. "A toast to Iris and Herbert." Iced-tea glasses and coffee cups come together above the center of the table. "And to living life to the fullest."

I sense Nate's eyes still on me, but I'm too busy watching Mother and Oliver to return his look. Their fingers brush, and they stare at one another with such tenderness my heartbeat speeds up and all the muscles in my body spring to attention, on alert for impending disaster.

"And to CiCi and *Penelope's Passion*," Stanley McDougal booms, his deep voice at odds with his scrawny, stoop-shouldered body.

"Here, here!" the group cheers in unison.

My gaze stays glued to Mother and Oliver. Their gazes stay glued to each other.

The party breaks up soon after the peach pie is served. (I allow myself one bite. No ice cream.) I walk Nate out to his car, an old white Porsche, obviously restored by loving hands. After a glance in the window, I look up at him. "Wow. You're full of surprises. I expected you'd drive a SUV." Or ride a white stallion.

"You like it?"

"Yeah, I do." I skim my palm across the glossy paint. "The old ones are classy, aren't they?"

"The very definition of class," Nate answers when Stanley McDougal toots his horn and pulls his truck out of the driveway with Jane sitting next to him, center seat.

I realize Nate's not only referring to the Porsche, and I like him all the more because of it.

"You think I should call Bill Burdette and tell him to guard the gazebo?"

Nate chuckles. "That's quite a group of friends you've got there."

Watching Stanley's taillights shrink into the darkness, I shiver and smile. "I started out thinking I was doing something to help them stave off boredom and stay active, but it ended up the other way around. They're the highlight of my week. Or were. We don't meet anymore."

"I think you did more for them than you realize. It's clear they're all a lot happier since they got together. And better off. They seem pretty darn grateful to you for giving them the nudge they needed to go after what they wanted in the first place."

"You mean a little hoochie-koochie, as Herbert said?"

Nate's laugh is uninhibited. Just hearing it makes me feel good all over. "He makes sense, CiCi. By starting that reading group and bringing a book they could actually have fun with, you helped break the ice. It got 'em to really talking instead of just saying 'hi' in the hallways. That's a good thing."

"Please tell me you can convince a jury of that."

"You worry too much."

"And I'm starting to think you don't worry at all. About anything."

He shrugs. "Why waste the energy? It won't affect the outcome. Only action'll do that." With a jerk of his head, he motions me toward the car. "Come on, I'll take you for a ride."

I bite my lower lip, hug myself, glance over my shoulder at the house. "I'd better not."

"What? Afraid I'll go too fast for you?"

Terrified, I think, sensing we're talking about more than a drive in his car. But I don't want to admit I'm chicken, so I drop my arms and stand straighter, my pulse thumping loud in my ears. "Me? No way.

Speed's my middle name."

"Okay, then." He reaches out a hand to me. "Let's hit the road."

When Nate drops me home again, Oliver's restored Studebaker still occupies the driveway. I feel too good to stew about it.

Nate did drive too fast. We went out of the city to a stretch of back road seldom traveled, then he cut loose.

For once, so did I.

The chilled wind blew out all the tension I've stored up inside of me these past months and carried it away through the car's open windows. (Nate insisted we keep them down, despite the weather.)

Invigorated, I step from the Porsche and lean down to look at Nate through the window. "Thanks. That was fun. Freezing, but fun."

He tips a nonexistent hat. "My pleasure, Speed. See you at my office next Friday at five."

"Did we schedule an appointment?"

"Don't tell me you forgot already."

"Refresh my memory. Why are we meeting?"

"I'll think of some reason before then." He winks and takes off, leaving me standing in the cold looking after him. And laughing, which is such a relief.

Now, as I enter the house, Mother's delighted shrieks drift to me from the kitchen. Oliver is singing, if you can call it that. It's a rap tune, I think. I listen closer. Truth is, he's not half-bad.

I walk through the dark living room to the kitchen door and peek in. His arms are out in front of him forming a circle, holding an invisible partner, and his hips grind slowly left then right then forward to the beat of the song.

My mouth drops open.

Across the room, Mother is doubled over, clasping her stomach. "Ollie! Quit! That's terrible."

The singing stops. The dancing doesn't. "This is how the youngsters do it, Belle. See? Dirty dancing, they call it. I've been paying attention. I've got it down." He does a shuffle across the tile floor and grabs her. "Here, I'll show you."

Oh, no you don't, old fool. I start to barge in and interrupt them, then stop when his hands settle at her waist and she raises her arms to encircle his neck. Mother's laughter quiets and they sway gently; she smiles up at him, he smiles down. Such intimacy in the look they share, so much revealed in their sudden stretch of silence.

My eyes fill; so does my heart. With tangled emotions I can't unravel. I press one hand to my chest, step backward into the darkness of the living room where they can't see me.

Beneath my palm, the beat of my heart slowly steadies.

What's happening to my mother is a miracle . . . a gift. Difficult as it is for me to see her with another man, I know that Oliver is good for her. I know and, for the first time, feel a bittersweet twinge of pure joy for my mother.

Not long ago, I watched her heart break.

Now I'm watching it mend.

Chapter 18

To: Erin@friendmail.com
From: Noah@friendmail.com
Date: Friday 01/05
Subject: us

Erin,

why won't you answer my calls? i know you have caller id on your cell. would you listen to me? what you said last night about me finding someone else when i go away to school is bullshit. and it will piss me off if you think i will because i am not even interested in anyone else but you. OK? OK! and that is final. i love you and only you. it will be hard being apart, but we can last. i don't care what anybody says. we're not 'most people.'

I'm wearing the necklace you gave me for Christmas. i sleep in it and shower in it and everything. if you don't talk to me soon, I'll go crazy. i don't think i can stand it. new year's eve was the best night of my life. i love you so much erin. i need a kiss from you, to know you're ok. call me. i love you, noah

When my bedroom door creaks open, I close my eyes and pretend I'm asleep. I knew I should've locked it. Mom still thinks I'm twelve, that if the door's not locked, she can just walk in without knocking.

I smell her perfume; the same scent she's worn always. Not too flowery or exotic or mysterious. Sort of crisp and fresh and no-nonsense. Like her. It makes me remember a thousand hugs, days of playing dress-up when I was little. Mom would let me wear her shoes, her perfume, her jewelry. She'd fix my hair and make up my face.

The bed shifts from her weight as she settles beside me. Her fingers brush hair from my cheek, which is wet from about a million tears.

"Erin?"

A sob shudders out of me. My shoulders shake.

"Sweetie, what's wrong?" She strokes my head.

I open my eyes, roll onto my back and scoot up in the bed. I open my arms and so does she. For a long time, she holds me and lets me cry. We don't say anything, just rock back and forth.

"I'm so sorry, Erin."

"You knew?"

"Yes."

"How?"

"He called me this afternoon."

Leaning back and wiping my eyes, I frown at her. I can't believe Noah would call Mom about our breakup. "What did he say?"

"That he didn't want you to be upset."

I kick off the covers and climb out of bed. "Well, what did he expect? I mean, I'm happy for him and everything. It's just —" I sob. "I'll miss him so much."

"Oh, Sweetie. This isn't going to change the way he feels about you. You can still see him. You can go visit whenever you want."

What? I stop pacing and stare at her. This must be a dream. "You wouldn't freak out?"

Mom looks confused. "Why would I freak out? I understand that you need to spend time with him. You love him and he loves you. I know that. I wouldn't want it any other way."

Wow. I am totally not believing this. Is my mother on drugs, or what? "Thanks, Mom. You're awesome." I circle the bed, sit and throw my arms around her neck. "Thanks for understanding. I didn't even think you liked Noah."

"Noah?" She breaks free of my hug.

"Yeah. I'm surprised you'd let me go see him without throwing a fit." I laugh. "Not that I'm complaining. I mean, it's about time. I *am* almost eighteen."

"Erin . . . what are you talking about?"

"Visiting Noah in Montana. What are *you* talking about?"

"Montana?"

"When he goes away to school there in the fall. I thought you said he called?"

Mom places a hand across her forehead and pinches her temples. "Shit."

"*Mom.* What is going on?" I knew this was too easy, too surreal. She was being way too nice.

"I was talking about your father, Erin. You visiting him and Natalie after they get married and move to Amarillo."

"Dad's marrying Natalie and moving?" She nods and I burst into tears again. I pick up a pillow and throw it across the room. *"Fuck."*

"Erin! That sort of language won't help anything."

Never mind that she just said "shit." I pick up the other pillow and throw it, too. "You don't know how it feels. You had your dad your whole life. He acted like a real father. Not some stupid —" The words choke me. I bite my lip, lower my chin to my chest and stare at the mattress as tears roll down my cheeks.

"Maybe not. But I do know how it feels to love someone and have them leave." She dips her head down to see my face. "Noah got one of those scholarships, didn't he?"

I nod. "But it's different than you and Dad. I mean, we're young." Right after the stupid words leave my mouth, I wish I hadn't said them. I know how much the divorce hurt her.

"Believe it or not, Erin, I was young once, too, and in love with someone other than your dad. He left. And it hurt so much I thought I'd die. I still remember how that feels."

I can't believe what I'm hearing, or how sad Mom sounds for me.

She lifts my chin and wipes at my cheeks with her fingertips. "It's not that I don't like Noah. It's just that I guess I'm more like Grandpop than I want to admit. He never thought any guy was good enough for me, and I feel the same way about you. Because I love you so much."

"I love you, too." I lay my head on her shoulder. When I was little and something was wrong, just being this close to her always made me feel better. Some things don't change, I guess. "I know you've been upset about Dad for a while," I say. "I'm really mad at him for lots of reasons but mostly for making you so sad. If I knew how to make things right again —"

Mom squeezes my hand. "I know. Just be you. That's all I need you to do." She stands. "How about some hot tea? Maybe it will help you sleep."

Sniffing, I smile up at her. "Now you sound like Nana."

"I'll take that as a compliment." She turns.

"Mom?"

Pausing in the doorway, she glances over her shoulder at me.

"So . . . you're still cool with me visiting Noah in Montana whenever I want, right?"

She crosses her arms, tilts her head and smirks. "Nice try, Sweetie. Nice try."

Chapter 19

Cecilia Dupree
Day Planner
Monday, 01/15

1. 7 a.m. — Weight Wackers weigh-in.
2. 8-noon — Leave open to study for continuing education course.
3. 3 p.m. — Pt. Appt. — Joy Cowles (divorcing).

At eight o'clock, I leave the Weight Wackers diet and exercise center after my workout. Showered and dressed for the office, I walk through the parking lot with my tote bag over one shoulder and my hands burrowed into my coat pockets, on the lookout for anyone watching me. Several days ago, a guy with a camera snapped my picture as I stepped from my car on this very lot. My nerves have been haywire ever since.

Willa's on the phone when I enter the office. She points to the receiver and widens her eyes at me. "I'll certainly give Ms.

Dupree the message. Yes, sir, I wrote down the number. We'll be in touch." She hangs up. "Girl, you will never guess who that was."

I set my briefcase beside her desk and frisk my palms together to warm them. "I won't even try then. Who?"

"*20/20.* They want to interview you about the Parkview Manor sex scandal."

"How many times do I have to say this? It isn't a sex scandal. It —"

She stops me with an upheld hand. "I'm just calling it what everyone else is."

"Everyone else?" Unbuttoning my coat, I sink into the chair across from her desk.

Willa lifts a second pink slip of paper with another phone number scribbled across it. "*People* called, too."

A tremor ripples through me. It isn't excitement. "You're kidding me."

"Nope. And it gets worse." After opening her center desk drawer, Willa pulls out a magazine then holds it up. *Newsflash.* She passes the tabloid across the desk to me. "Page six. I marked it."

The article talks about the "scandal" but is predominantly about me. The therapist who gives others advice on how to live their lives successfully while her own spirals out of control. And there are pictures.

Me in my car in the Weight Wackers parking lot, scarfing a doughnut before my workout. Bert and his bimbo fiancée kissing in front of his condo. Mother and Oliver dancing at a nightclub, the only two gray heads in a room of gyrating teens and twenty-somethings. A blurry Erin dressed in a skimpy outfit, body painted à la Goldie Hawn in her *Laugh In* days. The breasts are too large to be hers, though I swear I see nipples poking through the clingy fabric of her top.

I start to shake. "Where did they get these?" I meet Willa's sympathetic dark gaze. "They've invaded my privacy . . . my family's. I'm going to murder somebody, I swear to God, Willa, I am."

Tossing the magazine on the desk, I stand, grab my briefcase and start for the door.

Willa stands up so fast that her chair, which is on rolling casters, bangs into the wall behind her. "Hold it, CiCi. Calm down." Her phone rings. "Don't you go do something stupid you'll regret. Gulp down some air while I take this call." Her eyes never leave me as she lifts the receiver to her ear. "Cecilia Dupree's office." She pauses. "Let me check." Placing a hand over the mouthpiece, she whispers, "Your ex. Are you here?"

I take the phone. "Hi Bert." He's yelling. "Yes, I saw . . . no, *you* listen . . . *I* didn't take the pictures. I'm as pissed off as you are. I — no, Erin hasn't had a boob job . . . I don't know, I can't be with her every second of the day and night. I guess I could bar all the doors and windows in the house and hide the key."

Drawing a breath, I let him rant uninterrupted for a minute, then I start yelling, too. "Well, poor little Natalie. I'm so sorry she's humiliated. I'm sure it's not the first time, and I doubt it'll be the last since she's marrying you." I slam the receiver down and grab my briefcase again.

Willa comes around the desk, takes my arm and herds me into my office. "Sit down. Give yourself a minute, then call your attorney and see what he says about this." I slip off my coat. She hangs it on the rack in the corner. "Girl, I'm telling you, you won't do yourself any favors by killing Erin or that photographer outside."

Slouched in my chair, I blink at her. "What photographer?"

"You didn't see that bozo lurking in the bushes out front? He's been there ever since I came in this morning."

I shake my head and blow out a breath. "What a mess." Propping an elbow on the desk, I cover my face. "Erin . . ."

"Don't be too hard on her. Kids her age all do stupid things. I sure did. Just didn't get caught on camera, thank you, Jesus."

"It's me I'm mad at, not Erin. What kind of mother doesn't know what's going on with her own daughter?" I look up at Willa. "Where have I been?"

"Don't be too hard on yourself, either." She smiles, her teeth flashing white against her caramel skin. "I'll get you some coffee."

"Thanks. Put a shot in it, would you? There's some Southern Comfort in the top kitchen cabinet."

"You sure? It's eight-thirty in the morning."

"I promise I'll get an earlier start on the drinking tomorrow."

"Girl, if tomorrow's anything like today, I'll join you."

The Colby brothers' secretary finally made it back from maternity leave. She answers when I call for Nate, and in her raspy smoker's voice, informs me cheerfully that he's out of the office for most of the day on a mediation.

"Figures," I say. "Men are never around when you need 'em."

She laughs and agrees, then promises

Nate will return my call.

At noon, fearing a run-in with photographers or reporters if I leave, I order lunch to be delivered and hide in my office. I watch *The Scoop* on television. Somehow I just know there will be a tidbit about the case, and I'm right. Their "Update" segment practically repeats the article in *Newsflash*, complete with identical photographs, making me suspect that the same people own the program and the tabloid.

The phone rings at twelve-thirty. Willa's out for lunch and I don't want to answer, so I let the machine pick up. It's my three o'clock appointment calling to cancel.

I spend the next couple of hours doing paperwork, then leave before three to drive to Erin's school. There's no orchestra practice today, and I want to be waiting when she comes out so I can warn her about the photos, if she doesn't already know.

When I spot Suzanna's Honda Civic in the high school parking lot, I pull to the curb across the street. Suzanna gave Erin a ride this morning since Erin had a flat tire. I wait, my gaze on the door I think they'll exit.

Sure enough, they emerge side by side, surrounded by a swarm of other students. I grab *Newsflash* from the seat beside me and hurry across the parking lot to meet them.

"Erin!" By the time I reach her, I'm out of breath.

She stops walking, her books clutched to her chest. "Mom? What are you doing here?"

I don't want to make the hike back through the now-crowded parking lot to my car and drag out Erin's worry, so I turn to Suzanna and nod at her vehicle. "Could we have a minute alone inside?"

"Oh." She tucks her long blond hair behind one ear and looks from me to Erin and back. "Sure." Placing her books on the hood, she digs through her purse and produces a set of keys. She unlocks the Civic then leans against it. "I'll just wait here."

The inside of Suzanna's car smells like a mix of stale corn chips and perfume. I settle behind the wheel eyeing my daughter, who sits on the passenger side. Her face is pale, her eyes dark and wide.

"Is Nana okay?"

"Nana's fine. It's nothing like that." I swallow my sudden nervousness. "The publicity about the lawsuit has gotten out of hand, Erin. I wanted to warn you before anyone says something to you about it. It's been all over television today." I hand her the tabloid, already open to page six.

Her breath draws in so quick and sharp, I

hear it. She doesn't look up from the pictures.

"I'm sorry, Sweetie. To have your privacy invaded and displayed like this . . . it's unfair. I'm just so mad I could —" I blow out a breath. "I'm worried, too. About you. Where was that picture taken? Why were you dressed like that?"

"It doesn't matter, Mom." She glances up at me then quickly down again. "I don't go there anymore. Don't worry about it."

"But I am worried."

"It's not a big deal."

"Not a big deal?" I point at her breasts in the photo and struggle to stay calm. "You're right. They aren't big — they're enormous! Don't you realize how you look, dressed like that?"

She turns and stares out her window. "Why do you have to make a federal case out of everything? Who cares how I dress?"

I lose the struggle. "Me, that's who. I want you to tell me right this minute what's going on with you."

"Or what?" Her sharp glare pierces me. "You'll ground me? I might as well be already my curfew's so early. You'll forbid me to see Noah? Well, we broke up, remember? And he never felt comfortable coming around anyway. You made him feel unwelcome, no matter how nice he was to you. What's left? No moving out in the fall? You already struck that down. Taking away my keys? My phone? Fine. Go ahead. I have friends, Mom. You're not the only person in my life. They'll come get me if I ask them to, and you can't stop me from leaving." She tosses the tabloid at me and opens her door.

"Erin, wait."

"Why don't you get your own life, Mom, and stop trying to run mine?" She gets out. The door slams.

Too numb to move, I grasp the steering wheel, my knuckles bone-white. Outside, Suzanna stares in at me, her mouth forming a circle as round as her eyes. After a minute, I force myself to open the door, to step out. With a choked voice, I thank Suzanna. Erin stands beside her friend, her back to me. I want to say something to her, too, but what? I feel like a twisted dishrag, every word, every good feeling and ounce of hope wrung out of me. Nothing's left.

Turning away, I walk to my car and drive home.

Nate's Porsche sits in my driveway. I find him with Mother at the kitchen table, laughing, mugs of something hot and steamy in front of them. Their laughter fizzles the moment they see my face.

Mother scoots back her chair. "There you are."

"When I called your office," Nate says, "your secretary said you'd gone home for the day. She told me what's going on and said you were pretty upset, so I dropped by on the off chance —"

"I'm sorry." I toss my copy of *Newsflash* on the table between them. "I just . . ." Turning, I start from the room. "I can't talk right now."

In the living room, I sit on the floor and lean against the couch. Max climbs into my lap and licks my cheek. Closing my eyes, I bury my face in his soft, sleek neck. I feel the throb of his heart against my hand. The calm, faithful beat of it steadies me.

After a few minutes, I look up to find Mother and Nate standing over me. "Oh, Sugar." Mother wads up the tabloid. "This is nothing but a big ol' bunch of trash. What they say about you is untrue. You're a wonderful therapist. You've helped so many people."

"That doesn't bother me as much as having our privacy invaded. Yours and Erin's. Even Bert's."

I stare into Max's sad eyes. "Let's not talk about this now. It makes me too crazy."

Nate squats beside me. "I have an idea

that might make you feel better. Will you come with me?"

I shake my head. "Thanks but, right now, I don't think anything can change how I feel."

"Sitting around here mulling over your troubles certainly won't," Mother says.

Nate offers his hand. "When I want to pound someone's head in, this always does the trick. Keeps me out of jail, too."

Doubtful, I blink at him. "What?"

He winks. "Trust me."

Relaxing my shoulders, I hold the bowling ball out in front of me, bend my knees slightly, focus.

"Okay," Nate calls from where he sits at the scorekeeper's table behind me. "See that center pin? Imagine it's the *Newsflash* photographer. And the one to the right of him? That's the reporter from *The Scoop.* You see them?"

I squint. "Yeah, I do. The plaintiffs who filed suit on me are there, too." An evil laugh bubbles up from my chest. "Doris Quinn's son is on his knees begging. Sue Kiley's trying to hide behind the ten pin."

"You going to take pity on 'em?"

"Are you joking? Like they took pity on me?"

"Good girl. Give 'em hell."

I count to three then take off. My arm pulls back, swings forward, the ball leaves my hand and hits the polished wooden lane with a smooth and satisfying *thump.* It seems to gather speed as it moves up the center and crashes into the pins, scattering all ten of them.

I squeal and jump, pump the air with my fist. "All right!"

"Beautiful." Nate claps as, dancing a jig, I make my way toward him.

I pause to bow. "Who'd have thought I'd have a knack for this? I haven't bowled since Erin was little, and then I mainly helped her."

Nate hands me my beer when I stop beside him, then clinks his bottle against mine. Earlier, he informed me that bowling without beer was like fishing without bait. "Feel better?" He stands to take his turn.

"As a matter of fact, I do."

"Works every time."

"You do this a lot?"

He gets up and holds both palms over the air blower to dry them, then hefts a glossy black ball. "Like I said, it keeps me out of jail."

Two games later, we drink another beer in the adjoining bar. In the corner on a tiny stage, a cowboy strums a guitar and sings of unrequited love. He's far too good for this smoky dive. His voice sounds pure and is filled with such longing the melody pulses like heartache.

When the song ends and our bottles sit empty, we bundle into our coats and head outside to Nate's Porsche. He opens my door for me. "You did great in there. Both games were close."

I climb in. "Next time I'll beat you."

A minute later, we're on our way. I thank him for the evening and apologize for my earlier negative frame of mind. "I've had a difficult few months. A difficult year, really. Too much change in my life, I guess."

"You don't like change?"

"I'm not good at it."

Since he's an attorney, I expect him to interrogate me. He doesn't. But I find I want to tell him everything anyway. If he has this effect on witnesses, it explains why he's so good at his job.

"My dad died a little over a year ago. Mother sold their house in Cleburne and moved to Parkview Manor to be closer to us. Not long after, my husband and I separated. Then Mother moved in. She wasn't happy at Parkview and I was worried about her failing eyesight. I thought she needed me."

All at once I realize my true motive for moving Mother in, and the admission slips right out of me. "Really, I needed her. Bert was gone. Erin started to declare her independence and wasn't home as much. The house felt so empty." *I felt empty.* "Now Oliver and Mother have fallen in love and she's preoccupied, too." I glance across at him and feel myself blush. "I didn't mean to go on and on. God, I sound pathetic."

"No." His eyes hold sympathy. "That's not only a lot of change, it's a lot of loss. You've had a tough time. Change opens new doors, though." He shrugs. "Might lead to good things."

"I'm too scared to find out what's on the other side."

When we pull into the driveway, Noah's cycle is parked out front of the house. I shake my head. "He doesn't give up." Nate frowns and I point to the cycle. "Erin's boyfriend. She broke up with him."

"Smart kid, that boy. Your daughter's a good-looking girl. Just like her mother." He leans across to kiss me. When I turn my head, he hesitates, then kisses my cheek. "Erin's boyfriend isn't the only one who doesn't give up easy," he mutters.

His mouth hovers close to my ear, and his quiet, deep voice vibrates through me, raising goose bumps on my skin, bringing all my long-suppressed needs to the surface where they hum and shimmer and ache like that love song the cowboy crooned in the bowling alley bar. And I'm tempted. So tempted. And so afraid. To move my head just a fraction, to let his lips touch mine.

"Isn't this unethical?" I ask, my voice hardly more than a whisper.

His breath warms my cheek. "What?"

"An attorney on the verge of kissing his client." I risk facing him and smile. "His client on the verge of kissing him back."

"I'm not sure. Maybe."

Oh, help. I'm dizzy. "I don't want to get you disbarred."

"I promise that's not going to happen. And even if it did, I'm dead sure kissing you would be worth giving up the practice of law." He leans closer.

I start to go for it, then waver and scoot nearer to my door. Even if I weren't his client, kissing Nate would be wrong. I'm not ready to get involved. Not with him or anyone.

I offer my hand. "How about a hand-shake, instead? Just in case a kiss would be breaking some lawyer oath you took and don't remember."

Nate leans back, shrugs. "Sure," he says,

286

"whatever you want." The smile in his eyes tells me he's well aware that it wouldn't take much coaxing to change my mind.

He reaches for my hand, but instead of taking it, his fingertips brush mine. So soft, that touch, yet it makes the muscles in my stomach tighten. He slides his fingers up my palm and when our thumbs lock, he clasps my hand gently, strokes the pad of his thumb over the top of mine. And all the time he does this, he stares into my eyes, looking very sure of himself. Which he should be, since I'm melting; if I don't get out of this car in the next few seconds nothing will remain of me but a puddle on the floorboard. No doubt about it.

I grab the door handle, pull it, climb out of the car. "Good night, Nate." My knees almost buckle as I bend down to look in at him.

"I'll see you at Friday's appointment. Five o'clock. Don't miss this one."

That again. "What's with you and imaginary Friday afternoon appointments? We don't need to meet. You said yourself the suit's in waiting mode."

He holds my gaze so long I don't feel the chill in the air anymore. "Listen to your attorney, ma'am. He'll keep you out of trouble."

"Or get me into it."

"That depends on your definition of trouble."

"I'm looking at it."

"I hear some things in life are worth it." His cheek twitches. "Trouble, that is."

Chapter 20

To: Erin@friendmail.com
From: Noah@friendmail.com
Date: 01/20 Saturday
Subject: hi

Erin,
thanks for letting me come over the other night. have you decided if you'll play with us? i know you love Cateye. whatever happens between you and me, you're still part of the band. just show up by eleven. we'll be there. i promise not to push you about anything else. love, noah

Suz and I get to The Beat at ten forty-five. We take a quick walk around the club, squeezing through the crowd, saying hello to people we recognize. Noah's e-mail isn't the only reason I decided to come tonight. Ever since I saw those pictures in Newsflash I've been freaked out about being followed. And not only by reporters, by Nana and Mr.

Winston. I'm sure that picture of them was taken at The Beat. I can't believe I didn't have a clue. If anyone's following me tonight, I plan to catch them in action.

Suz tugs my arm and leans close to my ear so I can hear her over the noise. "Come on. I'm dying of thirst and you need to get on stage. Besides, no one's watching you."

"Not yet. Or maybe they're just hiding. Obviously they're good at it."

"You are so paranoid."

"And you wouldn't be? You saw the pictures. I'm completely humiliated! In more ways than one."

Her face squinches up. "I think it's funny."

"You only think it's funny because you aren't the one getting teased."

"I'm sorry," she says, but keeps on laughing. "I promise while you're playing I'll keep an eye out."

Noah, Tonto and Reese are tuning up when I get on stage. "Hey, girlie!" Tonto nods at me and smiles. "Glad you could make it.

"Relieved, too," Reese adds. "The crowd complains when you don't play with us."

Noah stays quiet, but his expression tells me exactly how happy he is that I'm here. His eyes say I'm the only person in the place who matters, the only person in the world. Which makes it really hard for me to stay cool toward him. Not that I'm mad or anything; I'm not. I just want to stop caring about him, so it won't hurt so much when he leaves for good.

The entire time we play, I search the crowd, but it's hard to see faces since we're in the spotlight, and they're in the dark. The dance floor is a sea of swaying bodies, heads bobbing like buoys.

At midnight, we take a break. Suz has soft drinks waiting for us at her table. While she flirts with Tonto, I gulp my Coke, then take off to pee. A long line stretches from the door of the women's restroom. At the head of it, I spot someone who doesn't fit in with this crowd.

"Do you mind?" I'm half angry, half nervous as I weave my way through the line. "Sorry. I'm in the band. I have to hurry." A few people grumble, but most seem to understand as I push toward the bathroom.

Once inside, I glance beneath each of the four stalls, pausing on black polyester slacks scrunched around ankles above a pair of flat shoes. Black leather lace-up *Naturalizers*. Cushiony soles. Shoes made for comfort, not fashion. Easy on the bunions.

Facing the stall, I lean against the sink

across from it, my arms crossed. A girl comes out of stall number three and glares at me since I'm blocking the only unoccupied sink. She starts to say something, but I press my finger to my lips and point at the shoes.

The girl's forehead wrinkles and she gives me a have-you-gone-insane? look. But I guess she wants to see what happens, because she stands beside me, her eyes on stall four. Humming starts behind it. A church hymn. I cover my mouth and smile. Sure, I'm pissed, but I can't be *too* mad.

The feet shuffle. The polyester pants unscrunch. The toilet flushes. After a couple of seconds, the stall door opens and Nana steps out. Her magnified eyes pop wider when she sees me. "Oh, Erin. Hello, Sugar." Her eyelids flutter like moth wings and she fidgets with her blouse, fanning it away from her chest. "It's hot in here. I've never heard the band sound better. You and the boys are really rocking."

The girl beside me snickers as Nana nods at the sink. "Excuse me. I'd better wash up."

I don't move. "What are you doing here, Nana?"

"Why, dancing, Sugar. What else?"

As if. "We don't play the kind of music people your age dance to."

She looks all offended. "Says who? Since when, Erin Dupree, did you become an expert on people *my age?*"

"Nana."

"I'll have you know, Oliver and I come here often and we have the time of our lives. And I can't speak for my own dancing, but that old man puts some of those young dudes out there to shame."

Laughter erupts. All at once I realize the restroom is packed with people. Heads poke through the open door. Everyone watches Nana and me.

I grab my grandmother's hand. "Come on."

"But I didn't wash up." She glances back at the sink. "Neither did you."

I pull her through the giggling crowd. Oliver stands outside the door, sweating like a rock star. A really old balding one. "Well, hello there, Miss Erin." He chuckles. "I was starting to worry about your grandma she'd been gone so long."

"How are you, Mr. Winston?"

"Exhausted." He lifts a foot. "My dogs are howling. How about a slow tune in the next set?"

"Sure," I say. He's so funny, it's hard to stay annoyed.

"Cateye's in top form tonight. The

crowd's hopping like cold water on a hot griddle."

"Thanks, Mr. Winston." I nod toward my table. "Come meet the band."

As we work our way through the crowd, I'm totally shocked to hear kids call out to my grandmother and Oliver like they're old friends.

"Hey, Belle. Ollie," a guy wearing a ball cap yells.

Nana waves. "Trey! You shaved your beard. You look so handsome."

A girl rubs the guy's cheek. "The kissing's better, too."

Oliver chuckles. "Now, didn't I tell you she'd think so, Trey?"

I'm not believing this. I turn to Nana. "Who are they?"

"Our friends Trey and Megan."

"Where'd you meet them?"

"Why, here, Sugar."

When we reach the table, everyone stops talking and looks up. Suz says, "Oh." Noah's mouth drops open. I make introductions. "You guys keep Mr. Winston company while Nana and I go outside to the car to talk."

The guys pull out my empty chair for him, and Suz tosses me her keys. Oliver launches into a story as Nana and I head for the exit.

At the door, a two-hundred-fifty-pound tattooed bouncer in leather, stops us. "How ya doin, Belle?"

"Fine, Bongo," Nana gushes. "And you?"

He rubs his temples. "My ears are ringing again. I got another headache."

Nana plants fists on her hips. "You didn't buy those earplugs like I told you to, now did you?"

Bongo looks all sheepish. "No, ma'am."

"You'd better, young man. There's no such thing as an eardrum transplant, and working around all this loud music night in, night out, is bound to ruin your hearing if you don't do something."

He opens the door for us and grins. "You're right, Belle. I'll buy some tomorrow. I promise."

As we walk outside, I don't know what to say, so I don't say anything. Once inside Suzanna's car, I turn on the ignition and crank up the heater.

"Now, I know you're not happy with me, Erin, but —"

"How long have you been following me?"

"Since the second night I watched you climb out your bedroom window."

My stomach does a somersault. No wonder everyone here knows her. My grandmother's a regular. I feel defensive, but ashamed, too. I know she must've been worried about me. And tired of following me around to make sure I'm okay.

"This is not a safe place for girls your age to come to alone. Especially if no one knows where you are."

"Nana . . . things have changed since you were seventeen."

"Yes, they have. The world's even more dangerous now. I couldn't just sit back and hope for the best while you stayed out until the wee hours. If anything happened to you, I'd never forgive myself."

"I know that." My throat aches, like a pebble's stuck in it. "You didn't tell Mom?"

"No." Folding her hands in her lap, Nana lifts her chin. "That's probably a mistake on my part. But I don't want to be the one to tell her, Erin. I want you to."

"I can't."

"I know your mother seems unreasonable at times."

I huff a laugh.

Nana surprises me by laughing, too. "Her mind's as closed and locked tight as a safe at the bank, isn't it? Especially when it comes to allowing you to grow up." She stops laughing and gets all serious. "Your mother went through some things when she was hardly older than you. She wants to spare you the same hurts she suffered."

"Was it a guy?"

"That's not for me to tell. Go to her. Ask her your questions. Tell her how you feel. I'm sure the two of you can find some middle ground. Just try not to lose your temper while you're doing it."

"Tell *her* that."

"I have, and I will again." Nana heaves a sigh. "I understand your need for more freedom, it's just your method of getting it I don't like. I hate that you haven't spoken to your mother since those photographs hit the news. That's not good for either of you. You need each other. I know things haven't been easy for you since the divorce, but they haven't been easy for her, either."

Outside my window, cars speed past on the street, like it's early instead of after midnight. Where are they going? Are the people inside them as confused as me? Are their lives as big a mess? "I'll talk to Mom," I say. "I promise. Just give me some time. It won't be easy."

"Until you do," Nana points a finger at me, her voice teasing but firm, "I'll have my eye on you, young lady."

I laugh. "You just don't want to give up the dancing and the music. You like it. I can tell. Just don't break a hip or something."

"Don't worry about that. My hips are well-padded." Nana smiles. "You, your mother and I are more alike than you might think."

"I've never heard you lose your temper like we do."

"When I was your age . . . well that's a story for another time." With a nod at the building she says, "Better get back inside. Your fans are waiting, and I've got my second wind."

As we start toward the entrance to The Beat, I feel lighter than I have in weeks, like I'm walking on air without the big burden of my lie weighing me down. But then I think of the promise I just made, and the air turns to quicksand. Nana expects me to do the impossible.

Talk to Mom.

Chapter 21

From The Desk of
Belle Lamont

Dear Harry,

I've been under the weather today with a stuffy nose. Well deserved, I suppose, for staying out so late and in such cool weather.

Harry, I'll just speak my mind and be done with it.

Oliver Winston asked me to marry him. I haven't given him an answer yet. But I won't lie to you; I want to say "yes."

What's wrong with me? How can I feel like I do? Happy with another man? Excited about a new life? A life without you in it? I think of our years together, how full and rich they were, and I tell myself that should be enough. That I'm selfish to want more when we had so much.

I'm ashamed to admit that, when I'm with Oliver, for a time I can almost forget the pain of losing you. I feel alive again. Is that wrong? Am I betraying you by loving him?

I do love him, Harry. I'm finally happy again. It's been so long.

At Christmas, I asked that you give me your blessing to move on, that, somehow, you let me know you accept my decisions, whatever they might be. I've watched and waited, and you've yet to give me a sign. Please don't make me wait forever. Time is passing, and I'm not a young woman. Until then, please know I'll love you forever.

As always, your yellow rose,
Belle

Chapter 22

Cecilia Dupree
Day Planner
Tuesday, 01/23

1. 8:30 — Ask Willa today's schedule — forgot to write down.
2. Resume training Max.
3. Ask Erin out for Tex-Mex tonight, just the two of us.

Mrs. Stein is sweeping her front porch when I go out to get the morning paper. "CiCi!" she calls. "I'm so glad to see you." She props the broom against the house, scoops up Pom Pom, then starts across the yard in her slippers and long flowery caftan robe.

Oh boy. I grab the paper and force a smile. One good thing about starting my day with Mrs. Stein, the hours ahead can only improve. "How are you?"

"Fine, hon." She purses her poofy lips. Strange. I'm sure she's always been thin-lipped. No, make that lipless.

Mrs. Stein must notice me staring because she purses her mouth and turns her head left, then right. "Well, what do you think? I had them done last week. I've always wanted Cupid's bow lips."

Poor Mrs. Stein. Her lips look more like Cupid's buttocks than Cupid's bow. "Wow," I say. "They're incredible."

Pom Pom licks the topic of conversation, making me shudder and Mrs. Stein squeal. She ruffles the puff of curly hair atop the poodle's head and says in a high-pitched tone, "Pom Pom likes them, too!"

After a moment, her expression shifts to one of concern. She places a hand on my wrist. "How are you holding up?"

"I —"

"I don't blame you for hiding out." Her brows aren't penciled on yet, so I can't be sure, but I think one hikes.

"Well, actually —"

"How in the world did you get yourself in such a situation?" She scans the block, as if the neighbors might hear my dirty little secret. "The things the media's saying . . . how humiliated you must be. I can't imagine."

"Mrs. —"

"I don't understand it. Neither does Henry Bocock. You remember Henry. The patient I sent you? Strapping bear of a man?

Rugged? Nice jewelry?"

She means You-Can-Call-Me-Hank, but since it's against the rules for me to acknowledge seeing someone, even though she referred him, I only blink and smile.

Leaning closer, Mrs. Stein gives me a woman-to-woman grin. "I do so love a man with a little hair on his chest, don't you?"

A little? The man was Teen Wolf grown up.

"Well, just so you'll know, Henry said that after only one meeting, he's certain you're too much of a lady to be involved in something so sordid, and I agree."

"I appreciate your support, Mrs. Stein. Mr. Bocock's, too. I hope you'll tell him."

"You can do that yourself. He plans to make another appointment."

Lovely.

"So, CiCi." Her eyes blink sympathy as artificial as her nipped and tucked face. "I'm here for you, hon. Tell me what started all this nonsense."

"It's a long story."

"I'm not busy. Come on over for coffee. I have a fresh pot on."

"Another time, maybe." I glance at my watch. "I have to get to the office. But thanks." I make my escape.

Willa's on the phone when I arrive. Since

I never book anything prior to nine, I know I'm not late for an appointment, but I've been so scattered lately, and I hate not knowing what's ahead in my day. I grab a diet shake from the kitchen fridge, then head for my office, mouthing for Willa to join me when she finishes on the phone.

After a couple of minutes, she comes in. "Good morning, boss." She eyes my breakfast. "What? No coffee and Southern Comfort?"

"Not yet. Check in with me again in a couple of hours. Do I have a nine o'clock?"

"Not anymore. The toe sucker just cancelled." When I scowl, she says, "You know, girl. The foot-fetish guy?"

I laugh. "Darn. He always keeps me posted on the best shoe sales. Why'd he cancel?"

"Didn't say." The phone rings. Willa stretches across my desk and grabs it. After a short conversation, she hangs up. "That was Mrs. Smythe, your two o'clock. She and her daughter Halee can't make it this afternoon." Worry creases her forehead. "Or any other Tuesday, apparently. She canceled their standing appointment."

My stomach stops growling; I'm suddenly too filled with anxiety to be hungry. "Did she say why?"

"She mentioned the scandal."

That word again.

"Said she heard about it on *LIVE With Regis and Kelly* yesterday."

"*Regis and Kelly*?"

"Don't you know?" Willa plants a hand on her hip. "You're famous, girl. They talked about everything on the program yesterday. Parkview. That poor old guy taking too much Viagra. You and that book."

"I don't want fame, I want patients. Get me Mrs. Smythe's number, would you? I want to call her back."

When Mrs. Smythe answers, I ask her straight out if she's dissatisfied with the progress Halee's made since we started meeting.

"This is difficult for me to say to you, Ms. Dupree. Maybe I'm wrong to judge, but with all I'm hearing on television and seeing in the papers and in magazines, I've lost trust in your advice. Face it, your daughter's as big a mess as mine."

She's dead wrong about that, but no way am I going to beg this woman or anyone else to continue using me as a therapist. Don't get me wrong, I want to, at least a part of me does. For the sake of my career, my mortgage and Erin's college fund, I want to plead and reason and grapple until Mrs. Smythe takes pity on me. Instead, I grasp on to the threadbare remains of my dignity, wish her well, and hang up.

The second the receiver is down, the phone rings again. Willa looks as antsy as I feel when she picks up. "Cecilia Dupree's office . . . yes, sir . . . I'm sorry to hear that. Would you like to reschedule on a different date?" She looks away from me. "I see . . . No, I understand."

Willa lowers the receiver to the cradle and her butt to the edge of my desk. "Tomorrow's ten o'clock just cancelled." Her troubled gaze meets mine. "Lord, girl, what's going on?"

"They're pulling out because of all the negative publicity."

"Surely they know you better."

"Can you blame them? My marriage fell apart, my mother is acting like a teenager, my seventeen-year-old daughter sneaks around behind my back and lies to me, my dog needs Prozac and I can't stop stuffing my face."

Shoving the diet shake aside, I open the bottom desk drawer, revealing my secret stash of Reese's Chocolate Peanut Butter Cups. "If I can't solve my own problems, why should anyone believe I could help them solve theirs?"

After dinner alone yet again, Max and I sit in front of the TV and channel surf. Mom and Oliver went out to eat and to a movie. Erin opted for fast food with Suzanna over Tex-Mex with me. I'm just glad she's stopped the silent treatment. We still haven't talked things out, and I know I should insist she either confess her sins or be grounded the rest of her life, but I've decided to ease up. Bide my time. She's had a lot to deal with lately; we both have. I can't force her to talk to me. Nor can I watch her every second of the day and night, like I informed Bert. And I refuse to bar the windows.

I pause on *Extreme Makeover* and watch until the first commercial.

"Tonight at ten," a familiar local newscaster announces, "join us for all the latest on the Parkview Manor sex scandal. . . ."

All the latest? There's more I don't know? I turn off the set.

Picking up a magazine that came in the mail today, I flip through pages of ads for cosmetics, articles about facial peels, lip enhancements, Botox injections. Soon the world will be full of Mrs. Stein clones. A scary thought.

I read a couple of paragraphs about the

Botox, then go look in the mirror, scrutinizing my laugh lines, the deepening frown groove between my brows. Maybe if I didn't go overboard, a quick trip to the plastic surgeon would be okay. A little touch-up couldn't hurt, could it? Especially if my current trend continues and the only men who interest me are so young they've never seen or even heard of an eight-track tape.

Sick of myself, I leave the mirror and head for my closet for warm clothes. A walk, that's what I need. What I *don't* need is to look twenty-something again. I was a confused wreck back then. Forty-one is a much happier place. At least it would be if Bert hadn't screwed up. Or, more accurately, if he hadn't screwed the Butterfield girl.

Bundled up in a coat, earmuffs and gloves, I leash Max and head out. It's been a while since we walked and it shows on both of us. I decide on our usual route, down to the end of our street, turn left to the park, circle it, then return to our street and head back to the house.

A chill nips the air, but it's more invigorating than uncomfortable. Max must disagree. He's sluggish as we run through the training manual routine. After once around the park, I decide to walk a couple more blocks rather than head home, hoping to perk him up. When I try to pass by our street, though, Max puts on the brakes and glues his butt to the sidewalk.

I tug his leash. "Come on, boy. We're adding some variety to our routine."

He tugs back, looks at our street, then back to me.

"Don't be such a fuddy-duddy. I swear, I must be rubbing off on you." I tug again and, when he doesn't budge, I walk over to him and squat so that we're eye-to-eye. "Look buster, I'm the boss here, and I say move it. Understand?"

He lays a slobbery dog kiss on my cheek.

I stand. "Look at us, Max. Out of shape, lethargic." *Scared to death of all these changes in our lives.* "It's time we stop moping around and get back on track. What do you say? Come on. Let's do it."

Again, I tug the leash. No deal.

"Fine then. Be that way. I thought I could at least count on *you* not to make my life difficult." I drop the leash and start walking the direction I want to go. "Run home if that's what you want to do," I yell as I walk away with my back to him.

Max barks, so I look over my shoulder at him while I continue to walk. He's still perched right where I left him. "Sit there until your butt goes numb. See if I care."

I turn in time to see the curb, too late to stop my next step off of it. Stumbling, I cry out. My right ankle twists as I fall.

Max comes running, dragging his leash behind him. He circles me in a prancing panic, barking and licking my face. I try to stand, but it hurts so much that I sink to the ground and squeeze my eyes shut tight to stop the tears.

Pushing to my hands and knees, I crawl to the corner and grab hold of the Stop sign pole. I pull myself up onto my left foot, take a breath, try my weight on the right one. I jerk my hurt foot up again. "Ow, ow, ow!"

Max barks and stares at me.

"Sure, now you're sorry." Holding tight to the pole, I bend and grab his leash. I hop three steps on my left foot, put my right foot down to rebalance, wince and squeal, pick it up, hop three more steps. Headlights turn the corner and approach. A welcome sight, though I feel like an idiot.

Nate's Porsche pulls to a stop alongside me. He rolls down the window and I hop over and lean against the trunk. "What happened?" He gets out and helps me around to the passenger side. Max jumps into the floorboard at my feet.

"I twisted my ankle."

Nate goes back around and slides behind

the wheel. "Want to tell me about it?"

"Not really." Crossing my arms, I stare out the window and sulk. "So, you just happened to be cruising my neighborhood?"

"Haven't heard from you lately. I called your office. Willa said you went home early again."

"No reason to stay. All my patients are bailing thanks to my sudden sorry reputation."

For several seconds, he doesn't say anything, then, "I tried your house. The phone's been busy all afternoon and evening."

"It's off the hook. Too many calls wanting my side of the story."

He takes off in the direction of home. "I want to talk to you about the case." When I shoot him a skeptical glare he says, "No, really. I have an idea." He pulls into my driveway. "Are your mother and Erin home?"

"No. Some people in this family actually have a social life."

"My, we're in a cheery mood, aren't we?"

"Sorry. Mother's out with Oliver. Erin's studying at Suzanna's."

I'm close to tears as Nate helps me into the house with Max at his heels. It's not just the ankle. Everything in my life feels out of my control. What happened to the together woman I was two years ago? I'm tired of this gloomy cloud hanging over my head, tired of getting pelted with grapefruit-sized hailstones.

Nate checks out my swelling ankle and decides no bones are broken. I direct him to the bathroom cabinet for an ice pack and an Ace bandage.

When I'm settled on the sofa, my ankle wrapped, iced down and propped on a pillow on the ottoman in front of me, Nate sits at my side.

"I've been talking to Everett about your case."

"Your brother?"

"Yeah."

"What does he say?"

"He'd like to represent you."

"But that's your job."

"The ethics, remember? It's clear you're not comfortable mixing business with pleasure. And when I think about it rationally, I know you're right."

"Nate . . ." He smells like shaving cream. God, I love that scent on a man. I want to bury my nose in his neck and take deep breaths. "I thought we agreed to keep our personal relationship at a handshake level?"

"CiCi . . ." Nate scoots closer, hooks a strand of hair behind my ear. "As much as I want this case, I want you more. Everett and I aren't legally partners. We're sole proprietors. There isn't anything unethical about getting involved with your brother's client. And Everett's a great attorney." He grins. "Almost as brilliant as me."

He keeps talking. I listen, but my mind returns again and again to three little words. "You want me?" If he doesn't say yes, I'll be forced to eat an entire carton of double-chunk chocolate.

Nate shuts up and grins wider. "That's what I said. So . . . what do *you* say?"

I place my hand at the back of his neck, bring his face close to mine. "I say, you're fired."

Chapter 23

When the alarm goes off at seven, I cover my head with a pillow and swing blindly at the radio to stop the buzzer. Why get up? Yesterday, all my appointments for today cancelled. Other than my three o'clock, that is. You-Can-Call-Me-Hank. What a guy. The only patient I have left, and he doesn't even really want therapy, or need it. What he wants, and thinks he needs, is a sparkly woman on his arm to match his sparkly gold neck chain.

With the buzzer silenced, I burrow deeper into the covers and clear my mind. Or try to. Music flows into my room through the ceiling vent. Erin's alarm. I press the pillow tighter against my head.

A memory of Bert surfaces. The two of us in this very bed when we had the old mattress, muffling our laughter while trying out every position we can think of that won't make the springs squeak so Erin won't hear us through the vent.

Groaning, I throw the pillow aside and sit

up. No more thinking about Bert and the old days. Get over it. Be a big girl and move on. Quit being a victim. That's what I'd tell a patient. Not so bluntly, but the message would be the same.

The phone rings as I limp into the bathroom on my sore ankle. I decide to let Mother or Erin pick up. I've just stuck my toothbrush into my mouth when someone knocks at the door.

"Mom, it's for you."

I poke my head out the door. "Who is it?" I ask, the brush still in my mouth.

"Nathan Colby," she whispers, extending the cordless phone.

I stare at it and continue brushing.

Erin frowns. "Where's Nana?"

"Isn't she cooking breakfast?" I say around the brush.

"No, and she isn't in her room. The bed's made."

"Go look out front. Maybe she went to get the paper and ran into Mrs. Stein."

Glaring, Erin jabs the phone at me. "*Mom,* I'm going to be late. Here."

Choice time.

Three nights ago after I fired Nate, we ended up in my bedroom. Wouldn't you know it? Erin picked that night as the first one in months to be home by eight. The slam of her car door interrupted us before any clothes came off. I'm thankful for that. And not. Thankful, because getting in over my head with him so soon, before we really thought it through, would've been a mistake. Not thankful, because right or wrong, I *wanted* to make that hot, sweaty, irresistible mistake.

Turning, I spit into the sink, rinse my mouth, then face Erin again. She fidgets, huffs, rolls her eyes. I take the phone and close the bathroom door.

"Hello, Nate."

"Okay, what's the deal? Am I that bad of a kisser?"

I recall the feel of his mouth on mine and a hot wave of want almost makes me stagger. I lean against the sink. "You're the best kisser I've ever kissed."

"You sure? Because if I'm not, we can practice until I get it right."

I smile. "In that case, you're terrible."

He chuckles. "How's the ankle?"

"Better. Still a little tender, though."

"Why haven't you answered my calls?"

I stare into the mirror at my less than radiant complexion, spot a gray hair at my temple, fumble around in my top drawer until I locate the tweezers. I put on my reading glasses, lean closer to the mirror and see that the hair is pale blond, not gray. A ridiculous surge of relief shoots through me. "How old do you think I am, Nate?"

"I don't know. Thirty-seven? Thirty-eight?"

"Try forty-one. And you're . . . what? Thirty?"

"Thirty-three. So, what are you saying? I'm not experienced enough for you?"

Erin knocks on my door again. "Mom, open up. Look at this."

"Just a minute," I say to Nate, then open the door. She hands me a note with Mother's handwriting scrawled across it, then shrugs and leaves.

Ran an errand with Oliver. Nothing to worry about. Home soon. Left warm sweet rolls in the oven for your breakfast.

Nothing to worry about? Ha! Please tell me they didn't elope.

Still staring at my mother's perfect script, I say into the phone, "Sorry about that."

"Anything wrong?"

"Mother's AWOL. She left a note saying not to worry. So I won't." Yeah, right. "Where were we?"

"You said I'm not experienced enough for you."

"I didn't say that." I slip the reading glasses off of my nose and frown at them. "I

317

was about to say I'm too old for you. You probably never even saw *Footloose* or danced to the Bee Gees. You probably have perfect up-close vision. What could we possibly have in common?"

"Lust?"

I bite the inside of my cheek. "Seriously. You're a young, interesting, sexy, unencumbered guy. You've got it together. You could have any hot babe you want. Why me?"

"Because —"

"I'm middle-aged, boring, chubby. A divorced single mother. My life is a mess right now."

"Boring? The Parkview Manor madam? You're kidding me, right?"

"Very funny."

"And you're not chubby, you're curvy. I like curvy." When I start to interrupt, he continues, "I don't care if you're forty-one."

I close my eyes. "My ex is making a fool of himself with a girl seventeen years his junior. I don't want to follow in his footsteps."

"I'm eight years behind you, CiCi, not seventeen. So what are you really afraid of?"

Of risking my heart again. Of screwing up. Of getting hurt. I could go on.

"I'm not afraid of anything."

"Good. Have dinner with me tonight. It's

Friday. No work in the morning. We could go to a movie, too."

A real date. I squeeze my eyes shut tighter. "I can't."

"Tomorrow night, then."

I chew the earpiece of my glasses. "I'll think about it."

"I'll call you in the morning. Answer the damn phone. If you don't, I'll just come over. There's no hiding from me. I know where you live."

An uneasy laugh ripples out of me. "I'll answer. I promise."

At eight-thirty Mother's still not home. I call Willa to tell her I won't be in until Hank Bocock's appointment this afternoon. I plan to spend the morning worrying while painting the sunroom daffodil-yellow.

The moment Willa picks up, I hear a television in the background. "Do you have your feet on my desk?" I ask in lieu of a greeting, knowing she's in my office.

"Girl, you are not going to believe what's happening around here. The phone was ringing when I walked in a half hour ago and it hasn't stopped since."

My heart does a swan dive to the pit of my stomach. "More cancellations?"

"What do you mean? You didn't have any

appointments left to cancel."

"Didn't?"

"Now you're booked solid through Wednesday of next week. Not a one of them under the age of seventy." Willa hoots. "They've been reading about you and the scandal, hearing about you on television. They all say the same thing, CiCi. That they're behind you."

"I can't believe this."

"I'm telling you, these people are thrilled about what you started at Parkview. They say no one ever takes their matters of the heart seriously. One old gentleman's driving all the way from Oklahoma City just to bend your ear."

I sink into a kitchen chair, lift a sweet roll from the pan Erin left on the table, take a bite and wash it down with my diet shake. "So, what? Now I'm the geriatrics' Dr. Ruth?"

Willa laughs. "Is that so bad? I think — oh . . . sweet Jesus . . . oh, my . . ." She shrieks.

"What? What's going on?"

"Get to a television set and turn it on channel four. Hurry! They just cut in with a live report."

Still holding the phone, I run into the den and switch on the set. I flip to four. It must be a job requirement that female news reporters be blond, I think, as the perky, young bombshell appears on screen, microphone in hand.

"I'm standing in front of the accounting office of Donald Quinn, a Dallas C.P.A. and one of the plaintiffs in the lawsuit against Parkview Manor Retirement Village and licensed therapist Cecilia Dupree."

The camera pans out, and there, standing beside the reporter, are Mother and Oliver. Behind them, elderly picketers bear signs and pace back and forth in front of the office door. Among the crowd I see The Frans. Mary Fran's sign reads, Senior Citizens Should Not Be Censored. Francis's sign, End Senior Oppression.

"I have with me," the reporter continues, "Belle Lamont and Oliver Winston, members of the Parkview Manor reading group and the organizers of this rally." She turns to Mother. "Mrs. Lamont, your daughter, Cecilia Dupree, is being sued along with the retirement village for exposing the Parkview reading group to soft pornography and, as a result of that exposure, inciting some of the members to engage in rash, potentially harmful acts. What do you and your group hope to accomplish here today?"

Mother clears her throat as she faces the

camera. "I want Mr. Quinn and the other plaintiffs to realize how silly they're being. My daughter has devoted her life to helping people. She didn't hurt us, she brought us together, gave us something else fun to look forward to each week. It's true that one of our members had a medical emergency, but it wasn't Cecilia's fault, or Parkview's, either." Mother lifts her chin. "I'm very proud of my daughter. *Penelope's Passion* is not pornography. It's an adventure. A lovely romance."

Willa and I groan at the same time as the reporter lifts the book and the camera zooms in on Penelope's naked back and the captain's hand touching it. "A lovely romance with quite a bit of sex," the perky blonde responds in a bedroom voice.

The camera shifts to Mother, who doesn't flinch. "Since when did sex become a four-letter word?"

Willa shouts, "You go girl."

I cover my mouth and laugh. I guess I never took a long enough look at my mother to see how truly gutsy she is. She always says I'm like her and don't realize it. Right now, I hope it's true, that her strength lives inside me. Lurking. Waiting for me to find it.

The camera moves to Oliver who points to the words on his sign, We're Old, Not

Dead, then at the picketers behind him. "We aren't kids. Not a one of us is senile. We don't need our grown children to shelter us." He looks directly into the camera, directly at me. "We may be a little worse for wear on the outside, but inside . . ." he taps his fingers against his chest, right over his heart, "inside, we're no different than we've ever been. At least Cecilia Dupree seems to be figuring that out, if no one else is."

Willa's sigh travels across the line. "That sweet old man."

My eyes fill. "Sweet old conniver's more like it. Damn him. He's going to end up making me love him."

Mother and Oliver step back and Doris Quinn steps forward. The camera zeroes in on her sign — Seniors Need Love Too. When the scene widens again, Doris waves a hand at the building and twitters, "This office belongs to my son. If you're watching, Donnie, I just want to say that it's time for you to give up this ridiculous lawsuit. Quit being a bully. Straighten up and act right, for heaven's sake. Make your mother proud."

The live report moves to a male reporter on the sidewalk in front of a house he identifies as Sue Kiley's residence. A similar rally is in progress there, led by Sue's father,

Frank Rayburn, now fully recovered from his Viagra incident, his blue Paul Newman eyes sharp and gorgeous as ever. The sign he waves at the camera says, Free To Read, Free To Love, Free Parkview & CiCi. I watch until the report ends, then turn off the set.

"Wow," Willa says.

"My thoughts exactly."

"Those folks are something else. Your mother's one feisty lady. She's got gumption. You must be proud of her."

"I am." So proud I could pop.

No painting for me this morning. Instead, I pace, channel surf and wait for Mother. I consider driving to Donald Quinn's office to see her, but the thought of a possible face-off with reporters keeps me locked in the house. Okay, I know what you're thinking. Where's that gumption I supposedly inherited from my mother? Nowhere to be found at the moment, that's for sure.

Midmorning, I flip to *LIVE With Regis and Kelly,* and my heart beats in double time when I hear Regis speak my name. It seems that since their earlier program where they discussed the "Dallas retirement village scandal and therapist Cecilia Dupree, who allegedly instigated it," senior citizens from all over the country called in to voice their support for me and what I "started."

When my phone rings, I check the caller ID, see that it's Willa and pick up.

"You're on *Regis and Kelly*, again."

"I'm watching. I got in on the middle of it, at the part about all the calls coming in. What else have they said?"

"Seems book groups of retirees all over the country are reading *Penelope's Passion*. Kelly suggested they invite you on the show, girl. Maybe the author, too. And Bill Burdette."

"Me? On television?" Somehow I always imagined celebrity would excite me, not make me sick to my stomach. "That's not going to happen. I'd be a wreck."

"That's not all," Willa continues. "Sela Summers? The lady who wrote the book?"

"What about her?"

"She called a minute ago. She wants you to call back. *Penelope's Passion* just went into a third printing. It's selling like crazy because of you. Ms. Summers wants to thank you."

"Since I've made her rich and famous, did she offer to pay my legal fees?"

"Shoot. Who are you fooling? The only payment Nate Colby's gonna want from you is —"

"Funny, Willa. Anyway, I fired him."

"You did what?"

"Long story. Relax. I hired his brother."

"Is he as cute?"

Before I can answer, the front door slams and Mother and Oliver walk in, both pink-cheeked, animated and talking nonstop.

"Gotta go. Mother's home."

"Give her a high-five from me."

"Will do."

"Oh, and CiCi? I booked the rest of next week and through Tuesday of the next. All new patients."

"Any of *these* under seventy?"

"Only one." She chuckles. "He's sixty-nine."

Chapter 24

The next day, Saturday, is rare and wonderful. Erin is home, Mother's home, I'm home. No one has anywhere to be until this evening when we all have dates, although my feet are getting colder by the second at the thought of mine.

Calls from television shows wanting my interview have come in nonstop the past twenty-four hours. I take the phone off the hook, and we spend the morning washing and drying loads of laundry while watching a couple of movies; Erin's favorite, *Finding Nemo*, then an old dramatic tear-jerker Mother and I both love, *Imitation of Life.*

When we break for lunch, Erin fills Mother and me in on everything from school, to Suz's latest crush, to Noah's plans for college. I have a feeling she's headed toward something touchy and important, but she never arrives. After we finish eating, I slip off and call Nate to cancel our dinner date and am relieved that his machine picks up. I leave a message.

Back in the den, Mother puts her Glenn Miller album on the ancient turntable I never got rid of, cranks up the volume, then the three of us fold all the clean clothes we dumped center floor earlier. Not once does Erin complain, which surprises and pleases me. She seems content to pass the day with us. Yesterday on the six o'clock news, she saw a replay of the protest rally outside Donald Quinn's accounting office, and she's as proud of her nana as I am.

When "In The Mood" starts to play, Mother drops a towel and grabs my hand. We jitterbug like she taught me when I was a girl, hands waving, feet slapping the carpet to the beat of the song. Erin laughs and shrieks, then finally joins in. Nothing else matters as we dance together, my mother, my daughter and me. Nothing intrudes. No problems. No fears. No differences, age or otherwise. There is only our laughter, the pulse of our feet, the energy flowing between and around us.

Later, they leave with Oliver and Noah, and I'm still so alive with the joy of the day that I almost reconsider and call Nate to say I've changed my mind. But I tell myself this is all I want in my life now, enough to fulfill me for the time being. My family under one roof, the three of us learning to relate to one another as grown women, not merely mother and daughter, grandmother and granddaughter.

I admit, I'm the one who's had the toughest time adjusting. Even tonight, when Mother left with Oliver and Noah led Erin out the door, a twinge of worry and resentment and, yes, jealousy too, crept up to try and tug me down from my high. They'll break your heart, I wanted to warn them. They'll turn your life upside down, let it crash and then leave you alone to pick up the pieces. One way or another. Death, divorce, dreams. Something will take them away. Erin, I know, will have to learn that the hard way, there'll be no convincing her. But Mother's been through it once already. It's hard to see her set the stage for another broken heart.

I'm painting the sunroom, looking lovely in daffodil-yellow-splattered sweats and wool socks, hair in a ponytail, no makeup when, at eight, the doorbell rings. It's Nate. Surprise, surprise. He holds a sack in one hand, two bottles in the other.

"If I can't tempt you with myself," he says, "I thought maybe a little merlot and Chinese might do the trick."

I cross my arms.

He smacks his lips and lifts the sack.

329

"Beef with oyster sauce and mushrooms. Yum, yum. Spring rolls. Fried rice, too."

Hunger gnaws at my stomach. A hunger not only for food, but also for his company. Sighing, I step back to let him through.

I grab a couple of wineglasses from the kitchen cabinet and scrounge up an opener. Nate whistles in the next room. A Paul Simon song. Listening closer, I recognize the tune. Something about making love with a woman named Cecilia up in a bedroom. How subtle. Laughing to myself, I join him in the den where I put one of Mother's Frank Sinatra albums on the turntable to shut him up. We sit side by side on the floor and eat off the coffee table.

"One of your neighbors must be having a party. I had to park down the street," Nate says between chews.

"Mrs. Stein next door. She's upset that I didn't come. She wanted to introduce me to her lesbian niece, Cleo something-or-other. Since I've refused every setup she's tried to arrange with men, I guess she's decided I'm gay."

Nate grunts and keeps on eating. "Everett said he scheduled depositions for the week after next."

Sipping the wine, I nod. "He called this afternoon and we coordinated the date."

I wish we didn't have to discuss the lawsuit and risk spoiling the meal. The beef tastes so tender and delicious; I want to concentrate on that, on Old Blue Eyes crooning on the stereo, the spice-scented air, the nice hum of awareness skimming just beneath my skin, caused by the wine and Nate's nearness. If we have to talk, I'd rather talk about him. Since we've met, my problems have taken center stage. It occurs to me I know next to nothing about his life. Just that he's a lawyer. That he has a brother. He enjoys fishing. And he likes older things; sports cars, rock and roll. Me.

"After that news segment yesterday, it wouldn't surprise me if the plaintiffs dropped the suit," Nate says, refilling our goblets. "Doris Quinn seemed madder than a wet hen at her son for starting the thing in the first place. Nothing like a mother's wrath to set a son straight."

We clink our glasses together. "You saw?"

He nods. "Belle and Oliver were great. They all were."

Pushing my empty container aside, I shake my head and laugh. "Who would've thought reading a romance novel would cause such a stir? You wouldn't believe the calls I'm getting at the office. Every senior citizen in the greater Southwest seems to want an appointment with me. Suddenly I'm Masters and Johnson for the Geritol crowd."

"Good for you. They obviously need your services. You took a bad situation and turned it to your advantage. And theirs."

"I'm not sure I had anything to do with it. The whole thing just happened. And I'm not sure how I feel about it, either. I've pretty much focused my practice on troubled teens, troubled families and troubled marriages up until now."

Nate reaches for the opener and goes to work on the second bottle. "Well, maybe it's time for a change."

"I told you, I'm not good at that." Groaning, I take a long drink. "How much change can a person stand? In the space of less than two years, my husband started going down on women half his age, my stud bulldog's so depressed he can't get it up, my mother's moved in and my daughter wants to move out." I lift my glass for a refill. "Oh, and on top of all that, my dad died and my mother's in love again. Now you're telling me my career focus should change, too?"

"You said yourself the members of the reading group were the highlight of your week. That they did as much good for you as you did for them."

"That's true, but . . . I don't know." I start laughing and can't stop.

He watches me, a look of delighted surprise in his eyes.

"I'm sorry. I think I'm a little drunk." I try to compose myself, but it's no use. "I'm sorry," I say again, giddy for no particular reason. "It's just, I mean . . . me? A senior sex therapist?"

"I'm sure they have other issues to discuss with you besides sex." Nate takes the wineglass from me and sets it on the coffee table. "Now, I, on the other hand . . ." He slides his fingers into my hair, against my scalp, and kisses me. The awareness beneath my skin stops humming and sings along with Frank.

As I push Nate to the carpet and kiss him back, the music crescendos.

The bed is spinning when I wake in the middle of the night. I blink to look at the clock. The numbers glow green in the darkness — 4:12 a.m.

Moaning, I close my eyes. They hurt. So does my head. I can't move my body. It feels like a weight presses me into the mattress.

I lift my right hand to cover my gurgling stomach and touch something else. A weight *is* pressing me into the mattress. I pat my palm against it. A leg. A hairy leg.

My eyes pop open again as I raise my left hand to my breasts.

Oh, God. I'm naked. I'm going to throw up.

I slide my right hand up the hairy thigh . . . up . . . up . . . pause . . . jerk it away.

Oh, God. He's naked, too. I'm going to have a coronary.

He. Nate.

It all comes back to me. The wine. The laughter. The kissing. More wine. More laughter. More kissing. And finally, no wine. No laughter. Only kissing and . . .

Oh, God. We did it. Tell me I dreamed it, then let me go back to sleep.

I lie perfectly still; my eyes don't even blink. The only thing moving in my entire body is my heart. Boy does it move. Like a tap dancer on speed. Images flash through my mind. Everything.

Oh . . . It was fun. Fun and thrilling and sexy and . . .

A sneeze sounds somewhere else in the house.

Erin? Mother?

In a panic, I squeeze from under Nate's leg. My head pounds, but my heart pounds harder. I shake his shoulder.

"Wake up!" I plead.

He stirs. A satisfied sound rumbles up from deep in his chest, sending a shiver down my spine. When he reaches for me, I bolt from the bed and scramble around in the dark, searching the floor for my clothes, desperate that they be here in the bedroom instead of in the den where Mother or Erin might've seen them.

Out of nowhere, a scene appears and plays through my mind. Nate undressing me, piece-by-piece, clothes flying over his shoulder, landing on the rocker in the corner.

I run to the rocker. Sure enough.

After struggling into the sweatpants, I tug the sweatshirt over my head and run back to my bed.

"Nate! Please!" I shake him again. "You have to get out of here."

He bolts straight up. *"What?"*

I cover his mouth. "We fell asleep. You have to go before Mother or Erin catch you here."

We don't speak as we move around in the darkness. I wasn't as tidy as Nate when I undressed him. The clothes landed everywhere. His shirt on the dresser. Pants at the foot of the bed. One sock on the nightstand, another in the corner. Underwear? No underwear. I'm sure he wore them. I vividly remember taking *them* off. Boxer briefs. Gray. Snug.

Oh, boy.

I drop to my hands and knees, reach beneath one side of the bed, then crawl around to the other. Nate trips over me, falls against the wall with a loud thud.

"Shhhh!" I rise to my knees. He seems okay. Closing my eyes, I tilt back my head and take several deep breaths. When I open my eyes again, the first thing I see is the shadow of the ceiling fan and something hanging from one blade. I stand and reach up. Nate's briefs. How did that happen?

Nate sits at the edge of my bed and dresses while I pace. Seconds later, as we leave the bedroom, I say a silent thanks to Mrs. Stein next door for having a party. With Nate parked down the street, surely Mother and Erin didn't notice his car.

We tiptoe down the hall toward the entryway. Halfway there, I hear a noise behind us and pause. Dizzy with dread, I look over my shoulder.

Oliver is at Mother's bedroom, his back to us, closing her door. His shirt is untucked, and he reaches to remedy that as he turns. His startled eyes meet mine, but before either of us can react, Erin's bedroom door opens and Noah, sleepy-eyed and rumpled, backs out on tiptoe.

My heart does a quick slide to the floor, hits it, then bounces back up to my throat.

"What in the *hell* do you think you're doing?" I glance from Noah to Oliver and back again, every cell in my body poised for battle. "Both of you! Do you know what time it is?" Anger burns through my body like a shot of whiskey. I shake from the force of it.

Neither of them move; it's as if they're frozen in place. Suddenly, Mother and Erin are in the hallway, too. I see them through a red haze. All of them.

Erin's face is white and wary. When I start toward Noah, she steps in front of him. "Mom. Don't."

That's all it takes. I lose it. "Get out of here!" I scream at her boyfriend. To his credit, Noah moves Erin aside and faces me. "Get out of my daughter's bedroom and out of this house. Do you understand?"

"Yes, ma'am. I —"

"If I ever see your face here again, I'll —" I pause for a breath, feel Nathan's hand on my arm, shake it off. "I'll have you thrown in jail. Don't think I won't. She's a minor, did you know that? She's a minor, and I could get you into a lot of trouble, young man."

Now Erin's screaming back at me, crying and screaming words that don't penetrate the roar of anger and fear and worry in my head. And then there's Mother, her arm around Erin, tears in her eyes, saying, "Don't do this, Cecilia," and Oliver behind her, his hands on her shoulders, and behind me, Nathan's on mine.

The roar subsides enough that I finally hear Erin.

"We fell asleep," she screams. "We were watching a movie."

"You expect me to believe that?" I scan her clothing. "Look at you." She wears a T-shirt, no bra, baggy flannel drawstring sleep pants.

Erin crosses her arms. "Believe what you want. I don't care anymore."

"How can I believe you, Erin, when photos show up in a tabloid of you dressed like a slut, out at some bar, and you refuse to even talk to me about it?"

Mother tightens the belt of her robe and shakes her head at Erin. "Oh, Sugar. You didn't tell her?"

I go still. Mother knew? They kept this from me together? I can't say anything, can only stare at them both, feeling like I might explode into a million tiny pieces and splatter the walls.

"Okay." Erin bites her lip, pushes hair from her eyes. "You want to know? I'm in a band." She glances at Noah. He looks like he might pass out. "It's called Cateye, and

I've been sneaking out a couple of nights a week to play at a club called The Beat. They pay us, Mom, and I'm saving the money so I can move out of here in the fall when I go to college. So I can get away from you and finally have a life."

So she can get away from me. A fist in the stomach would've felt like a kiss compared to those words. "You're not eighteen. How do you get into a club?"

"I have a fake ID."

I narrow my eyes at Noah.

"He didn't get it for me, Mom. Judd did. Do you want me to call him so you can yell at him, too? No guy is ever going to be good enough for me, is he? You told me that once. I should've known you really meant it. You'll never let me go. Never. You just want me to stay here and hide, scared of everything, suspicious of everyone, bitter and mad at the world. Like you."

"We used to talk." I choke back tears, my voice quiet now. "What happened?"

"You stopped hearing me, Mom."

Nate rubs my shoulders as I take deep breaths to steady myself. "I just want to know one thing. Did the two of you use protection?"

"See? You're not hearing me now." Erin looks up at the ceiling. "We fell asleep

339

watching a movie."

"Answer me, Erin. Did you use protection?"

"We would've if we'd done anything. How about you two?" She pokes a finger at Nate and me. "Did *you* use protection?"

I feel Nate tense, and shame washes over me. What was I thinking? I *wasn't* thinking. "We're not talking about me. We're talking about you."

Mother steps between us. "Now Erin, Cecilia —"

"You knew about this, didn't you? You knew Erin was sneaking out of the house."

Mother shifts a nervous glance Oliver's way, then meets my gaze. "We've been following her, making sure she's not in any trouble. I —"

"You had no right to keep this from me. She's my daughter —"

"I was wrong, I know that now. I urged Erin to tell you, Sugar. But I guess I should've given her an ultimatum to either tell you, or I would. You just made it so difficult for her with your overprotective —"

"Don't you *sugar* me. So, I'm overprotective? Maybe if you'd been a little more overprotective of me when I was her age, things would've been different. Maybe —"

"CiCi . . ." Oliver clears his throat. "I'll

ask that you not talk to your Mother with that tone."

I turn on him, glaring. "You're not my father. I'll talk to her however I want." Returning my attention to Mother, I say, "You and Erin have been conspiring against me, haven't you? What are you trying to be, Mother? Her friend instead of her grandmother? Look at you and that horny old man . . . acting like a couple of teenagers. What kind of example is that?"

Everyone glances from me to Nate and back. My knees go weak. So. I get it. I'm a bad example, too. They're right. One night. I slip up once, and look what happens.

I draw a breath. "At least I didn't stand back like you did and watch without saying a word while my seventeen-year-old daughter, your *granddaughter,* let her raging hormones overrule her good sense."

"Shut up!" Erin screams. "Leave her alone! I told you we didn't do anything." When Nate steps forward, she points at him and adds, "And you aren't *my* father, so you keep out of this."

The hallway goes quiet except for the sound of staggered breathing and tears. Mother's the first to break the silence.

"I've made mistakes, I admit that." When I start to interrupt, she lifts a hand. "I'll have my say. I'm seventy-five years old, and I've earned the right to speak my mind. I've been quiet too long, hinting and encouraging and hoping for the best for you, Cecilia. For you and for Erin. Well, I'm through beating around the bush." She blinks again and again, her eyes tired and misty. "I've learned some things over the years, through trial and error. Oh, yes, CiCi, we made lots of errors, your father and I. I'm well aware of that. We weren't perfect. But blind as I am, I see some things more clearly now that I'm an old woman. And here's what I see."

She links her fingers with mine. I don't pull away, just stare at her knuckles, the protruding blue veins on the back of her hand, her long, thin fingers. Fingers exactly like mine.

"You've allowed Bert's escapades and your own regrets to make you close-minded and cynical. Terrified of life. That attitude, my darling, will sabotage not only your relationships with the people you already love," she glances at Nate, "if you let it continue, it will sabotage any chance of a new relationship with a man, as well. Don't you see that? Don't you understand that you're hurting yourself? Hurting Erin?"

I can't speak; I can only stare at our joined hands.

"You've been unwilling to accept Oliver in my life or Noah in Erin's because you're afraid. Isn't that true?"

I tuck my lower lip between my teeth, look up and into my mother's gentle eyes. I am afraid. Afraid of losing them, of being alone. Afraid they'll get hurt. And that I will, too. Again.

"Mother . . . I haven't been fair to you. I'm sorry," I say quietly. "It's just so hard to see you with a man who isn't Daddy. And I can't stand the thought of you caring so much for Oliver then losing him, too, some day."

She squeezes my fingers as I turn to Erin. "I'm scared to death you'll repeat my mistakes, that you'll fall in love too soon, before you're ready. That he'll be the wrong person, and you'll end up shattered, like I was."

Tears stream down my daughter's face. Her brows pull together, and her eyes are filled with so many questions. When we're alone, I'll have to tell her about Craig, the boy I loved before her father. And maybe, too, about the baby we lost. That's a decision I'll have to make soon.

"So I guess that in my attempt to protect you, I've gone overboard with restrictions. But it backfired. It forced you to take foolish risks to get what you want and need. What you deserve. The chance to grow up." I take a breath. "But we need some middle ground, Erin. You can't just run wild, doing whatever you please, no matter what."

Erin nods.

"We can get through this, Cecilia," Mother says. "All of us. Together."

I want to. So much. I don't want to be the woman my mother described. I'm tired of being unhappy. Closed off. I don't want to push my family away. I need them now more than ever.

A sob escapes me as Erin steps toward us. She takes her grandmother's free hand in one of hers, then mine in her other. We form a circle. And I have hope. With their help, I can move on. And let them do the same.

After Oliver and Nathan leave, Mother makes coffee. Then, despite Erin's horrified protests and Noah's cringing embarrassment, the four of us sit down to discuss the responsibilities and risks involved in having sex at any age, but especially as teenagers. Maybe they aren't sleeping together, as Erin has implied, but I still have my doubts. Either way, it won't hurt for them to listen to the facts for an hour, instead of their hormones.

Stars still wink in a navy blue sky when Noah leaves on his cycle. Shivering, I stand on the front porch and watch him drive away. I've realized in the past hour that he's a nice kid; I should've known that all along. Should've trusted that my smart daughter wouldn't care so deeply for anyone who didn't have a good heart.

Despite the cold, I don't go in for a while. I hug myself and watch the horizon. When morning dawns, so does the truth, and I accept it. My daughter is growing up and must be allowed her own mistakes and triumphs. My mother has found true love again. Their lives are changing and so is mine. I think of my evolving counseling practice, of what happened last night with Nate, and smile.

For the first time, excitement trickles through me as I wonder about my future, the next chapter of my life. Some of it won't be written by my hand; I know that. But most of the blank pages are for me to fill.

However I choose.

Chapter 25

I have plenty of time to reflect during my flight to New York City, but I'm too nervous and excited to take advantage of it. So I just sit back and endure the bumpy ride.

Bill Burdette, on the advice of his legal counsel, declined an interview. Everett left the decision up to me. He thought telling my side of the story couldn't hurt, and Nate agreed.

So, here I am.

LIVE With Regis and Kelly put me up for the night at the Omni Hotel. At 8:00 p.m., I meet Sela Summers, author of *Penelope's Passion*, in the lobby, and we go to dinner at Tavern on the Green. We've become phone friends over the past three weeks, and I find I like her even more in person. She's smart and ambitious, yet friendly, funny and down-to-earth, too. Sela's giddy over her newfound success, and thanks me with every other breath. Last week, she sent each member of the Parkview Reading group a copy of her new release, *Irma's Indiscretion.*

The next morning, a limo picks us up and takes us to the studio. After that, everything's a blur of excitement until, finally, Sela and I walk onstage serenaded by music.

Regis is funny and warm and witty, while Kelly is gorgeous, enthusiastic and funny, too. Soon I'm at ease, or at least as calm as I'm going to get while on national television. Anyway, I'm relaxed enough to enjoy the conversation with Sela about her book.

I expect jokes about the sex at Parkview, and sure enough, they soon begin.

"Can you *blame* the residents?" Regis asks. "What would *you* choose? Shuffleboard or steamy sex in a gazebo overlooking a *pond?*"

"But the temp that day in Dallas was close to freezing!" Kelly shivers. "Talk about shrinkage!"

The audience roars.

"They had to do it *someplace* cold to stay *awake,*" Regis says. When Kelly slaps his arm, he continues, "Come on! The couple were in their *eighties,* for crying out loud! They need their rest."

I take my cue from Sela who, when teased about the sex in her book, laughed, then set the record straight.

"Like Sela's novels, what happened at Parkview was about relationships, not sex. It had everything to do with human needs, no matter a person's age."

I tell them how Mother came to live with Erin and me after Bert and I separated. How we are three women at three different stages of life with three different sets of issues and points of view. How, despite all that, I've discovered in our hearts, where it counts, we're as much the same as we're different on the surface.

"Through my mother and my daughter, I've come to understand that it doesn't matter if you're young, middle-aged or older, people are alike at the core. Everyone has dreams, fears and desires. Everyone needs love, laughter and acceptance. None of that stops just because children grow up and leave, hair turns gray or faces wrinkle."

Heads nod in agreement all around.

"Life is full of risks, and love is one of them. But, at seventeen or seventy-five, it's a risk worth taking, don't you think? People should be allowed to live until they die, not just exist."

The audience claps. So do Regis and Kelly and Sela.

I feel vindicated.

Sela puts an arm around my shoulders. "I just wish the grown children who filed the lawsuit against you and Parkview Manor would realize the same truth about their own parents. If a steamy novel, be it mine or someone else's, added romance to their lives, that's great!" She relates a quick story about her own mother starting to date after being a widow for the past two years.

Kelly mentions hearing that my counseling practice nose-dived when the so-called scandal hit the news, and I explain that, though I did lose prior clients, I gained new ones, that senior citizens from all over the Dallas metroplex and beyond have been making appointments.

I face the camera and take a deep breath. No one knows the decision I've made. Not Nate, not Mother, not Willa, Erin or any of my friends. I didn't know it myself until right this second. "In fact," I say, "I'm shifting the focus of my practice away from marriage and family therapy. From now on, I plan to address the needs and concerns of senior citizens exclusively."

A week later, it snows. Fat, wet flakes fall during the night, and Mom, Erin and I awake on a Saturday morning in early February to a sight seldom seen in Dallas: the city blanketed in pristine white.

As we drive to Cleburne in the afternoon to attend a wedding shower for the daughter of a family friend, we discuss my new weekly radio show, *Sex and the Senior,* which will air in selected markets starting in the fall. I'll take calls and answer questions on issues affecting senior citizens. After my appearance on *LIVE With Regis and Kelly,* I received offers of every kind. The radio program worked out best for me since I can do it from a Dallas station and still maintain my practice.

Sue Kiley, Donald Quinn and the other plaintiffs dropped the lawsuit against Parkview Manor and me. Though no one ever said, and I didn't ask, I can only assume they saw me on television, too.

We arrive in Cleburne early. I ask Mother, who sits across from me, if she'd like to drive by the old house. At first she says "no," then changes her mind. She's been quiet most of the drive, listening to Erin and me talk, not adding much to the conversation. As we turn into the old neighborhood where I grew up, where she lived with Daddy for so many years, I find out why.

"Did I tell you Oliver asked me to marry him?" Her words are spoken casually, but I notice her head trembles, that her hands are restless in her lap.

For weeks, I've dreaded hearing this news. But I don't feel the resistance I expected, the need to stand up for my father, the fear of this major adjustment ahead in my mother's life. And mine. I imagine her living the rest of her years with Oliver. Somehow, it seems right.

I turn to her with a little laugh of surprise, then look back at the road. "No, you didn't tell us that." Emotion wells up in me. I smile at her. "Oh, Mom . . ."

"Nana!" Erin squeezes between the bucket seats and gives her grandmother a hug. "When's the wedding?"

Mother blushes and blinks. "I haven't given him an answer yet."

The uncertainty in her voice alarms me. Is this thing with Oliver just an attempt to help her through her grief over Daddy? "Maybe it's too soon, Mother. It's only been a little more than a year since Daddy died."

She shakes her head. "It isn't too soon, Sugar. I'm ready."

I turn the corner onto our old street. "So, you love him?"

"Of course I do."

"Well, what are you waiting for, then? If it's my blessing, you have it." I take one hand from the wheel and cover hers on the seat between us.

"Mine, too," Erin echoes.

Mother's eyes mist. "I know this isn't easy

for either of you. If I marry Oliver, things will be different for all of us, I won't pretend otherwise."

"What do you mean, Nana?"

"Well, holidays for one. It won't be only our traditions anymore. I'll have to embrace his, too, of course. And his children, as difficult as they sound, they'll be a part of my family, too. Then there's —"

"Mother . . ." I squeeze her hand. "Everything's already different. Life changes all the time. We can either adapt, or we can be unhappy. I've spent way too long nursing misery. From now on, I plan to adapt. But if you're not sure about Oliver, then please, please, don't marry him."

"Oh, I'm sure about him." She looks down at her lap. "It's myself I question. Am I wrong to love him? I feel as if I'm betraying your father."

"If you are, then so am I. I care for Oliver, too. Not that I didn't fight it." I laugh. "The sneak. He has a way of working his way into your heart, like it or not."

She laughs with me as I pull to the curb in front of the house. Still, I sense she's not convinced.

"You're not wrong, Mother. You have to go on. We all do."

"So," Erin says when the silence stretches

too long, "When are you gonna say 'yes'?"

Mother sighs. "I wish I knew. It's your grandfather I'm waiting on. I talk to him, you know. All the time. Through letters. I asked him for —"

"Nana, look!"

Mother gasps as we glance in the direction Erin points.

At the side of the house sits the only one of Daddy's rose bushes the new owners didn't pull up. Barren from neglect the last time we were here, it's now covered in snow. And in the center of the frosty white bush, as lush and beautiful as if it were spring, blooms one perfect yellow rose.

"Harry . . ." Mother whispers, and I turn to see tears streaming down her cheeks. She opens the van door and climbs out.

Through our own tears, Erin and I watch her walk across the snow-covered lawn toward the bush, then bend forward to smell my father's last flower.

Chapter 26

From The Desk of
Belle Lamont

Dear Harry,
Thank you.

From the first moment we met, I loved you, and I never stopped. I will always remember our wonderful years together. I will never forget you.

Goodbye, my love.

As always, your yellow rose,
Belle

Chapter 27

To: Noah@friendmail.com
From: Erin@friendmail.com
Date: 08/20 Friday
Subject: Miss you and other stuff

Noah,
It was great to hear your voice last night. Thanks for letting me know you and your parents made the drive safely to Montana. I'm glad you miss me as much as I miss you. And that you love me. I MISS YOU!! How is MSU? How is your dorm? Have you met your roommate? I hope he's okay. I'm glad I have Suz. I would be so nervous to move in with a stranger.

I am e-mailing you from my dorm room! Suz has clothes everywhere already. We are gonna be tripping over each other, but I'm excited! I MISS YOU! If I wasn't so psyched about school starting, I don't know what I'd do.

I wish you could've been at Nana's wedding! It was beautiful! Not stuffy and dull like Dad's to Nat the brat. Nana looked so pretty in her cream-colored suit. Oliver looked handsome and proud. Mom gave Nana away. Or, as Nana said, walked her "into the next season of her life." Isn't that sweet? When it was over, and she and Oliver started down the aisle, some old guy shouted, "that-a-boy, Luther!" Everybody cracked up. Oh, and the funniest part — a few kids Nana and Oliver met at The Beat were there. Reese, Tonto and I played at the reception. (WE MISSED YOU!) Nana and Oliver can really dance! I've never laughed so hard. Anyway, they are in Hawaii now on their honeymoon. When they get back, they'll rent a little condo close to our house. I can't wait until they see the surprise Mom and I have waiting for them. It's a really awesome brass bed. Mom paid a fortune for it but she said Nana's always wanted one, and she deserves it.

Guess what? Maxwell is gonna be a daddy. The mother is our neighbor's poodle, Pom Pom. Mrs. Stein isn't too happy. She thinks Maxwell is a "brute" and not good enough for her precious, prissy poodle. She says Max "took advantage" of Pom Pom. As if. Pom Pom dug the hole and came over to Max. The hoochie. Mom thinks it's hilarious because Mrs. Stein has been trying to fix Mom up since the day Dad left and, instead, the dogs got together. Anyway, we wondered what had perked Max up, and now we know.

Well, tonight is my first night away from home. Mom cried when she left me here, but I think she'll be okay. She's really busy with her work and her new radio show starts soon. She and the Margarita Martyrs have started walking in the evenings and she's lost most of the weight she put on when she was stuffing her face 24/7. Oh, and she and Nate are still on. That dating-other-people-for-a-while-just-to-make-sure thing she suggested to him lasted about five minutes. They're together all the time. It's still weird for me to see her with another guy besides Dad, but Nate's nice and he doesn't try to act like my dad's stand-in. I'd rather see her with him than someone else.

So . . . have you met any girls? Do they have hairy armpits and legs? Never mind! Suz told me to ask that! Still, I secretly hope they are as hairy as King Kong. And as big, too. <grin>

Well, gotta go. Next time I write, I'll have gone to class and, hopefully, met some people. I'll tell you about everything. Write or call me soon and tell me every-

thing that's going on with you. I MISS
YOU!!

Love and miss you bunches,
Erin

Chapter 28

Cecilia Dupree
Day Planner
Monday, 08/23

1. 8 a.m. — First Sex & The Senior radio show.
2. 9:30 a.m. — New pt. appt — Maevis Carlyle (struggling w/staying active).
3. 11:00 — pt. appt — George Godfrey (grief counseling over wife's death).
4. Noon — lunch @ home (salad). Check on Pom Pom. Decline date w/ Mrs. Stein's husband's cousin's son. Excuse: incest (we're now related through granddogs).
5. 2:00 — Parkview Reading Group. Start new Sela Summers novel, *Daphne's Desire*. (save copy for Mother and Oliver.)
6. 4:00 — pt. follow-up — Iris & Stanley McDougal (marriage counseling over Iris's continued phone relationship w/obscene caller).

7. 6:00 — Walk w/Martyrs, then put away Erin's baby photos & stop crying.
8. 8:00 — Dinner w/Nate. Accept invite to weekend in Cozumel next month. These conditions:
   (a) pressure about the scuba (maybe, maybe not);
   (b) iffy on bikini for me (no promises);
   (c) definitely no Speedo for him (Pu-leese!);
   (d) no wine (well, maybe a little);
   (e) separate rooms (extremely negotiable).